The Light Behind
Blue Circles

by **Robert Louis DeMayo**

1/2013

1

Cover design: Andrew Holman, Tom Fish
and Robert Louis DeMayo
Cover art: Tom Fish

Available from <u>Amazon.com</u>
and other retailers.

for

Patricia DeMayo

my mother and inspiration.

I would like to thank some of the people who helped me craft this story: notably Nina Rehfeld, whose insightful edits brought the tale to life; my proof reader, Dave Egan; and Deb DeCosta and Jody Phillips, who helped with earlier versions of the novel. My thanks also to Mark Patton, who advised me on a screenplay version; and several friends who read it and encouraged me to turn the screenplay into a novel, among them: Penelope Bodry Sanders, Derek Lillesve and Briana Robbins, and Catherine Robbins.

I am indebted to my readers whose insights have been priceless: Lucinda Sylvester, Monica Shaw and Shannon Shaw, Mark Mathus, Jessica Johnson, Josh Robbins, Sherri O'neil, Brian Walker, Joanne Sheehan, Heidi Benson, Kathy Kallfelz, and David DeMayo. Andrew Holman helped with the cover design, and the cover drawing was completed by Tom Fish.

And lastly, I'd like to extend my thanks to some of the people I encountered while on various trips to Africa: notably, Fritz Swart, for saving my butt several times; James Shawcross; Mama Rosch, whose guest house was my home for several periods; and Wayne & Sparky at the Rocks, in Harare, Zimbabwe (*or wherever they are now*).

Chapter One

The Serengeti Plain
(1983)

By the foot of a low hill a fire smoldered; next to it lay two occupied sleeping bags. A parked Land Cruiser stood a few feet off. Dawn was still distant and the only movement was a wisp of smoke as it slowly curled from the fire pit. A lone dove crooned shyly from a flat-topped acacia tree just behind the vehicle.

Far to the east the sky was just starting to glow, lit by the promise of a new day, but on the African plain that meant life or death for some living thing—and here death came on fast and hard.

Slowly, morning spread over the veldt, subdued and patient in a thousand shades of blue and green.

The expansive view of the savanna was one of the reasons the campers had picked the site. It felt like the entire world could be contained in this wilderness; nothing but swaying yellow grass and lone acacia trees.

The Serengeti plains cover almost six thousand square miles of grassland plains and savanna, and it is here that the wildebeest breed from December to May. *Serengeti* is a Maasai word that means *endless plain*.

Here, at its northern end, it did indeed appear endless.

The rainy season had come and gone, leaving the earth parched once again, and the few animals that were visible were all slowly moving north, to the Maasai Mara—there the grass was green and the plains were full of activity.

Behind the camp a woodland clung to the land. It rose up in a great plateau—one side of the Great African rift. A dirt road ran into it. Although the tree line was a good fifty feet away, smaller bushes spread forward, right up to the edge of the camp.

Around the campsite the bush now slowly came to life. Although the sun had yet to peek over the horizon the twittering and fluttering of singing birds was beginning to fill the air.

Far back in the woods a monkey barked a warning and everything quieted down for just a moment before the symphony of insects and birds ramped up again.

In the east the glow grew stronger.

Through it all the two campers slept, but then a lion coughed—from fairly close by—and one of them sat up abruptly.

His name was Peter.

He was thirteen, had a head full of brown hair in need of a haircut, and striking blue eyes. His face was lit with curiosity and enthusiasm as he looked around for the lion. The cool morning air carried sounds well and he could clearly hear the cat growling as it circled behind them in the forest.

While he observed the woods, listening more than looking as they were still full of gloom, he nervously touched a large blue marble suspended from a thin leather string around his neck.

Peter and his father Simon—the man in the other sleeping bag—hailed from Pretoria, in South Africa. They had come to Kenya together for his father to attend a conference on poaching. His father, Simon, often worked as a veterinarian in the national parks of South Africa and whenever he could he took Peter along on his calls.

Until about a year ago Peter's mother came along as well.

Father and son had always been relaxed around each other, and it felt natural and easy when they camped. Both had a knack for identifying birds by their calls so even when they silently sat by the campfire listening their minds moved in unison with the sounds around them.

They didn't seem to need words. A bird would call out, Simon would cock his head and listen, and a simple nod would acknowledge its recognition. When in the bush they each shared a silent understanding of one another and the world around them.

At least that's the way it was until Peter's mother died.

Ever since then Simon had found excuses to remain out of the bush and close to home. He stopped socializing and just moped around the house. Peter had been desperate to get away with his father for months now, and when he overheard Simon's supervisor mention a conference on poaching in Kenya he jumped at the chance.

His father was hesitant when Peter urged that this was their chance to see something that they'd often talked about. Together they had explored many of the parks in southern Africa, but Peter had never seen the great wildebeest migration.

"You realize we'll be away for the anniversary of your mother's death, don't you?" asked Simon.

"Well," said Peter, hesitating. "I think she'd like it."

Simon lowered his gaze and nervously ran his fingers through his hair. Peter knew his father was afraid he'd want to talk about his mother when they were camping and added, "Don't worry, dad. On this trip we'll discuss nothing serious."

Simon nodded, but his mind was flooded with images of his wife and of their time together. She hadn't been born in South Africa, but had fallen in love with the country the moment she arrived.

They had met while she was stationed at Kruger National Park, doing field work on conservation techniques, and every day he'd found some excuse to bring her into the bush.

His enthusiasm was contagious and soon they spent every moment they could exploring the wilderness areas of southern Africa. Simon liked the big cats and loved to follow a pride on its wanderings; she preferred the gazelles—all of them—from the enormous eland to the delicate dik dik.

The animal encounters had been so integral too their relationship that even today, whenever he saw a sable he thought of her. Once they'd woken to find one standing a short ways from their tent, lit up in the morning sun.

It had watched them, unafraid, as they crept to the tent entrance and observed. The sable was male with a black coat; and the underbelly was white, as were its cheeks and chin. Two enormous, ringed horns arched back over its neck which was covered with a shaggy mane.

He watched her looking at it with such fascination in her soft brown eyes that it might as well have been a unicorn.

He knew he would feel her shadow by his side in the bush, and the prospect of going on safari again terrified him. He dreamt of her continuously since her passing and knew if he closed his eyes he would believe it to be true—that she was standing next to him.

But he could only close his eyes for so long. He was still struggling to deal with the reality of life alone, and didn't want to be reminded of her painful absence in the bush where they had shared so many serene moments.

Yet, when he looked into Peter's desperate eyes he could not say no. The boy had lost her as well, and maybe the trip would help them both move on. Reluctantly, he began planning the trip.

Now they were in the bush, on the verge of witnessing the migration. Giddy with anticipation, Peter hadn't been able to sleep for weeks before their departure, and now that they were on safari he was electrified when he heard the lion's call.

He knew the cough he'd heard was what lions used when they tried to find each other. The cat must have skirted the savanna and followed the woodland to circle behind their camp. If the pride had hunted in the night the chase was long over; he knew the lions were now regrouping before sleeping away the day.

Peter had slept in his jeans and T-shirt and wiggled out of his sleeping bag. He grabbed his boots, checked them for scorpions and pulled them on. Then he picked up the light jacket he had folded into a pillow and shook it before slipping into the sleeves.

Taking in the day, he listened to the birds and picked out a Bush Cuckoo, whose sweet song lingered over the morning, each note as liquid as a drop of water.

He breathed deeply, the air luscious and tropical.

Slowly his eyes searched the gloomy wooded area, scanning again for the lion. In the heat of day the land had felt parched and arid, but now the grass was covered with dew and the morning was cool.

He pictured the wetness of the lion's scruffy yellow fur as he trod through the woods, head and tail down, back straight, flashing dew drops in its wake.

A monkey again barked a warning, this time deeper into the woods, and Peter sensed the lion had moved away from the camp. Grabbing his binoculars, Peter scanned the woods.

As he stepped behind the Land Cruiser to relieve himself, his eye caught something at the top of a nearby hill which stopped him in his tracks.

On the hill stood a young warrior peering at the horizon — judging the progress of the sunrise from the look of it. Even before he'd found him in his binoculars, Peter knew he was Maasai.

The warrior was muscular and tall, his black skin dulled by gray dust. His long hair was tightly braided and smeared with a paste of fat and red clay; he wore a short toga and a blood-colored robe. His wrists were ringed with wooden bracelets and two wooden circles filled his elongated earlobes.

A gourd hung from a cord around his waist on his left, and a short Maasai sword, a *lalem,* on the right. Numerous bags and satchels were also attached; enough to hint that he was more than a warrior.

His name was Lekai, and he was barely an adult. Five summers had passed since his initiation into the warrior caste. He pulled the eighteen-inch blade from the concealed safety of a red sheath made from cowhide and fingered the sharp edge.

He crouched low and moved through the brush. The warrior appeared focused on his surveillance of the horizon, and that concentration drew Peter in—he had to see what this young man was up to. The hill he stood upon sat away from the woodland; a lone island that seemed to have drifted into the yellow sea of grass. Peter saw that by following the perimeter of the woodland he could get closer, undiscovered.

He felt for his binoculars. His father had taught him not to use them in the open as the reflection might announce you to your subject.

From what Peter could make out with the naked eye the young warrior was tying two spears together into a cross. He nervously glanced at the horizon, as if the sunrise might come before he was ready.

A dense shrub with a dug-up depression under it provided the perfect spot for Peter to stop and observe. He was still about twenty feet away, but all that stood between them now was swaying yellow grass.

Lekai was unaware that he was being observed. In the stillness of the morning Peter could hear Lekai softly chanting. The warrior picked up his war club, a *rangu,* and pointed it determinedly to the east.

In the shaded depression Peter picked up his binoculars and trained them on the young warrior. Just then he heard the lion cough again in the distance, this time from the other side of the hill.

The warrior looked in that direction and did a good imitation of the cough. Then he stuck a spear end into the ground, a cross of spears now standing in front of him. He draped a faded red toga over the horizontal spear, creating a scarecrow.

Lastly, he grabbed a handful of yellow grass and tied it into a bundle. This he placed on the end of the spear that pointed skyward.

From his left side he lifted his throwing club. It was made from a root and had a hard, polished knob at the end. Lekai ran his hand over the smooth weighted end as he examined the scarecrow.

He smiled at it and said, "Soon you will greet the day."

Peter didn't understand the words, but he knew something mystical was going on. He tried to crawl closer through the high grass, but his necklace had gotten tangled in a branch and held him fast.

He yanked it, and the shaking limbs drew Lekai's attention. He stared at the bush for a moment, but in the early light of dawn he didn't see the boy.

Suddenly the sun poured over the horizon and illuminated the scarecrow. Both Lekai and Peter marveled at the plain lighting up with the flood of golden rays. A warm breeze came with it and made the scarecrow look alive as it twisted in the wind.

Lekai stepped back and proudly observed his creation.

Back at the campsite, Peter's father, Simon, emerged from his sleeping bag. He was in his mid-forties, dressed in a khaki shirt and pants. He glanced at his son's sleeping bag and saw that it was empty.

"Peter!" he shouted.

When he got no response he called again, this time louder and with a trace of concern.

Simon's call startled both Peter and Lekai.

Peter jerked backwards, and his necklace — still caught in the branches of the shrub — broke and slid to the ground.

Peter nervously glanced at the warrior to see if he'd given away his location.

Lekai turned and stared into the thickets. The sun's sharp rays were now piercing the shadows and he could see Peter clearly.

The warrior smiled and said to himself, "Peter."

He turned to his scarecrow, and then back to the boy, as if comparing them.

Peter and Lekai made eye contact and for a silent moment they just stared at each other. The wind had picked up and the tall grass between them swayed erratically.

Simon's call rang out again and Peter yelled back, "I'm here, dad!" He held Lekai's gaze for another few seconds and then returned to the campsite.

While Peter helped his dad break camp below, Lekai spotted the necklace beneath Peter's hideaway.

He picked it up and stared at it.

He said, "I have been waiting for you, Peter."

He took the marble off the string and dropped it into a leather bag that was tied to his side.

Simon cranked the wheel and backed up the Land Cruiser. He put the vehicle in gear and stepped on the gas, and then slammed on the brakes as he saw Lekai blocking his way.

"Bloody hell!" shouted Simon.

Lekai stood his ground, lifted his war club and pointed it at Simon.

"I did not mean to startle you."

He spoke in a British accent, but his words were softer and more melodic.

Simon shifted the Land Cruiser into neutral and stood, glaring at the Maasai, but before he could speak the warrior held up his right hand, palm forward, in a sign of friendship.

"You will speak with me before leaving."

Peter looked into Lekai's eyes and was startled by how direct he was.

Peter had been exposed to many black people, mostly servants—he had grown up under Apartheid rule—and although they were friendly and appeared to like him, they were never as self-assured as Lekai appeared.

Simon barely concealed his impatience.

"What're you doing there? What do you want?"

Lekai again pointed the war club at Simon as he said, "My name is Lekai."

Simon glared at him and said, "Well, Lekai, I'd like it if you could stop shaking that club at me."

Lekai nodded and broke out a disarming smile.

"I have a problem—help me with this."

Simon glanced at his watch, and then at Peter.

"I don't want to buy anything, Lekai," he said. "We have plenty of supplies."

The Maasai shook his head.

"No, I do not wish to sell you anything. What I talk about is a matter of life and death."

Simon looked skeptical as he asked, "Whose life or death?"

Lekai said, "It is my dearest friend, Kiboko. Without my help, this one—my friend—he will surely die."

Simon slowly shook his head.

"I don't want to get caught up in anything political."

Lekai leaned forward and laughed with his entire body and he snapped his fingers for emphasis. He continued to giggle as he spoke but then became serious.

"My friend is an animal—a big one—and he is in danger."

Peter stood on the passenger seat and looked at Lekai. Simon looked up at his son and saw the grin on his face.

He said, "You found the right man, my father is a veterinarian."

Simon turned off the engine.

"Tell me what the problem is," he said.

13

Chapter Two

The Maasai Mara

Simon drove the Land Cruiser with the soft top down. Lekai sat up front with him and set his two long spears by his feet so that they extended out beyond his right shoulder into the air above them. From their campsite they had followed the dirt track through the woodland and as they neared the top of the plateau they encountered puddles from the recent rain.

They drove casually, skirting several flooded sections of road. The morning was fresh and cool. The forest deepened and soon they were surrounded by tall silver trees that shimmered in the early morning light. Some of the tree trunks bore marks from elephants rubbing against them, but none of the giant animals were in sight now.

On the plateau the view was commanding with the Serengeti stretching off to the south, and the green grass of the Maasai Mara to the north; there, the rains had prepared a feast for the massive herds that would soon arrive.

Peter was leaning forward from the back seat, eagerly listening to the Maasai and his father talking; whenever he saw a large pothole approaching he stood on the seat, held onto the roll bar, and let himself be launched into the air.

His father glanced at him in the mirror and said, "You better quit fooling around or you might end up impaled on one of Lekai's spears."

Lekai and Peter both looked at the sharpened tips, pointed safely to the side of the vehicle.

Peter feigned indignation. "Jeez, Dad, I thought we were leaving the serious stuff behind—at least until we get back to South Africa."

For one uncomfortable moment Simon was stung by Peter's words when he thought the boy was referring to his mother, but before he could reply, Lekai cut in. "You are from South Africa?" He shook his head in amazement. "South Africa is a long way from Maasailand. How many days did it take to drive that far?"

Peter laughed. "We didn't drive here."

Apologetically, Simon explained, "We didn't have a lot of time. I came to Kenya for business and decided to bring Peter with me."

Lekai nodded. "It would have been a noble journey." He seemed a little disappointed. "Next time you should come overland. We Maasai, we love journeys."

Peter said, "Dad got us this Land Cruiser so we could see the wildebeest migration."

He looked around. "I thought there'd be more animals."

Lekai laughed. "Oh, you will see many animals, very soon you will."

He indicated for Simon to pull over.

Peter excitedly pulled himself out of his seat by the roll bar again.

Simon steered the Land Cruiser to a pullout with an expansive view to the north. There the plain extended, with a dark river cutting through a belt of green.

Even from a distance the river looked swollen.

Lekai pointed to a bend in the river where the game was gathered. From their vantage point the animals appeared as small dots that bunched along the river.

"Wildebeest," Lekai said. "Many more are coming."

Peering into the distance, Simon ruffed up Peter's hair and said, "And not just wildebeest—there are 250,000 zebra; 500,000 gazelle, 97,000 topi, and 1,800 eland."

Lekai looked skeptical.

"How do you know these numbers?" he asked.

Lekai looked over the plains, laughed and added, "How could there be numbers that big?"

Peter smiled and added, "Yeah, dad, how'd you count them all so fast?"

Simon smiled at his son and replied to Lekai, "These are only estimates, but they were available at the conference I just attended."

Lekai shook his head in disbelief, "I always believed there were too many to count."

Peter asked, "How many wildebeest are there?"

Simon replied, "One and a half million."

Lekai whistled through his teeth, then grinned at Simon. "I am thinking you are having fun with me. You are joking. Is right?"

Simon said, "No, why would I do that?"

The Maasai said, "Who would have time to count all these animals?"

Simon shrugged. "Someone must have."

Lekai laughed and pointed over the Maasai Mara below them. "My people were grazing our cattle here for generations before Europeans arrived and we never had time to count them. When the migration is on you will see animals all over the plain below—then you will see why we named it "Mara" which means *spotted*."

Lekai shrugged. "I still do not believe that someone could count all of these animals. All I know is there is as many as there are stars."

"Agreed," replied Simon. Then he looked at Peter. "This is it, Peter. This is what we've been waiting for."

Peter nodded. He wanted to get closer.

Before they left the viewpoint Simon addressed Lekai again, asking, "Now where can I find your friend?"

The Maasai pointed all the way across the valley to the far north.

"In the foothills," he said, "There he will be."

Simon looked at the distance and shook his head.

He said, "That's too far, son. I'd guess that'd be at least two days travel. "

Lekai nodded enthusiastically.

"Yes, we could be there in time."

Before Simon could protest, Lekai added, "We camp tonight by the river, and the next day we are there. If I do not help Kiboko he will surely die."

Peter looked at his father.

"Dad, we've got to help him," he pleaded.

"We would be moving away from the migration," Simon said. "You might even miss it."

"I don't care," stated Peter. "I want to help."

The three sat in silence.

Lekai finally said, "The deeds of one's life are greater than the facts of his birth."

Peter looked confused. "I don't understand."

His father looked at Lekai as he spoke.

"I think Lekai is saying that the things you do in life are more important that who your parents were or how rich you are."

The Maasai nodded emphatically.

"Yes! That is it," he said. "And some of the things you do in this life are worth risking your life for, also. They are worth dying for. Do you feel this way too?"

Simon hesitated.

"It would depend on what I was fighting for."

Innocently, Lekai said, "It is simple. You fight for what you believe—for justice—justice will show you the way."

Peter proudly said, "My dad was in the army—Special Forces."

They both turned and stared at Simon, but he just scratched his head and stared off at the river below them before replying.

After a long pause he asked, "How do you know your friend, Kiboko, is even in danger?"

Lekai's expression became solemn, "The Great Laibon has seen it."

Simon exhaled and looked at his son. When he spoke it was with skepticism.

"His witch doctor told him."

Lekai sensed the doubt in his voice.

"You question Laibon's words?" he asked.

When Simon didn't reply, Lekai added, "Have you not heard of the Great *Emutai*?

Simon nodded, "Yes, I have."

Peter asked, "What's he talking about, dad?"

Simon answered, "*Emutai* means 'to wipe out.' The 1890's were a difficult time for the Maasai—for most of Africa for that matter. Several contagious bovine diseases swept through Africa, pleuropneumonia and rinderpest among them. Most of the buffalo and cattle died during this time."

"Many people died, also, during the Great *Emutai*," added Lekai sternly. "And the Maasai would have been wiped out if the Laibons had not seen it coming."

Hesitantly, Simon continued, "That's true, tribes like the Maasai who lived so closely to the animals were especially hard hit. Two-thirds of the Maasai died of smallpox."

Sadly, Lekai continued, "One hundred years ago our greatest Laibon saw this coming, but could not prevent it. There were years when it did not rain at all and many wild animals died."

A far-off look had descended over Lekai's features, and Peter and Simon could feel his connection to the elders who had passed down the story since the dark days of the Great *Emutai*.

Lekai said, "The proud warriors were scarcely able to crawl on all fours and the madness of starvation glared from the skeletons of the women. Over every village swarms of vultures circled."

Simon scratched his head again, and then looked at Lekai and asked, "What exactly did your Laibon say about your animal friend?"

Lekai answered, "He said that danger was approaching for both of us, and that soon we would see the end of things."

Peter gasped. "He said you were in danger, too?"

Lekai nodded. "Yes."

Slightly confused, Peter asked, "Then why are you going?"

The expression on Lekai's face was compelling.

"Because Kiboko needs me," he simply said.

It only took one glance at his son's face for Simon to confirm that they were going to find Kiboko.

He said, "Well, I guess we better get going. We've got some distance to cover."

Peter and Lekai both cheered as he turned the ignition.

Several hours later Simon parked the Land Cruiser on a high bank of the river, next to a fire pit. They had to weave their way through a herd of wildebeest and zebra to get to the campsite. Simon had honked and yelled, careful not to hurt any of them.

He strategically placed the vehicle so that it blocked off the campsite toward the open plain. The riverbank and the fire pit secured the other sides. About thirty feet further downstream the bank dropped away on each side, and it was there that the animals were coming from after crossing the river.

When they exited the car they could hear splashing and the high screeches of crazed wildebeest as they attempted to cross the river. The bank and a row of trees shielded them from the commotion, but the muffled sound still came through.

They walked to the high bank next to their camp and looked down at the river. The recent rains had flooded off the steep banks and turned the water brown with mud, a menacing impression that became even more disturbing when Peter realized that the bubbles that seemed to float on the water were the eyes of the crocodiles that watched the shore, waiting for one of the creatures to cross.

Most of the animals lining the shore in nervous anticipation were wildebeest, but there were zebras and gazelles as well. They were all getting ready to cross the muddy river from the far side of the campsite, but an angry herd of African buffalos were blocking their exit route. The stakes here were considerable: A swirling current and the lurking crocodiles made the crossing a treacherous undertaking. Yet there was no alternative if the animals hoped to reach the lush fields of the Maasai Mara.

"The buffalo are not happy now," said Lekai. "They live here always and do not like the new visitors."

Peter looked and saw that on his side of the river the buffalo were indeed holding their ground and intimidated any animals that did cross. Those that did reach the shore had to force their way through the herd in an awful gauntlet where they were kicked and gouges by the sharp horns.

Most only reluctantly entered the river after being forced from behind. They plunged in only to frantically resurface and fight desperately for the far shore.

"I've read that the crocodiles prefer the wildebeest to the other animals," said Peter.

Simon said, "They do have the numbers on their side."

Lekai shook his head.

"There may be more wildebeest, but I think the crocodile doesn't like the kick of the zebra."

On the far side of the river another herd of wildebeest congregated and eyed the crossing nervously. They swished their tails over their backs in a circular motion. Among them, a group of zebras bellowed high-pitched screams as they hesitated on the far bank, some stood frozen in fear with their ears forward. The smell of manure was strong in the air.

On this side, animals that had crossed just before the buffalo had congregated slowly trudged by, exhausted and restless, trying to shake off their brush with death.

While they watched the herd of buffalo began to back away from the river, moving along the bank.

"I knew they would not cross," said Lekai. "They only stay at the river to cause trouble—there is no food on the other side—why would they cross?"

"Look!" said Peter as he pointed to a huge crocodile on the bank below them, a good eighteen feet long, its dark bronze back freckled with black spots. Its legs were splayed out and its yellow-green flanks looked ready to burst.

"I think this one has eaten enough for two years," said Simon.

As they watched they saw the herd of buffalo coming in their direction. The trail the animals followed led off beyond their camp, but who knew where the chaos might spill over.

"We're gonna need a good fire to keep the animals away from our camp," said Simon.

The three of them scanned the area for anything burnable. Simon gathered a handful of dead twigs and dropped them in the fire pit. He reached into his pocket and found a lighter and handed it to Peter.

"Get the fire started," he said. "I'll collect some wood."

Lekai followed Simon.

"I will assist you."

Almost as soon as Simon and Lekai disappeared into the bush the herd of buffalo began backing into the camp. From the Land Cruiser Peter grabbed a few pieces of paper which he balled up and placed under a handful of dried twigs.

Although the paper took right away, the flame was small and grew painfully slow. Peter scrambled to add more kindling, panic rising inside him.

And then a solitary, rogue bull bumped into the Land Cruiser, shaking it violently.

Already agitated by the intruding wildebeest, the bull spun to confront the vehicle. It lowered its head showing the fused horns; beyond, its wet black coat extended across a frighteningly wide neck and broad back. Peter could see a gouge on one flank.

The bull shook his head angrily and bellowed.

Then it spotted Peter crouching over the fire pit with eyes that were highlighted by whitish circles.

Peter froze under the deadly stare.

The fire had begun to take; Peter didn't dare to break eye contact with the bull. It seemed that this was the only thing that held the buffalo at bay. But the bull moved around the bumper of the Land Cruiser, lowering its deadly horns even further. Its dark eyes watched Peter coldly.

Peter listened for sounds of Simon and Lekai returning, but only heard the splashing and grunting below. He was alone and the thought of it turned his mouth dry.

Slowly he picked up a burning stick and nervously stood.

The fire snapped and the bull stepped back bewildered. Behind him the herd scattered in a drifting cloud of dust.

The bull snorted, and then turned and in a few seconds was lost in the herd.

Peter let out his breath and dropped the stick.

"Yeah, you better run," he called after the bull, but then his knees went wobbly. He leaned against the Land Cruiser until his nerves steadied.

Although the immediate danger had passed, other buffalo were being shoved around the outskirts of the camp and Peter quickly set about adding more fuel to the fire. So focused was he on his task that he didn't hear Lekai as he approached from behind.

Lekai almost fell down with laughter when Peter jumped with a scream.

Then Lekai noticed the buffalo tracks near the fire pit.

"*M'bogo* was here!" he said. "It is good you stayed near the fire—I told you the buffalo are not happy now." With a shrug he added, "They know that death is coming back to the area—they sense that bad times are coming."

Lekai sniffed the air for a moment.

"We will have company tonight," he said. "I must collect more wood."

Chapter Three

Laibon

*L*ater that night Lekai sat alone by a bright fire. Peter and Simon were sleeping nearby. Although the buffalo had left, he kept adding wood to the flame, stoking it.

He stared into the shadows apprehensively.

Every so often, from the darkness animals slowly came forward into the fire´s glow and disappeared again; the night hid most of them, but the occasional sound of their hooves scraping against rocks betrayed their vast numbers. Their smell was heavy in the air, too.

Since he was young Lekai had a way with animals. They came to him, and he was not afraid of them. Laibon had sought him out because of this. As he observed them lurking in the shadows Lekai noted that they seemed agitated, or spooked, yet they were moving closer to the fire—like moths to a flame.

Laibon encouraged Lekai's education in many fields. Part of the training Lekai received from Laibon was in tending small wounds; as Laibon he would be responsible for healing his brother's injuries as well as leading them spiritually.

He also spoke three languages fluently. His first language was *Maa*, the language of a million people that made up his tribe, but at school he also learned Swahili and English, the two national languages of Tanzania.

He watched the animals' eyes glittering in the dark with the reflection of the fire, and in this quiet hour of the night he remembered his last visit to the Great Laibon's compound, just a few nights earlier.

A dozen Maasai warriors were standing nervously outside a mud-covered hut. Their eyes glittered in the dark with the reflection of the fire.

The men were all dressed in *shukas*, the traditional red togas of the Maasai that were wrapped around the body and then thrown over the shoulder.

They wore their hair in long, thinly braided strands — as only warriors were allowed to — and they each carried an assortment of spears. They were ready for battle.

Lekai faced them.

"Sendeyo, Kulet, all my brothers", he said, "I told you, Great Laibon has summoned only me. You must wait here."

One of them — Sendeyo — stepped forward; he was tall and strong, a leader of men, but he spoke with respect when he addressed Lekai. Two round discs of ivory pierced his elongated earlobes.

He unconsciously rubbed his war club as he said, "It is only right for the Great Laibon to summon his apprentice. I only ask that we accompany you on this journey that he has spoken of. To go on a journey like this alone is unheard of."

The others seconded this protest, but Lekai held up his hand.

"I must go alone."

With reluctance he added, "You cannot protect me."

The warriors listened to his words, but their expressions showed frustration. Lekai was moving into danger, yet Laibon's word overruled their concern for the young man.

"Why is this?" asked Sendeyo in a voice thick with authority.

Lekai shrugged. "I am only an apprentice and I don't always understand the ways of the Great Laibon."

Sendeyo shook his head. "You understand more than us. Please tell Laibon that we will not let you go alone."

Inside Laibon's hut it was dark. Lekai bent low as he entered the hut and then crouched and waited as his eyes adjusted.

The air was thick with the odors of vegetables cooking with garlic and cloves. In the far corner a blackened pot sat on a bed of coals, and a stew simmered in it; the smell lingered and mixed with the older, more dangerous scents. Lekai picked out *Acacia nilotica* and wondered if his seer was simply adding the plant to his stew for flavoring, or if he intended to boil down the roots to access the special—magical—properties. Hanging from pegs throughout the hut were herbs and satchels; a peg by the door held a cow's tail.

The low fire lit the inner framework of the hut: built to a height of four feet, the interior frame resembled a lobster-pot's ribbed structure; with a layer of grass set down over the ribs. A final layer of cow dung had been mixed with earth and smoothed over the entire structure making it weather resistant.

After a while he could make out the elderly seer sitting in a corner.

Laibon's wrinkled skin was covered in a thin layer of white powder. Over his shoulder he wore a rough tunic made from cow hide. His head was shaved and his chin was adorned by a light beard which had turned white over the years.

Lekai stood before him, his head bowed in respect.

"Greeting, Laibon," said Lekai, "I came as soon as I received your summons."

He hesitated before added, "My men are waiting outside as well; they would not stay away."

Laibon chuckled. "You are a good apprentice, Lekai, and they know it. After our discussion you can tell them of the approaching dangers."

Lekai looked at the ground nervously.

In a soft voice he said, "Laibon, you said I must go on this journey alone. My men do not understand this."

The Great Laibon shook his head.

"Not alone, Lekai. Not alone."

Then he added, "But I have looked into the future; any Maasai who leave with you will not return. Your helper must not be Maasai."

Laibon then gestured for Lekai to sit by his side.

But Lekai remained standing. "But if this help is not from one of my brothers than who could it be?"

Again, Laibon chuckled. "You will be helped by a white man, and of course, by Kiboko."

Lekai look puzzled.

"A *wazungu*?" he asked. "How can a white man know our ways? How could he help me?"

The old seer patted the ground by his side, and when Lekai had finally sat down, Laibon leaned forward and touched Lekai's head. He whispered, "Everyone has a lesson to teach. Do not worry, I have seen it."

He smiled at Lekai's distraught expression. "A blind sheep sometimes stumbles into a pool of water."

Laibon's words were echoing in Lekai's ears as he watched the animals hovering just outside the circle of light cast by the fire at the campsite. He peered into the shadows and then uttered a low growl that sounded exactly like a lion.

A zebra replied with a high-pitched bark of warning, and a frantic clattering of hooves ensued.

Lekai smiled as he grabbed another branch from the pile he had collected earlier and began breaking it down to smaller fuel.

Chapter Four

The Great Migration

*T*he first thing Peter noticed when he woke up the next morning was that the ground seemed to be vibrating. The second thing was that his face was covered with a fine layer of dust.

All night he'd listened to the commotion; although none of the animals tried to cross the river once it was dark. Still, he knew he camped in the middle of what had to be thousands of animals, and through the night their numbers had grown.

He stepped out of his sleeping bag and shook out his boots. He'd slept in his jeans, knowing he might have to move quickly if anything happened. Using a hand kerchief and a water bottle he wiped his face clean while he tried to glimpse the river.

Lekai had risen with him and stood by his side.

Simon rose as well, and nodded to them when they indicated the view point. As soon as the sun had risen the commotion had started as large numbers of animals gathered on the far shore, and within minutes it was almost deafening.

They walked to the spot where they could see the crossing, and with each step the sound grew louder. Although the riparian growth obscured any views of the herds on the plains, every bit of shoreline they could see was crowded with hoofed animals.

Peter looked down and saw that the ones in the front had spotted the crocodiles and were doing everything possible to keep out of the water. They stomped defiantly, and snorted, but with each movement they lost their footing and they were forced further into the water.

Once across the river the grass was lush and green, and the vast numbers sensed only that, not the ravenous crocs in the river. Hunger had started them on this migration, and with the end in sight the massive herds of wildebeest, impala and zebra would not be put off. They pawed the ground restlessly, stirring up great clouds of dust.

Lekai and Peter watched the scene; the tension building as the sky lightened. Meanwhile Simon organized their gear: taking the kettle off the fire and pouring coffee into a thermos; stowing their sleeping bags and putting out the fire.

He walked over once and looked down at the standoff.

Simon blew on his steaming coffee and asked, "How much longer?"

"They will all be swimming soon," answered Lekai.

As if on cue, one of the wildebeest in the front slipped and sank underwater. It only rose for a few seconds before a crocodile locked onto its head and rolled out of sight. Its legs kicked madly and then they disappeared as well.

A dozen wildebeest took advantage of the distraction and tried to make it across the river, the crocs went for them, but their movement had set off a signal and now the herd surged forward as one.

Soon hundreds of animals were crossing at once and the crocodiles were forced to the outskirts where they still slaughtered recklessly.

Once across, the animals looked beaten as they slowly marched up the bank and by the Land Cruiser. The bright light of day lit them up and their exhaustion was evident.

The noise and dust was overwhelming.

"I told you they would come," shouted Lekai.

The boy nodded enthusiastically.

"You sure did."

After a while they went back to the campsite where they could talk. Simon sipped his coffee, and then checked to make sure the coffee pot had cooled sufficiently before stowing it in a crate in the back of the Land Cruiser.

Lekai playfully grabbed Peter's shoulder and said, "I think I am with you too much. Last night I dreamt I was a white boy. I was Lekai, but he was white."

The Maasai took some white ash from the fire and smeared it over his forehead.

He continued, "And in this dream the Earth swallowed me. The great Earth ate me and I lay in his belly and felt his hunger as he growled."

Peter looked into Lekai's eyes and asked, "What happened?"

Lekai smiled.

"I said, 'God does not eat mankind' and so I was not eaten. But I do not understand why he rumbled so loudly."

He held Peter's stare and added, "Such a fearful sound."

Simon noticed that the numbers of animals on their side had grown and they were now overflowing. It was only a matter of time before they were overrun, and their fire was now out.

"We better get while the gettin' is good," he said to Peter.

As they climbed into the Land Cruiser Peter excitedly told him about Lekai's dream.

"Lekai dreamt he was a white boy."

Now, a bit shier, Lekai added, "It is a dream I have had before. Laibon says it is a face I will wear."

He made a gesture that encompassed all around him.

"The dreaming I will leave for Laibon." With a grin he added, "After all, I am only an apprentice—not a seer."

Peter watched his new friend with pride.

"Not yet," he said, smiling.

Simon put the land cruiser in gear and slowly cut the wheel into the animals as they tiredly passed. He had to honk the horn a few times, but most were still traumatized by the crossing and wanted only to get out of his way.

Within a few minutes they were away from the river and on a dirt track that led to the far side of the valley.

At a vista where they could look back at the river Simon pulled over and took out his thermos. He poured a cup and offered it to Lekai who accepted it, took a small sip, and then returned it.

Lekai pointed at Simon and said, "I see you know the Maasai ways — you know to offer me before you take."

"Excuse me?" said Peter.

Lekai looked blank for a moment. Then he explained, "We Maasai, we do not eat or drink alone, and when you are with someone you always offer him first."

He looked at Simon.

"How do you know to do this?"

Simon laughed.

"I do a lot of work in the game reserves in southern Africa," he explained. "There are a lot of different tribes that I come into contact with, but many of the customs are similar."

Lekai then took a long gourd that was tied around his waist and offered it to Simon.

Simon eyed it suspiciously.

He asked, "Is that milk? You know, *Kule*?"

When Lekai answered, "No," Simon thanked him, but refused the gourd. Lekai opened and took a long drink.

A smile spread across Lekai's reddened lips as he added, "It is *osarge*, it is blood. There is milk too, but maybe too much blood for you."

Peter's eyes grew, "You drink blood?

Simon put the Land Cruiser in gear and started driving again.

Peter was still lost on the concept of drinking blood.

Finally he asked, "Don't you feel like a bat?"

Simon looked uncomfortable and said, "Peter!" but Lekai smiled wider, showing reddened teeth.

"Blood is life," said Lekai, "the life of our herds, which passes into our body and gives us strength."

Lekai thought for a minute before adding, "And yes, in some ways the Maasai are like bats."

Lekai turned to Simon, "How many cattle do you own?"

Simon replied, "I'm afraid I don't own any."

A little embarrassed, Lekai asked another question.

"And how many children do you have?"

Simon smiled, "There is only Peter."

Looking at Peter, the Maasai said, "It is good you have him, because without him you would be very poor."

"What do you mean?" asked Peter.

Lekai explained, "A man's wealth is determined by how many cows and children he has. If you have many of one, but none of another, you are still considered poor."

"Is that why the Maasai were always such good cattle thieves?" asked Peter.

Lekai leaned forward, laughing hard and snapping his fingers. "Oh, so you have heard of this?" he asked.

The dirt road was smooth and as Simon drove he listened to their conversation.

Peter said, "In school we were taught that the British were afraid of the Maasai, but were often brought into conflicts because they were so good at stealing their cattle."

The warrior held up his hand in defense.

"We steal nothing! I was taught by my elders that God gave us all the cattle on earth."

"All the cattle on the entire planet?" asked Peter skeptically, but with a smile.

"Yes," said Lekai as he grinned back. "So we do not steal, we only taking back what is rightfully ours."

Simon pulled over again around noon and went through some of the supplies in the back. He returned with a sack that contained several plastic bags filled with jerky.

"Most of this is kudu," he said, "but there is a little impala mixed in."

He tore off a piece and gave it to Lekai, then tore off another and offered it to Peter.

"The South Africans always have the best dried meat," said Lekai.

"Well, I won´t take all the credit." said Simon. "The spices we use were introduced by the Dutch sailors on their way back from Indonesia—they always stopped at Cape Town on their way through."

They chewed quietly.

Peter asked, "Where is the belly of the Earth?"

Lekai grabbed his own stomach and laughed.

"Here!" he shouted.

Confused, Peter asked, "So what does it mean when your belly speaks to you?"

Now Lekai turned serious, as if a realization had sobered him.

"It means you must do something."

Chapter Five

Kakuta

*L*ater, they were making good time, when Lekai suddenly called for Simon to stop. He'd been looking to their left and as soon as they stopped he hopped out and walked to a cluster of bushes. Peter had seen a flash of something red in the bushes—something that hadn't looked like an animal.

Aside from a few acacia trees and the bushes the area was empty—just swaying yellow grass. About five hundred feet away several baboons watched them curiously, but they came no closer.

From within the bushes Peter heard a branch crack, as if whatever was in there was trying to climb deeper into the cover. Peter joined Lekai, curious to see what he'd spotted.

They stood motionless; but while they watched the bush remained still. Adrenaline raced through Peter's veins and he felt his heart pounding.

A white-bellied lourie called out with its warning, "Go away, go away."

Initially, Simon had thought Lekai had needed to relieve himself, but when he saw he took one of his spears with him he climbed out of the Land Cruiser and moved to join him.

Lekai slowly stepped closer to the bush, holding the spear ready in anticipation. As his right arm stretched behind his head, his left pointed forward with the war club held tightly.

He appeared unafraid and focused.

Just as the muscles of his arm tensed a scream erupted from the bush and a young boy jumped out.

Lekai instantly recognized his younger brother, Kakuta, and in anger threw his spear anyway — it landed inches from Kakuta's feet.

He held his hand up flat, motioning for Simon to relax.

"He is my younger brother, Kakuta," said Lekai.

The boy was around twelve and dressed in a *kanga*, a one-piece, red garment. His hair was short and his earlobes had not yet been elongated.

Lekai threatened him with the shaft of his spear.

He yelled at the boy, "You should not be here!"

He stomped the ground in anger and shouted.

"This is taboo; you defy Laibon!"

Kakuta stood his ground defiantly.

"You should not be alone," he shot back. "You know this. We are blind without you, brother."

Fighting back tears, he added, "You are our eyes."

Lekai knelt down and hugged him tightly. He took the boy's hand and put it on his heart. Then he made Kakuta look into his eyes and spoke to him softly.

Kakuta nodded, but before he departed he repeated his warning.

"You should not be alone."

When Kakuta had disappeared Lekai turned to Simon and Peter. His expression was distraught and Peter sensed the encounter had shaken him.

"He is right, I am their seer," said Lekai. "And I fear that by leaving them, I will make them vulnerable."

Peter tried to help. "But they have each other."

The Maasai shook his head.

"They have only the belief in our brotherhood. If that fades, then they are worse than alone."

"Is there no one else they could turn to in your absence?" asked Simon.

Lekai explained, "When we are young we are assigned to a *moran*. The *moran* I belong to includes all the boys I know that are near my age."

He looked at Peter, "The bond between us is very strong."

Lekai fumbled for words, "It is stronger than a brother."

"What do you have to do to get in? Is there an initiation?"

Lekai nodded, "As a young boy I was sent out with the calves and lambs. I could just walk, but even young boys cannot stay with the women who clean and cook. I learned to take care of the animals, and of myself. The older men gave me beatings to test my courage and endurance."

He winced as he continued, "Boys become men in the *Eunoto* ceremony. The worst part is *emorata*.

He picked up his short Maasai sword and made a quick flicking motion by his crotch.

As Peter crossed his legs, Lekai added, "The elders do it with a sharpened knife, and through the operation you must endure everything in silence."

Confused, Peter asked, "Why?"

Lekai explained, "Because expressions of pain bring dishonor."

Peter sat back and admired the proud bearing of the warrior, and he wondered how much pain he could handle before he would break the silence.

They drove through the rolling hills of the Maasai Mara for most of the day, but a few times they stopped when the road skirted a water hole, or something of interest.

At the first water hole they stopped at they spotted a herd of impala feeding amongst the tree trunks that sprawled to the river's edge. The gazelles looked delicate and skittish as they fed; often pausing and glancing around before they resumed grazing.

With their heads deep in the grass, Peter watched the dark curve and the points of their horns as they floated by. One stopped to lick its golden flank and caught sight of the Land Cruiser for the first time.

It barked a warning, and they all rallied together, startled, stamping their hooves and snorting at them.

Soon they quieted down again and Simon continued driving.

The second time they stopped it was because the pond they were passing appeared overflowing with life. After the rains came great hatchings of insects and the surface of the pond was dark with their droning. This place was far from the river, but it was full of food and now it attracted birds from all over.

The shore was lined with marabou storks who patiently patrolled the shallows on stilt-like legs; and behind them the emerald colored reeds were filled with numerous tiny birds that zipped around in the wind so quickly that Peter had a tough time following them with his eyes.

Sand-pipers and doves swooped over them, and closer to shore Peter spotted a few guinea fowl searching the shoreline.

While they watched Simon went into the back of the vehicle and opened the cooler. From it he produced some fried chicken which he offered to Lekai and Peter.

Lekai declined, but Peter took a drumstick.

In the center of the pond several Egyptian geese quacked, and were responded to by a large hippo that retreated to the far end of the pond when the Land Cruiser pulled up.

Peter stood in the back to get a better view.

He took a bite, and was about to say something when suddenly a large hawk—or kite—dropped out of the sky and snatched it from him.

It happened so quickly that he hadn't been able to respond. In fact, when he looked at his hand he saw that he still held the bone and the kite had simply grabbed the meat and flown off.

Lekai took a swipe at the departing bird, but it had been too fast.

Simon examined the hand, but found no damage.

"You were lucky," said Lekai with a smile.

Late in the afternoon Lekai announced that they were getting close. He directed Simon to a group of low hills, but they stopped short when they spotted a dead lioness in the dirt road. They got out and inspected the carcass.

Lekai sadly looked down at the body that was covered in bullet wounds.

Simon said, "These wounds were caused by military weapons. Who would do this?"

Lekai's face was angry as he answered, "Only Red Beret kills this way."

Simon looked closer at the underbelly of the lion and observed, "She was lactating as well; I bet there's a cub somewhere close."

He turned to Lekai. "How do you know Red Beret did this?"

Lekai looked away in disgust.

"This man," stated Lekai, "Red Beret, he kills only for fun; he does not take trophies."

Peter scanned the area and suddenly darted toward a small form a few yards away, half covered in dirt. It was a lion cub.

Simon followed him and examined the cub, checking for a heartbeat and then internal injuries once he'd found that it was alive.

"He seems to be breathing," said Simon.

To Peter he said, "Get the small wire cage from the back of the Land Cruiser."

While Peter ran off Simon wet the cats face and it stirred. They placed it in the wire cage and secured it in the back of the vehicle.

"We'll examine him tonight; he's too young to be on his own."

While Simon climbed in the front seat, Peter eyed the cub.

"Hey," exclaimed Peter, "one of its paws is all white."

"Not the best birthmark for a hunter," said Simon.

Peter gave him a confused look and he added, "Anything that makes a predator stand out isn't good."

Soon Simon pulled over by a cluster of thorny bushes that offered a little shade. The cub was coming around and Peter managed to get it to drink some water while Simon and Lekai walked the perimeter of their camp looking for snakes or other dangers.

Lekai returned with wood for a fire and said, "When the sun touches the land, Kiboko will be near. We will wait."

Simon was examining the cub when the Maasai noticed that Peter was getting sun burned and draped one of the sheets of his *shuka* over one of the bushes, creating a shade spot

"Laibon has seen things that only *Enkai Narock* can understand," said Lekai. "He is the God who is black; the good and kind God."

Lekai took a small bag from his side and held it up for Peter to see.

He said, "This is the *Eye of Enkai*; Laibon has given it to me as an aid in my trail. It is a great honor for without it even the Great Laibon cannot see the future."

Lekai then handed the *Eye of Enkai* to Peter who took it, but didn't dare open it.

"The keepers of this eye have witnessed great visions," continued Lekai. "My ancestors told of the coming of the white man. Many times Laibon has saved our warriors from defeat, and more importantly, he has saved our cattle."

He added respectfully, "The *Eye of Enkai* is large."

Lekai became quiet as he collected his thoughts. Peter sat respectfully, waiting for him to continue. Simon carefully rolled the cub over to examine its stomach and it let out a pathetic little meow.

"I fear for my brother, Kakuta," Lekai said.

"Laibon has told me he has seen my return, so I know it to be true. Today I promised Kakuta that I would return: it has been foreseen."

The Maasai stood suddenly and began pacing.

"But Laibon warned that they might not know my face when I returned. What does this mean? Why will they not know me?"

He paced some more, and then turned to Peter.

"We Maasai call God *Enkai*, but we believe God has two faces. In my daily prayers I talk to *Enkai Narock*, the Black God who is kind."

His face grew stern. "But if in the future I see trouble for my friend, Kiboko, then I will pray to *Enkai Nanyokie*. He is the Red God who is vengeful in nature."

He stared into Peter's eyes, "If anyone hurts Kiboko I will be vengeful."

The Maasai reached by his waist and untied a small package and said, "Tonight I will eat a special meal Laibon has prepared for me, and when I do I will see what path *Enkai* has set before me. I will step into the spirit world, the world of the dead."

Simon had been checking on the cub. He now approached them and handed Lekai a jug of water.

"When I walked our camp perimeter I found several other dead animals. We'll do our best to help your friend," said Simon. "Red Beret must be stopped."

Lekai pondered this and then said, "Maybe. The will of *Enkai* cannot be pushed. It is for him to decide."

"Don't worry, Lekai," said Peter. "We'll help you."

The Maasai nodded.

"It is strange to have a *wazungu* for a friend. All the whites I met before were missionaries; they did not like my words."

With a grin he added, "Not at all."

"And what words did you use?" Simon asked.

With a grin Lekai shouted, "Keep your good book!"

41

Chapter Six

Kiboko

The sky was red and orange, full of slanting rays and late afternoon sunshine, and in this light the animals mellowed. By the Land Cruiser a covey of guinea-fowl scratched in the dust, and in the distance two giraffes slowly moved through the bush.

Lekai had walked off and returned with a handful of some green plants. He glanced at the fading sun and looked around expectantly, turned his head and tilted it slightly. His ears seemed to have picked up something that Peter could not yet hear. .

Suddenly, Peter heard it, too. From the silence a powerful sound emerged: the scraping of padded feet as they slid over dry ground; twigs snapping, brush being whipped aside. Peter thought in alarm of a runaway steam train.

Onward it came, a thundering rhythm growing louder and louder. A loud snort gave the noise a direction, and then a giant horn emerged through the brush.

Peter's heart stopped as he saw a massive black rhinoceros heading directly at them. Its momentum made Peter's blood freeze, even at a distance of a hundred feet.

With a scream, Peter dove under the Land Cruiser. Simon jumped onto the seat, gasping.

Lekai didn't move. He simply smiled and called out: "Kiboko!"

The rhino lowered its head to charge, opening the view to a cloud of dust in his wake.

When he was only a few feet away Lekai nimbly jumped to the side and let the great beast rush past.

The rhino came to a stop and the dust obscured everything. Only after it settled could they see where the beast was. It turned and faced him again from only a few feet away. Its eyes were peaceful and held neither anger nor fear. It snorted through its flared nostrils and shook its massive head from side to side the great horn cutting through the air above Lekai's head.

Then it stepped forward and Lekai touched the horn. He laughed and said, "You still move like a hippo."

He scratched the rhino gently behind its ears as he whispered greetings. Then he took the green herbs he'd collected earlier and offered them to the animal.

While the rhinoceros chewed, Lekai spoke to it in a soft voice.

Peter watched from below the land cruiser, his jaw dropped.

It appeared that the rhino was actually listening to Lekai's words and Peter wished he could understand them.

Finally, Lekai bid the animal farewell; but it remained motionless with a questioning look in its tiny dark eyes.

"Go," said Lekai and pointed east. Kiboko remained motionless. Lekai began to shout at the beast and waved his arms in a shooing gesture. Kiboko instead turned his horn downward and dug up the ground, then turned and lumbered toward a clearing that lay about a quarter mile away and slightly below them — to the west.

Simon and Peter came up behind Lekai as he watched the rhino walk away.

Simon said, "I take it that was the friend you've been talking about."

Lekai's elongated earlobes shook as he spoke.

"His name is Kiboko—I tease him because the word means hippo. It was my friendship with him that first attracted Laibon to me."

He looked at Peter and said, "Laibon says I pick strange friends."

"With all the poaching that goes on here I'm surprised he's still alive," said Simon.

"Red Beret is no poacher," said Lekai. "He does not take trophies, not even tusks or horns."

Simon shook his head sadly and said, "There used to be black rhinos all over Kenya, but in the last ten years over ninety percent of them have been wiped out."

He added, "At the conference I just attended they estimated there were less than three hundred of them left in the country."

"All the more reason for us to save Kiboko," said Peter, trying to be positive.

Both Simon and Lekai looked at him with somber expressions.

That night, Simon, Peter and Lekai sat by the fire. They'd unpacked a few things and set up camp, but opted for sleeping in the open. Bats were flitting through the sky above, cutting in front of the stars that lay scattered across the sky like countless diamonds pinned to a black tarp.

Not far away a hyena called out with its eerie laughter. It sounded lonely—and surprisingly human—in the quiet night.

The Maasai nodded in the direction of the laughter.

"There is *Ondilili*. He will eat almost anything!"

He thought for a moment.

"But I do not think he would eat Red Beret."

Peter looked up at the stars. "Why not? Wouldn't they eat a human?"

Lekai laughed. "A human, yes, but maybe not any human. Animals can tell something bad when they come upon it."

"Even if they were starving?" asked Peter.

Lekai shook his head. "If a corpse is rejected by the scavengers it is because there is something wrong with it."

Lekai peered into the darkness around them: Then he spat into the night and said, "Who could not see the evil in Red Beret?"

Again, the hyena called out.

Lekai perked up and said, "They laugh when they get their food; eating makes them happy. In this way they are like the Maasai."

One or two hyenas were always near the outskirts of their camp, hovering in the shadows; Peter watched with distrust whenever one passed by with its loping gait.

"Do not worry," said Lekai, "they are only curious. They have much to eat and will stay away. It is Red Beret you should worry about."

The fire crackled and Lekai offered Simon a snort of his snuff, but he declined.

"You do not smoke tobacco either?" Lekai asked.

"No," answered Simon, "I stopped when I left the army."

"When was that?" asked Lekai.

"A few years before this one was born," said Simon as he grabbed Peter by the neck and affectionately shook him.

Lekai fell silent and stirred the fire.

His eyes reflected the glowing coals. "If Red Beret is near then none of us are safe."

Simon sighed and walked to his sleeping bag. He took off his boots, laid his jacket over them and climbed in. He rolled on his side and looked at Lekai.

"I'll do my best," said Simon, "but I am no longer a man of violence."

Lekai nodded, "Laibon has said I will be helped by a *wazungu*, maybe it is you."

Simon sat up and stared at Lekai for a long minute. "Let's get some sleep and we can make a plan in the morning."

The Maasai nodded, "First I must make the preparations Laibon has set for me." Pointing at a nearby hill he added, "I will go there so I do not disturb you."

He motioned for Peter to follow, and they walked to the top of the grass-covered hill.

Chapter Seven

The Eye of Enkai

When they reached the top of the hill Peter saw that Lekai had already gathered some firewood and built a ring of stones. He'd brought along a burning torch that flickered wildly in the wind; he placed it in the pit and started to break up the branches he'd collected.

He blew into the embers for several minutes until the flames took and spread with a growing crackle. Smoke rose from the burning wood and spiraled up into the night sky.

Lekai took one of his spears and planted it in the ground. He tied a short spear perpendicular to the main spear, added a bundle of yellow grass for a hair piece and draped a short toga over it — another Maasai scarecrow.

Peter said, "I saw you make this before. Why do you do it?"

Lekai examined his creation as he explained, "Laibon said to make this man so I am not alone. His name is Peter."

"You named it after me?" he asked excitedly.

Lekai gravely answered, "No. Laibon told me this name before I saw you. Peter is Maasai in his heart. Laibon has spoken of his coming."

The young warrior then looked down at the ground and Peter sensed his uncertainty when he said, "I do not know how he will help."

The scarecrow fluttered in the wind.

Lekai continued, "Do not worry. We may relax tonight because Peter watches over us."

As if to reassure himself, Lekai stared up at the night sky.

Then he held up the *Eye of Enkai*.

"You know this bag is very sacred to my village. I want you to hold it for me tonight when I enter the spirit world. You will know I am there when my body starts to shake.

"Peter took the *Eye of Enkai* reluctantly, almost afraid to hold it. "Maybe my dad should keep it for you," he said.

Lekai shook his head.

"No, Peter. This burden is yours."

Lekai faced the fire. He used a combination of red ocher and ash from the fire to cover his skin and he was now decorated as a warrior; the body paint made his limbs appear to be moving in the flickering light of the fire—even when he was motionless. His hair was plaited under another layer of ocher.

In the darkness, Peter thought he looked fiendish.

Lekai poured some water in one of the aluminum cups that Simon had packed and placed it over the coals. He took a root out of his leather pouch, broke it up and placed in the cup.

While it cooked he sat silently.

Eventually he stirred the concoction and took a sip.

His grimace told Peter something of the taste, but Lekai smiled as he sipped again, saying, "This tea is a gift from Laibon."

He looked around confidently. "It will make me fearless on my journey."

His eyes now burned with a strange energy, and his face quivered.

The Maasai scarecrow hovered in the night air above them, looking alive in its movements. Peter was edgy and it kept pulling his attention away from the fire, as if it were about to come to life.

Lekai took the *Eye of Enkai* from Peter and opened it. He scooped up the stones and let them fall through his fingers, one at a time.

And then, just as the last stone was about to slip through his fingers, he tightened his grip and held this one firmly.

For some time he sat silently, in a trance.

Suddenly, Lekai opened his hand and with a fearful look stared at the stone. Then he dropped it back in the bag. He handed the *Eye* to Peter.

Peter placed the *Eye of Enkai* by his side as Lekai closed his eyes and started drawing slow, deliberate breaths.

"I have seen the future through the stones, but I have only begun the journey that Laibon has intended," he mumbled in a voice that sounded very distant.

Lekai's breathing quickened. He started to sweat and began convulsing. Peter grabbed his friend by the waist and Lekai's eyes shot open.

"He would kill my friend," whispered Lekai. "He would defy the anger of *Enkai Nanyokie*, the red god."

Lekai tried to stand but Peter was worried he would hurt himself and held him down gently.

"He is not *Enkai*!" Lekai exclaimed. "I will not let him take Kiboko! He does not deserve this evil!"

Lekai fell back and his eyes rolled inward. He mumbled a few words in *Maa*, Peter could not make out.

Peter cradled his head and they remained like that for some time.

From their hill Peter could see his father sleeping below. Simon was curled up between the land cruiser and a low fire. He hadn't stirred, and again Peter wondered if he should get him. The thought of Red Beret, the talk of prophecies, Lekai, unconscious in his lap—all this overwhelmed Peter, and he yearned for his father's guidance.

But Lekai lay in a dream-like trance, occasionally mumbling, and Peter didn't dare to leave his side.

Suddenly the Maasai bolted upright and looked into Peter's eyes. "*Elala onu Ai,*" he stated, "The *Eye of Enkai* is large."

His eyes were wide open, but his gaze appeared turned inward. Then he scanned the horizon and seemed to focus.

He said, "You must drop your spear if you go for the lion's tail."

He looked around, but from his expression Peter knew he was in the spirit world.

Lekai whispered, "He will go for Red Beret, there will be no stopping him."

And then, with panic entering his voice, he added, "If you do not return the *Eye of Enkai* when it is time the tribe will remain blind."

Then he was silent as he lay back, closed his eyes and fell into a deep sleep.

Peter tucked his toga around him, monitored Lekai´s even breaths for a while, and then walked down to the campsite.

Chapter Eight

Red Beret

*L*ekai awoke and stared up at the predawn sky and saw there were long traces of red in it, as if smeared by a bloody hand.

He looked around, hoping for another sign.

An owl hooted once, and then remained silent.

By the edge of the camp a jackal was quietly looking for scraps.

He tried to listen harder, the way Laibon had taught him, but when he heard the partridge and the doves awaken he knew he'd delayed his departure too long.

Slowly, he stood and brushed himself off, and then walked off to the west, away from the rising sun.

Peter and Simon woke to the sound of gunfire; in the cool morning air the report was sharp and clear. They jumped to their feet and looked west in the direction of the shots.

In the clearing below them—the one Kiboko had headed for the night before—an army jeep was stirring up great clouds of dust. Four soldiers stood in the back, firing at several impala that were scampering into the savannah, while the driver swigged on a bottle.

He laughed at the feeble attempt the delicate animals were making to survive and tried his best to run them over before the others could shoot them.

In the front sat a white officer wearing a red beret. His face was mean and hardened.

Peter could clearly hear him shout at the driver.

"Turn around!"

The driver leaned hard on the wheel and headed back. An impala with a gunshot wound on its hind leg tried to limp away, but the driver ran it down.

As a gust of wind momentarily cleared the dust, Peter and Simon could see that the jeep was actually circling a rhino.

"Kiboko," Peter whispered, breathlessly.

Simon turned to get his boots but Peter couldn't look away. He watched in horror.

One of the soldiers raised his weapon to fire, but Red Beret grabbed the barrel firmly and yanked the gun out of the man's hands.

With a sinking feeling in his stomach, he saw how he aimed the gun at Kiboko and fired as the jeep passed the beast—a second later he heard the sound of the gun.

The men cheered as the rhino bellowed in pain.

Peter screamed and bolted barefoot for the clearing before Simon could stop him. "Peter! Stop!" Simon yelled and started after him, but then stopped and quickly slipped on his boots.

He turned to pursue and soon noticed blood in Peter's tracks. The thorny acacia branches that littered the ground were ripping his feet open.

Simon cursed himself for taking too much time with his boots and ran faster to catch his son. His lungs burned, but he had yet to catch a glimpse of Peter in the bush ahead.

In the clearing Red Beret was directing the jeep to go at the rhino again, but this time he was facing an angry, wounded rhinoceros.

Kiboko pawed the ground as his eyes searched the clearing.

54

As soon as the rhino spotted the jeep he charged.

The driver tried to steer away, but the rhino's shoulder smashed into the back right end of the jeep, projecting one soldier into the air.

The force of the impact threw the rhino's head up and its horn impaled a second soldier who'd been standing in the back. Kiboko shook the man's body off roughly, and then turned away, trampling the dying soldier in the dust.

The jeep veered into the bush and crashed.

Red Beret stood on the front seat and turned to locate the rhino; his face was bloody from a gash on his forehead. His eyes grew wide as Kiboko came charging straight for him.

He yelled at the driver, whose head was tilted at an awkward angle as if he was inspecting the pistol he wore in a shoulder harness. The man was dead.

Taking his horrified gaze from the driver, Red Beret sighted in on the rhino.

He shot once and the beast suddenly stopped.

He lined up his next shot.

And then he froze and stared at a tall figure coming into the clearing. The two remaining soldiers who'd been clinging to the vehicle didn't see the Maasai warrior. Their attention was focused on Kiboko, and they cheered when the animal sank to its knees.

Red Beret froze as he watched Lekai take two wide steps and throw his long spear.

For an instant it disappeared in the air.

Then one of the soldiers grabbed his chest and fell out of the jeep. The other spun around toward Lekai and raised his gun when Lekai's war club came down on his skull.

Red Beret raised his pistol to fire at point blank range, but the empty gun only clicked.

He turned white and his hand trembled.

The Maasai approached slowly and stared at Red Beret.

"You are not *Enkai*," he said.

Red Beret pulled the trigger again, and again it only clicked. Lekai knew that the man was considered by many to be a man beyond fear. Yet he seemed stricken with such dread in Lekai's presence that he could not move.

At the far end of the clearing Peter appeared. With bloody feet he stumbled forward.

He saw Lekai, and Red Beret's pointed gun, and he screamed, "Watch out, Lekai!"

Lekai turned and looked at Peter.

He smiled, and in that instant Red Beret grabbed the dead driver's pistol and fired into Lekai's chest.

Somehow he remained standing, a look of disbelief on his face as his smile faded. He slowly turned to face Red Beret.

Red Beret then raised his gun to Lekai's head.

He said, "As far as you're concerned I am God."

He fired again and Lekai dropped.

Peter let out a wail and fell to his knees.

Red Beret stared at him for a moment, but when he heard Simon shouting a short distance away he grabbed a water jug, and glanced at the three men who lay sprawled on the ground — and the two bodies in the jeep.

"Fucking amateurs," he said as he climbed out of the jeep and headed west on foot.

Simon reached the clearing running just as Red Beret disappeared into the brush. He grabbed Peter who was struggling to go after Red Beret.

"It was my fault!" cried Peter.

Simon hugged his sobbing son to his heaving chest and scanned the area to make sure the killer wasn't just circling them. He picked up Peter and carried him to a sheltered area underneath some bushes.

Then he walked around and looked over the carnage, a hand clutched to his forehead.

He stopped over Red Beret's tracks, heading west. Under the rising sun, Simon's shadow pointed like an arrow in the direction of the killer's escape.

He knelt to examine Lekai, whose eyes glassily stared at the sky. He was dead. The sight of the once proud warrior gripped him and he dropped his head, a wave of grief washing over him.

In a coarse whisper he said, "I'm sorry" as he closed Lekai's eyes and stood again.

Simon's limbs felt like they weighed a thousand pounds as he walked back to Peter who was still sobbing uncontrollably.

The boy was pulling spikes from his feet. They were covered with gashes, caked with dried blood and sand. Simon wondered how he'd managed to run with the big thorns poking into his soles. .

Simon was picking up Peter to carry him back to the campfire and their medical supplies, about a quarter mile away, when they heard Kiboko's anguished bellows. Simon carried Peter toward the jeep and set him by Lekai's body. While Peter sat there staring at the dead Lekai Simon briefly inspected the mangled men that were sprawled around them.

All were dead.

About twenty-five feet away Kiboko lay in the dust. He lifted his head painfully as he desperately heaved for a lungful of air.

Simon approached the rhino and Peter limped along behind him to the side of the rhinoceros.

Kiboko's eyes were dim.

"Do something, Dad!" pleaded Peter.

Helplessly, Simon stroked the rhino's snout. Then Kiboko's great head dropped. His mighty muzzle sunk into the sand, and his eyes went blank.

Peter wailed with grief.

Simon lifted Lekai and laid him against the rhino. Then he picked up Peter and started toward the campsite.

At the edge of the clearing they stopped and looked back on the bloody scene.

Peter blinked through his tears. For a moment it almost seemed to him as if the two friends were merely taking a siesta.

Chapter Nine

Revenge

Simon was cold and focused as he prepared. He reached into one of his bags and pulled out a pistol and stuck it in his belt. He also grabbed a long knife which he strapped to his leg. While he loaded the gun he kept glancing over his shoulder in the direction of Red Beret's tracks.

Upon reaching their camp he had tended to Peter's wounds, and the boy now sat in the front of the Land Cruiser with his head in his hands.

Peter lifted his head and watched his father. "Dad, what are you doing?" he asked, worried by the determined look on his face.

Simon looked directly at his son, but said nothing.

On the hill behind him the Maasai scarecrow fluttered in silence.

The sky above was solid blue without a cloud.

When he had finished his preparations, Simon said quietly to Peter, "You stay put—I'll be back."

Peter began to protest, but his father cut him off.

"Pack the Land Cruiser, put out the fire, and be ready."

It all suddenly hit Peter and Simon placed a hand on his shoulder.

"I'm sorry," said Simon. "It wasn't supposed to go like this. But I can't walk away from it now."

Simon stared in the direction of the mangled jeep, and then beyond. He looked at Peter and the cub in the cage behind them.

"Better let that cub go. I may be a while," said Simon. "Stay put, try to stay off your feet—and no fire!"

With his face set he headed west following Red Beret's tracks.

In the clearing Kakuta stared at his brother's body in disbelief. The sun was high in the sky now and burned on his head and on the back of his neck.

Kakuta had defied Lekai and followed him at a distance. Through the night he had walked, covering close to ten miles. He had just arrived when the shooting began, and had witnessed the event, but just like Simon and Peter, he'd been too far away to help.

His face looked deeply desperate.

He thrust his head up at the sky and yelled, "I curse you, *Enkai*, for taking my brother away! And I curse you, my brother, for breaking your promise of return!"

He looked down at himself and then up at the sky again.

"*Enkai*, hear me now!" he cried. "I curse myself and all that is Maasai, for not preventing my brother's death!"

Kakuta stood motionless for several moments. Then he took off his traditional jewelry and garments. Piece by piece he dropped it all in the sand and then walked off.

Later, Peter sat at the campsite alone. Sunset had come and gone with its soft colors and long shadows. Now he sat in the dark. His throat was parched and although there was a jug of water in the Land Cruiser cab, he hadn't moved. In his mind he replayed his last cry of warning to Lekai, over and over.

Suddenly two gunshots rang out—far off—and then one more.

Peter got up and walked to the cage. He stared at the cub, then opened the door to set it free.

The cub paused and looked at him, unsure of his motives. Peter touched the white paw, careful of the sharp claws. It hopped out of the cage and cried out as it wandered off. Peter felt his heart ache as he realized the cub's mother was dead.

In the dead of night, Peter was sleeping in the front seat of the Land Cruiser. He woke to the sound of something coming closer and peered into the darkness, holding his breath; and then he saw his father staggering toward the Land Cruiser.

Simon was wounded, bleeding from a gash near his ribs that had soaked his shirt with blood. The moonlight showed little detail, but when he opened the Land Cruiser door the interior light showed just how bad it was. Blood had flowed down his leg and soaked his jeans.

Simon winced as he reached for the medical kit and opened it.

Once he found bandages and tape he took off his shirt and lifted his T-shirt. With the shirt he wiped away the blood until he could see a gaping wound on his left side where he'd been nicked by a bullet.

Peter looked ready to pass out and his father paused. "It's not as bad as it looks, but I've lost a lot of blood and we have to get to a hospital."

The boy watched breathlessly as his father quickly applied several bandages to the gash. When Peter looked up at Simon's face he noted how pale he looked and saw that he was now beginning to fumble with the bandage.

"Can you drive, son?" Simon whispered. He had attempted to act calm, but Peter was suddenly hit by a hot pang of dread that they might not make it to a hospital in time.

Peter stared down at his own bandaged feet. There was so much gauze wrapped around them that he could not put on his boots.

All he could think about was saving his father.

Peter slid into the driver's seat and turned the ignition. "What happened?" he asked breathlessly.

"There's no time," slurred Simon as he fell forward into the front seat. "Drive!"

Simon pulled himself up into the seat and steadied himself. He attempted to put on another shirt and groaned as he lifted his arm to put it through the sleeve.

"Peter, I may pass out from blood loss." The boy nodded and put the vehicle into gear.

As Peter drove the dark road he watched Simon stow the pistol and knife in a bag by his side.

Peter noted that the knife had been bloodied.

Blood had already seeped through the bandages and he was now taking in short, labored breaths.

Pressing down on the accelerator, he grimaced, and he did it again when he stepped on the clutch.

Peter ground his way through a few gears but he managed to drive the Land Cruiser. His feet burned with pain, then went numb. He kept glancing worriedly at Simon who had gone quiet.

The moon had set and the headlights showed little more than tall grass lining the dirt track. In the dark hours of the night Peter wondered how many hours from sunrise they were. With the sunrise he knew he would make better time, but it felt like time had stopped and panic crept into his bones as he began to fear they would never make it to help in time.

Were they even going in the right direction? Again and again he cursed himself for not getting directions before his father had passed out.

Simon lay on his side and appeared to be sleeping; the dash lights lit his face with an eerie glow. In the middle of the night his breathing had become shallow, and beads of sweat stood out on his forehead.

When he saw Simon stir he asked, "Dad! Can you talk?"

Simon weakly lifted his head, then stared at his bloody hand and chest in confusion.

"How far are we from the park gate?"

Peter slowed to a crawl as his father painfully straightened up.

Sunrise was still more than an hour away, but the dawn sky had brightened enough for Peter to make out one side of the rift valley wall.

Simon passed a hand over his face and wiped away the sweat.

"You've done well, Peter," he whispered.

Peter stammered, "I...I don't even know where we are. What if I get lost?"

For a moment Simon faded, and Peter thought he was going to pass out again, but then he steadied himself and pointed at the high wall they faced.

"You just follow that wall and go left; the road will take you straight to the gate."

Peter accelerated, and then he asked how much further they had. "I think another few hours," replied Simon.

Seeing the panicked look on his son's face he added, "Don't worry, you'll make better time once it gets lighter out."

Peter nodded.

He looked to the east where the sky was beginning to light up a new day and said, "You know what day it is?"

His father stared at him and weakly answered, "Yeah, I know what day it is—it's been a year."

Suddenly four Maasai warriors appeared in the headlights. They were standing silently along the road. Peter slowed down as he passed them. They were all looking at Simon.

Then they stared at Peter as he slowly passed and he locked eyes with one of them. In those eyes Peter saw a question and he knew it concerned Lekai. It only took one look at Simon and Peter for the Maasai to know that something had gone terribly wrong.

"Those were Lekai's men," said Peter. "We have to tell them what happened."

Simon only moaned weakly and slid back to his side; Peter wondered if he should stop and ask the Maasai for help or just try to get to a hospital.

"Dad?" he said with panic.

One last time his father managed to open his eyes and look at his son.

"Just get me to a hospital, Peter," said Simon.

Then he passed out.

Peter hit the gas and left the Maasai in the dust.

By his side was the *Eye of Enkai* which he had all but forgotten.

Chapter Ten

Safe at Home

*P*eter limped into his room and tossed his bag on the bed. The drive into Nairobi and the stay at the hospital had the feel of a nightmare from which he had awoken back home in Pretoria.

Simon shuffled by in the hallway, and then paused in the doorway. His mid-section was heavily bandaged.

"How you holding out?" he asked with a forced smile.

Awkwardly, Peter unpacked his bag. He wouldn't meet Simon's gaze.

"Okay, I guess."

"We're going to be alright," said Simon.

"Yeah, we will, but what about the Maasai? What about Lekai's men? I have to go back and explain what happened. He died because of me."

Simon slowly moved to Peter's bed and painfully lowered himself onto it. He motioned for Peter to join him and, cautiously, he extended an arm and put it around his son and hugged him.

"Lekai died fighting for what he believed in. He died a proud death."

Peter shook off his father's arm angrily.

Simon stood.

His eyes pleaded with his son, but he couldn't find the right words.

"I cannot go back, Peter. Do you realize what I did?"

Simon had played that night over and over in his mind. He remembered coming up behind Red Beret and holding a knife to his throat. The man had struggled and fired twice into the air as the knife cut deeply into his neck.

Then, just when he'd thought the poacher dead, the man had spun and fired one last time at his mid-section.

Simon didn't mind his son knowing that he had killed the terrible man, but he couldn't tell him the details—ever. And he knew he'd always be haunted by the vision of Red Beret lying in the sand as the life drained out of him.

Peter sat back down and glanced up at his father.

He looked devastated as he said, "He was my friend."

When Simon left, Peter emptied out the remaining items in his bag. He paused when he saw the *Eye of Enkai*. Carefully he opened it and grabbed a handful of stones, letting them slip through his fingers.

The curtains fluttered, casting crazy shadows.

Peter's mind was filled with images of Lekai reading the stones and talking about life. He heard him discussing Maasai ways and certain quirks concerning the animals they saw.

The stones slowly slipped through his fingers.

He remembered when the Maasai scared him by the river—after his encounter with the buffalo, and then he thought of the first morning he saw him on the hill with the Maasai scarecrow.

With only a few stones remaining in his hand his mind continued to drift, and he heard drums beating and dogs howling.

Suddenly he looked around, as if he expected to find someone else in the room. He held one last stone in his hand.

Without looking at it he dropped it back in the bag.

"Is anyone there?" asked Peter.

The wind outside died down and he lay back on his bed.

Later, Peter was tossing in his sleep fitfully. The wind had picked up again and he dreamt of dark hands rubbing what looked like blood over a body in the blackness of night.

A gust banged the blind against the side of the window. Peter opened his eyes to see Lekai's face, decorated with war paint, staring at him.

Lekai smiled.

He said, "I have been waiting for you, Peter."

Peter screamed as he sat up, waking from the dream.

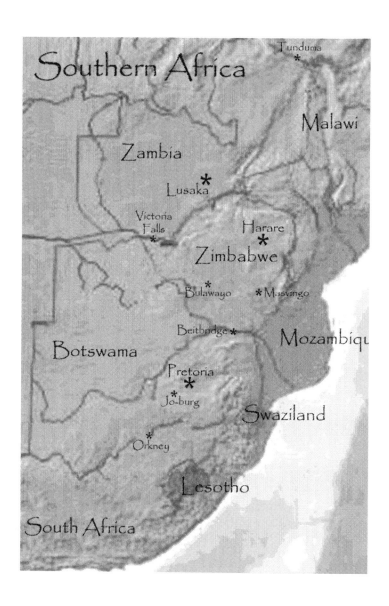

Chapter Eleven

The Belly of the Earth
(1993)

A bare bulb illuminated overhead metal netting, braced with steel to support great weight; it flickered momentarily as a slight vibration passed through the rock.

Beneath, a row of lockers was tucked against the wall and men covered in black dust quietly changed. The men moved slowly, like zombies in a movie, as if the grime on their skin had somehow trapped their souls and prevented them from feeling alive.

By the lockers hung a sink and they each thoroughly washed their face, forearms and hands in it. The water was hot, like everything else in the mine; and it swirled down the drain as dark as black coffee.

Once clean the men revived and grinned; as if the un-obscured view of each others´ faces made them more comfortable around each other. As they dressed to leave for the day their pace quickened. They came from different tribes of southern Africa, but having survived another day in the mine seemed to unite them.

One man made a comment about a quick drink after work, but before anyone could respond they all became subdued when another man appeared.

He was as dark as them, with a hard, lean figure developed under heavy toil—and he was tall.

His skin was streaked with lines of sweat; his dirty face was gaunt; and dust still spilled off his clothes as he passed the lockers and went straight to the sink and turned the faucet on full. Briefly, he stuck his hands under the flow and rubbed them together, then he cupped the water which was tinted grey by the remaining dirt.

But the man lapped up the water as if he had not had any in days.

The other men looked at each other knowingly and quickly collected their things.

He continued to drink as the men around him departed, and finally washed his hands and face thoroughly, dipping his head in the sink.

Behind him, locker doors slammed, and when the other men had left and silence had returned he lifted his face to a small mirror mounted on the wall.

The face that looked back at him was Caucasian, not black. It was young—early twenties—but the expression it wore was aged beyond those easy years.

Peter's blue eyes stared into the mirror, and they didn't like what they saw. He was now twenty-three and no longer a boy. He was dressed like the other men when they'd arrived, but there was something dark about him.

Unlike the other workers, Peter didn't change into clean clothes.

He grabbed his gloves and hard hat and headed back into the mine.

The hallway soon turned into a tunnel and as he walked down it bare bulbs lit up his face. He looked angry.

From a side tunnel two white men approached him. One of them was Christian, a manager in the mine. Christian was in his fifties and for some reason had taken a liking to Peter.

Peter didn't recognize the other man, who appeared overly enthusiastic as he looked over the lockers and changing area, smiling at the workmen that passed by.

Christian wasn't very tall, but he made up for it with attitude. Peter knew he'd worked in the mines all his life and had a natural confidence underground, but if he thought you were slacking, or hesitant in any way to do your job, he could be a hard man to work under.

He slapped his thick hand down on Peter's shoulder.

"Peter, I thought you worked the last shift."

Peter looked sternly at Christian; he knew the man meant him no harm, but he worked in the mines because he liked the solitude. He wasn't there to make friends.

It was easier with the blacks. They avoided him at all costs.

"I'm working a double today."

"Have you lost your mind?" asked Christian. "Get out of here, get some air."

He shook his head. "What's a young buck like you doing down here all the time?"

"Don't worry about me," replied Peter. "I'm just trying to put in some extra time."

Christian gestured to the man by his side.

"This here's Frank. He's doing a story on the mine."

Frank extended his hand.

"I just wanted to say how grateful I was to do this story. I've always wanted to document the terrible plight the black man faces when he goes down into these mines."

Christian held up his hand.

"Hold on there, Frank. Did you say an article on the black man's plight?"

"Yes," said Frank, although the look in Christian's eyes made him uneasy. "I've heard how dangerous the mines are and I'd like to document it."

Christian stroked the stubble on his chin.

"But you don't think it's dangerous for white men?"

Frank sensed that he'd offended Christian.

"Well, I assumed the whites would be in management positions and the blacks would be in the more dangerous jobs."

Christian stared at the ground for a moment and finally looked at Peter.

"What level you working on today, Peter?"

Peter answered, "I'm on level seventy."

This brought a smile to Christians face.

"Seventy! That's the bottom level—almost 8,000 feet underground."

Frank pinched his lips together.

Christian stepped back and pointed at Peter.

"Does he look like a black man to you?" he asked.

Frank meekly shook his head and Christian slapped his side as if he'd just had a great idea.

"You know what I'm gonna do for you, Frank? I'm going to take you down to level seventy to see just how easy a white man has it in this mine."

The reporter blanched at the suggestion.

"I don't see why we have to go down that far. My contact in your office said we'd most likely go no deeper than a few hundred feet."

Christian laughed deeply.

"How can you do an article on the mine if you stay near the surface?"

Frank paused for a minute, and Christian sensed his hesitation.

"That is if you're not afraid."

Now Frank began to squirm as he felt both sets of eyes on him.

"I still don't see how going all the way to the bottom would make a better article."

"Well," began Christian. "You said your article was about the black man's plight, and I want to show you the most dangerous part of this mine and show you that both black and white men work side by side there—I think it's directly related."

Christian then put a hand on Frank's shoulder.

"Like I said, if you're afraid then I understand and we can do something else."

Frank shrugged it off. "Okay, screw it. Let's go."

"Great!" shouted Christian.

As he led them down the tunnel, Christian leaned over to Peter and said, "He'll be with the drill team for two hours. How 'bout you come along when I take him down and then you wait and take him out?"

Peter jerked his head impatiently.

"It's easy work, mate!" said Christian, "And you'd be doin' me a favor—the wife wants me to get out early enough for us to go out to dinner for our anniversary."

Peter closed his eyes in annoyance.

"Thirty years married!" Christian shouted, "Can you believe that?"

Peter nodded slowly.

"Say you'll do it," pleaded Christian. "She likes you—you know she does. She can't stop mentioning you since you came over for dinner."

Peter thought back on the uncomfortable night. The happiness Christian and his wife displayed had tormented him. In his own life, such joy with a companion had been evasive.

"Alright," Peter mumbled.

"Good!" said Christian cheerily as he again slapped a dirty paw on Peter's shoulder.

Christian looked back at the writer, who was trailing a few feet behind and quietly added, "She'll also be relieved to know I was with you today—she thinks you're lucky."

Peter stared at him, dumbfounded.

"Me? Lucky?"

"W...well," stammered Christian, "you do seem to have a sense for danger down below."

Peter looked over some of the black miners they were passing in the tunnel.

"You're all too superstitious."

"Well, my wife certainly is," said Christian. "I'm approaching my thirtieth anniversary with this place as well, and the longer I'm down here, the more worried she gets."

He looked back at Frank again. The reporter was observing the details of the mine shaft. They had left the painted walls and paneled ceilings of the corporation building behind and were descending down several ramps to the underground levels.

"I don't know how to say it, Peter, other than that my wife is worried about me today."

For a brief moment Peter's features softened.

"Don't worry, you'll be fine."

Soon they were greeted by a hot blast of air that left them dry-mouthed. From deep under them they could now hear machinery pounding away; a low vibration in the floor became noticeable.

Christian's face broke into a grin as he looked over at Frank and said, "When we get out of the cage I'll get you set up with safety gear."

Frank nodded nervously and hesitantly asked, "What's the cage?"

Christian laughed and directed them down a tunnel.

"Well, this mine employs over seventy thousand workers. They suit up at stations on this level, and then take the cage down—you'll see it in a minute."

As they walked through the tunnel Christian looked at Peter repeatedly and finally asked, "You still havin' the nightmares?"

Peter looked down.

"Not so much lately. They seem to go away when I'm down here."

Christian laughed. "That's the craziest thing I've ever heard. This place gives even me nightmares."

Christian stopped and looked at Peter.

"You don't look like you're sleeping," he observed. "Now I feel guilty for trying to get you to cover for me. Why don't I do this and you get some sunshine?"

Peter shook his head.

"No, I'm good."

Christian shrugged. "Thirty years, can you believe that? I was your age when I first went underground."

Peter didn't like small talk and Christian had to have sensed it, but he continued anyway as they shuffled down the hallway.

"Of course, there weren't seventy levels then, but I was still scared shitless when I first went down."

They came to an open area with a sign that read, LOADING AREA. Here the tunnel merged with several others, each filled with men, mostly black.

They waited with the others by a large metal cage as men slowly loaded into it. When it was filled to capacity an attendant slid the metal gate into place with a loud screech and the lift rose.

"I guess we'll have to wait for the next one," said Frank with relief.

Christian laughed.

"There are actually three load levels on this lift," said Christian. "Each one holds about fifty men."

To Frank's dismay the lift rose to reveal another level underneath it.

Frank watched the loading of the middle level, horrified. "This looks like something you would move livestock with."

While they slowly shuffled forward another fifty men loaded into the middle level of the lift. As more and more men climbed in the weight set the cage to slowly bouncing and by the time Peter, Christian and Frank were loading into the bottom level with forty black men it was rhythmically rising and dropping by almost a foot.

Frank nervously stepped across the threshold into the bouncing lift, and all eyes were upon him.

Peter noted that Frank had already looked slightly claustrophobic at the changing area, even though that was at surface level and well ventilated. As he now stood in the lift waiting for the gate to be shut his eyes shifted uneasily, and he was breathing heavily.

The warm blast of air that rushed up at them from below felt like it could have come from a dragon's throat, and Frank's expression was that of someone being sent to his death. He'd come to the mine with the intention of doing a good, informative article, but now his only ambition was to make it out alive.

The gate was closed with another loud screech and then the entire structure descended, plummeting downward at a reckless pace.

Frank stood stiffly and his breathing quickened.

Christian cleared his throat and began to tell Frank about the mine. He had to shout over the screeching and groaning of the cage grinding against the supports as it dropped.

"There are seventy levels in this mine; each big enough to drive a large truck through."

All around them silent men were packed shoulder to shoulder. Their eyes were on Peter, who stood silently among them, staring down.

Peter was used to this kind of scrutiny; since his trip to Kenya, ten years ago, the tribal people he'd encountered had looked at him as if he were something primitive and vengeful.

He now appeared tired, but not overly concerned with this strange treatment. He'd grown used to it—even if he didn't understand it. Some days it seemed trivial, other days it really pissed him off.

They looked at him as if he could see through them.

He stared back at the men as Christian spoke.

"These men mine the gold-bearing rock. It is serious business I can assure you. They work so far underground that if there is a cave-in they have little chance of surviving."

The reporter nervously cleared his throat.

"Do we really have to go to the bottom?" he asked in a squeaky voice.

Christian grinned at Peter behind Frank's back.

"Well, you want your story based on the truth don't you?" said Christian. "Heck, if you didn't plan on going to the bottom you might as well have stayed in the parking lot."

"Okay," said Frank as he held his hand up and grabbed Peter's shoulder for support. "This is all just a little much for me. Why don't we start with the cage?"

Christian said, "Well, this lift is suspended over the longest vertical drop on the planet, and only a five-inch metal rope is holdin' us in place."

Frank glared at him.

The weighted cage screeched as it stopped to unload some men. The force of the stop set it bouncing even more and the men jumped off casually as it rose and dropped almost two feet now.

"This bounce is due to the length of cable doled out. If the rope broke now you'd drop seven thousand feet before you hit anything."

Peter eyed him and said, "Come on, Christian, lay off."

But Christian was enjoying himself.

"Oh, come on Peter. I just want Frank to see that we put in the same hard day as everyone else. He don't mind. Do you?"

Frank, wearing a sour face, went to reply but in the hot, dry air couldn't even croak out an answer.

The other workers were now watching the reporter and listened amusedly. They had never seen anyone this far into the mine that wasn't an employee.

Christian continued his lecture. "Many of these men come from tribal lands. They are very primitive."

Peter looked at the worn floorboards of the cage that were now visible as the crowd had thinned.

"They call the bottom of the mine 'the belly of the earth'."

Peter raised his eyes from the floorboards, and noticed that all the remaining miners were now surveying the reporter's reactions.

With a screech they plunged downward again.

"Don't worry, there hasn't been a lift accident in ten years," said Christian.

Sweat was forming around Frank's scowl. He didn't look well.

But Christian was on a roll, "No one survived the last one, of course, and the people who cleaned the wreckage were never the same."

The lift kept dropping like there was no bottom to the earth below them.

Christian suppressed a giggle, adding, "And once you hit the bottom don't forget there are a hundred men standing above us."

They continued to drop—stopping occasionally to unload more men—for the next half hour. The temperature was rising mercilessly.

Huge fans had been installed on some levels to relieve the noticeable lack of oxygen, and when the lift passed them they screamed like giants—each time Frank jumped in panic.

As they mentally prepared themselves, the men in the elevator hardened and their minds focused on the work ahead. This was what had attracted Peter in the first place—this solitude. But today was different. Today he had woken with an unquenchable thirst and a sharp hunger in his stomach.

When they stepped off the lift a densely hot environment embraced them.

Peter looked at the other miners as they set off. There was something wrong, he felt sure of it.

One look at the reporter and it was obvious he believed the descent would only stop when they plunged straight into the hot, molten core of the earth.

Eventually the cage came to a bouncing stop. A sign read: LEVEL SEVENTY.

The men shuffled forward, but Frank elbowed his way out of the elevator like a panicked animal.

Peter murmured, "Thanks a lot, Christian."

"Just tryin' to help," Christian replied.

The cage door slammed shut and the lift ascended up, out of sight—leaving them stranded and in silence. They were now in a room with a sign that read SAFETY AREA.

Frank staggered to a wall of naked, cut rock.

He briefly leaned against it, then jumped and cursed.

"The rock is hot!" he shouted.

Peter walked to a row of lockers and took some gear out of one of them. He handed Frank a hard-hat, jumpsuit, and some gloves.

Frank asked, "Shouldn't I have had this stuff on already?"

Christian laughed.

"Do you really think it would have helped if that cable broke?"

The reporter got to his feet and puffed up his chest.

"You really are a son-of-a-bitch," he spat out while staring into Christian's eyes.

Christian's dirty face broke into a wide grin.

"Now that's more like it!"

He grabbed Frank's shoulder and squeezed it as he added, "I was raised by a tough lot—I had six older brothers. I guess some of their bad habits rubbed off on me. They were a demanding lot and always made me prove myself.

Incredulously, the reporter asked, "This is all some macho test to you?"

For a brief moment Christian became serious.

"Well, yes and no. This is a dangerous place and if you didn't do well in the cage how could I bring you to see a drill team in action?"

The reporter wiped the sweat from his forehead while he steadied his breathing.

Christian stepped back, adjusted his hard hat, and turned on the lamp.

"Listen, mate," he said, "you've got nothing to worry about."

"How's that?" said Frank.

Christian nodded in Peter's direction.

"That kid has a sense for this mine. It's the damndest thing I've ever seen — and I've been down here most of my life."

The color began to come back into the reporter's face as he climbed into the jumpsuit, glancing expectantly at Peter, who was opening another locker.

There was a photo of him with his father posted to the door, and another, older, image of his mother. Inside, hung a change of clothes.

On the shelf above sat a lone leather bag — the *Eye of Enkai.*

Peter took the bag and reached in. He grabbed a handful of stones, and let them slip through his fingers.

When there was only one stone left in his hand he lifted it and examined it.

What he held looked more like a clump of dirt than a stone.

As he stared at it, puzzled, it crumbled away with a puff of dust.

Peter looked up nervously and then put the *Eye* away.

His stomach growled loudly.

"Maybe not the best time for a tour," Peter murmured.

Frank glanced around in alarm.

"What do you mean?" he asked.

Peter zipped up his jumpsuit, put on goggles, and turned on his lamp. Christian was waiting in a small rail car and motioned for both of them to join him.

"Let's go," he said.

"No, wait," Frank said. "What did he mean? What's wrong?"

Christian waved it away.

"Everything is fine, come on."

Frank shook his head.

"No. You said he had a sense for the mine, and he just said this wasn't the best time for a tour."

"Oh, I was just kidding about that," said Christian with a laugh.

"I don't feel so good," he said and crouched down again.

Peter hadn't moved and stood looking at the roof as if he had just discovered something.

Finally he snapped out of it.

"Nothing is wrong, relax," he said. "You stay here while I check things out."

"Sure," he said with an exhale. "I'll be right here."

Peter joined Christian on the rail cart and they started off into the tunnel. A long line of light bulbs scarcely illuminated their way — one solitary bulb about every thirty feet.

Christian put a lot of faith in Peter's hunches, and now even he proceeded cautiously. While they cruised along he stared at the ceiling.

"Looks fine to me down here," he said to Peter, "you're just down on your sleep, huh?"

He let loose a nervous laugh.

"You really shouldn't scare a man on his anniversary."

The rail car rolled on.

"Yes, sir, I'm gonna treat my wife nice tonight. Do you know she didn't even mind when I took off hunting last week?"

He wiped the sweat off his forehead.

"I think she was glad to have a little peace without me snoring next to her."

Christian looked at Peter and added, "Hey, I made some great *biltong* from some of that meat — I'm gonna give you some. In fact, I ..."

Peter cut him off. "You better stop."

Christian stopped the rail car and Peter got off.

Cautiously, Peter walked forward, looking up at the ceiling. He gestured for Christian to back up.

In the silence Christian stared at Peter.

"Now you're making me feel all superstitious," said Christian.

For a brief moment Peter thought he heard drums beating.

Suddenly there was a puff of dust, followed by a large rock falling directly in front of them. The rail car moved back just as more rocks fell into the safety wiring, but within seconds their weight proved too much, and the net collapsed. The earth groaned as it let loose a landslide of rocks and debris.

Christian shouted, "Peter!" and the young man managed to jump towards him just as a dust cloud came up behind and enveloped him. The last thing Christian saw was a large slab of rock that dropped directly where he'd seen Peter last.

The roof was in motion. And then all was black.

Emergency lights came on, dimmed by all the dust.

Peter saw a sly hyena approach a boy sleeping by a fire; followed by a Maasai scarecrow fluttering in the air; then Laibon blew a sad note on a Kudu horn; and an officer with a red beret drew his pistol.

Finally the image of a young Peter smiling at Lekai appeared.

He heard himself ask Lekai a question. "What does it mean when the Belly of the Earth speaks to you?"

"It means you must do something, "Lekai replied.

And then everything was black.

Chapter Twelve

North

*P*eter lay unconscious in a hospital bed; his head wrapped in gauze and his right arm pinned to his side in a sling.

He slept fitfully, twisting and squirming; as if he were still trapped under the rock.

In a chair beside the bed sat Christian with a bandage on his forehead and watched him with concern.

Peter opened his eyes and Christian moved closer.

"The nurse said you've been coming around," said Christian, obviously relieved. "I'm glad you're okay."

Peter nodded sleepily and took in the room.

Christian grabbed his unbandaged hand and squeezed it, "I'd be dead if it wasn't for you."

Peter looked him in the eye but didn't respond.

Nervously, he added, "And my wife thanks you as well—I was a bit late, but I did make my anniversary dinner."

He struggled to remain respectfully quiet, but soon blurted out, "How'd you know it wasn't safe?"

Peter thought for a minute before replying.

"Because God does not eat mankind."

Christian furrowed his brow and glanced at the gauze that covered Peter's head, hoping he really would be okay.

He shook his head and pointed to a box on the nearby stand.

"I cleaned out your locker and boxed it—figured you'd be wanting some time off."

Peter nodded; it took him a few moments to form his words. Christian nervously stood.

"Yes, I believe I am through with the mines."

Christian stared at the ground uncomfortably, shifting his weight from one foot to the other; he had some bad news but was reluctant to speak it when his friend was in such rough shape.

Instead he lifted a bundle from the night stand that looked to weigh about ten pounds. Heavy cloth was wrapped around several sealed plastic bags containing meat.

"I brought you some biltong! Wait until you taste it! I made it with my own family recipe."

Peter thanked him, but could tell there was something he was withholding.

Although his superior, Christian had always been uncomfortable when Peter's gaze was turned on him; now that this gaze was cast from a hospital bed he felt the need to relieve himself of the news he carried.

He said, "We tried to contact your father. I reached the game reserve, but they'd just received some bad news."

Christian hesitated.

"Well, out with it," said Peter.

"Your father has died," said Christian quietly. "It was an accident, in the bush, about five days ago. They said it was quick."

Peter closed his eyes and tried to pull air into what now felt like a frail body. He thought of how his father and him had drifted apart in the last ten years, how they had finally been more connected by their scars than their love. It seemed downright impossible to him that he was dead.

Christian had fixed his gaze to the floor and was cracking his knuckles.

He asked, "What're you goin' to do now?"

Peter opened his eyes. "I'm not sure."

He thought of his home and the places he knew, and they all were connected to his father. His chest felt like a great, empty cavern; and he suddenly realized how he'd wasted the last ten years by allowing the distance between him and his father to continue to grow. Tears welled up in his eyes.

There was a window on the far wall, and through it Peter could see the slag pile from the mine. He looked at the sky which was overcast. It was July, the middle of winter, and the morning was cold and damp.

"I think I'll go north," he said, "away from here."

Peter stared at the ground. "I thought I could hide underground from my nightmares, but it didn't work. Even there they plague me."

Christian looked at Peter. "If you don't mind my askin' — how long have you had them?"

Peter closed his eyes again.

"Ten years ago I was responsible for a man's death and it has haunted me since then. He was a friend, and I can't seem to let it go."

Christian waited for him to say more. But Peter remained silent, his eyes closed.

In an attempt to lighten things up a little, Christian said.

"Just north, eh? Well, that dried meat will be handy there. Yes, sir, you never know what you'll be stuck with on the road — especially up north."

Peter opened his eyes and smiled at Christian. "Ya, thanks. North should do for now. I'll check out Zimbabwe and see where that takes me."

Christian nodded.

"I once went clear up to Malawi and paddled the great lake — that's what I would recommend. It'll do ya good to get away."

He seemed suddenly inspired, "And I'm gonna send you off properly, Peter. Yes sir, you let me know what day you want to take off and I'll get you a train ticket all the way to Beitbridge, on the Zimbabwe border."

Peter began to protest but Christian cut him off.

"Save it, Peter. You saved my life—it's the least I can do. I'm sure my wife would insist on it as well."

He thought for a minute.

"It's about five hundred miles to the border—I'd drive you, but it'd be two full days and my car wouldn't make it."

Christian smiled. "You'll be on local transportation from there, but it'll get you started."

Reluctantly, Peter agreed.

"Take care, Peter, and try to find some happiness out there," Christian said. "A young fella like you shouldn't look so down all the time." Then he turned and left the room.

The day after they left the hospital in Orkney and Christian drove Peter to the train station. They said goodbye on the platform and Peter found a seat. It was a long day's ride as the train passed through Johannesburg, then Pretoria, and finally left the vast suburbs behind and continued into the bush.

Now they were far from civilization and he sat chewing on a piece of Christian's biltong as the train slowly made its way through the African scrub. Thorn trees and massive baobabs burst through the low scrub on either side of the tracks and reached toward the sky like giants.

Peter leaned forward over the cabin heater and stared out the window. He was traveling lightly and wore all the warm clothing he had—a light, black jacket over a button-up long-sleeved shirt. The sun was rising and it looked to be a nice day, but the morning had a chill and he had a hard time shaking it.

With both of his parents now gone he no longer felt anchored to South Africa, and the loss of his father had resulted in a feeling of being less connected to those around him.

Peter mostly wanted to get away.

He was still wearing the bandage around his head. He had no stitches, but the doctor had told him to keep it on for another week to help prevent the wounds from getting infected. The bandages on his arm, and the sling, had been removed, and the cuts and bruises were now merely covered with white tape.

A middle-aged missionary who was sharing his cabin smiled and nodded at the bandages. "An accident?"

Peter eyed him for a moment, weighing just how offended the man would be if he didn't reply at all. The man's bright-eyed enthusiasm didn't mix well with Peter's dark mood.

He answered anyway.

"In the mines."

The missionary leaned forward to examine the tape and bandages Peter wore and grimaced.

Annoyed, Peter said, "I'm fine."

The man held up his Bible and asked, "Have you ever thought that the reason you were saved was because someone was watching over you?"

Peter just stared at him until the missionary started to fidget.

His enthusiasm seemed to be stifled by the dark look in Peter's eyes. There was anger there, and frustration—and something else.

Something darker.

"Maybe," Peter finally said.

The missionary shook his Bible again and said, "Well, this book will tell you who that was."

Peter looked into his eyes for a solid minute while the cabin was filled with the click-clack of the wheels on the joints of the rail. He thought of Lekai and what he had said about missionaries. He had been dreaming of him every night and his words were never far from his thoughts.

The man gave his best grin, showing all of his front teeth, as he confidently waited for Peter's reply.

Finally, Peter said, "Keep your good book."

Then he smiled.

The missionary's smile dissolved and his brows folded together.

Just then the train jolted as the conductor applied the brakes. The train's whistle sounded loudly through the squeal of the wheels.

The speaker crackled. *"Beitbridge, Zimbabwe in two minutes. This is the end of the line."*

Peter stood and reached up to grab his backpack from the luggage rack. The missionary had sat back with his bible on his lap and hands folded on top of it.

The train jolted and Peter fell in the missionary's direction — and almost landed on him. The man glanced at him with nervous eyes that shifted back and forth. The eyes were different than they'd been a few minutes before, when there had still been hope of saving Peter's soul.

Peter stopped and smiled at the man who turned a shade of pale and looked away.

Peter exited the train and walked to the customs office, a building with faded yellow walls. People were lining up silently to have their documents stamped.

The immigration officer never looked up as he examined Peter's passport. One of the border guards watched him uneasily, but finally, the officer waved him through.

He exited the building to see a sign that read, *"Welcome to Zimbabwe."*

This side of the border was a colorful blur of faces and noise. The people here were mostly black and appeared different than those on the South African side — more confident and exuberant. They walked with pride and a bounce to their step.

Others had exited the customs office with him and he followed the crowd to the road, listening to the birds singing out from the trees around them, and stuck his thumb out for a ride toward the capital, Harare. It was still morning and he had the day ahead of him, although he wasn't certain he could cover the distance in a day as it was close to three hundred miles.

But his luck that day got him several short rides. The first to pick him up were a South African family on vacation in a rental car. Peter sat in the back with their son who looked bored with the journey. As they drove north toward Harare they took him past Bubi to the town of Rutenga, but eventually they turned off towards Bulawayo.

From there he rode in the back of a pickup, on top of a load of vegetables, to the edge of Ngundu. In the late afternoon — after waiting for an hour — he got a ride with a government worker heading to his office near Masvingo.

Inevitably, his chauffeurs would ask about his bandages and destination and each time he fumbled through an answer. Peter was grateful for the lift, but his father's recent death and the chaos caused by his nightmares weren't subjects he wanted to share.

The bandages had nothing to do with these things, but he'd been hiding in the mine to escape the nightmares and he felt it was somehow all connected.

None of the rides were long, yet the forced conversation had been painful to Peter and at the end of each lift he couldn't get away fast enough.

On the outskirts of Masvingo Peter stood on the side of the road as a dinosaur of a truck passed, enveloping him in a massive cloud of exhaust fumes. He had been travelling all day, yet he had only covered half the distance and was already running out of energy.

He shouldered his pack and continued on foot, pointing at the ground to signal his need for a ride whenever a vehicle passed him by. Peter guessed it was around five o'clock, and at this hour there was more traffic, but most people were busy getting home from work and barely seemed to notice him.

Just before sunset a dark van passed by, then braked and stopped to back up to him.

A man in a turban looked Peter over and said, "You give money for gas when ride is finished. We go to Malawi, but stop in Harare first."

Peter nodded and simply said, "Ya," and the door was slid open to reveal about ten men, all wearing turbans, crammed into the back. One tried to slide over to make room for Peter, but it seemed a futile gesture as the van was already packed tight, half filled with heavy sacks.

Peter squeezed in and they managed to shut the door. The men stared at his bandages, quietly, until one commented that it must be a new style of turban—and then they all laughed and welcomed him.

He had just settled in when the right front tire blew and they skidded off the road. The vehicle came to a stop with the men in the back half buried by the sacks they'd been sitting on. One man had scraped his arm, but no one was gravely injured.

They helped each other out, and then discovered that they had to unload the sacks to get to the tire jack. Then they had to push the vehicle back onto the road where they could use the jack.

All this took up precious minutes as the sun disappeared. Peter thought of trying for another ride, but once it got dark he knew he would have slim chance of being picked up.

An hour later Peter was still waiting as they finally got the flat tire off the van. The sun had set and it was now dark out and the men worked by the light of an ancient gas lamp. The driver pointed to one of the younger men who nodded, shouldered the flat tire, and ran back in the direction they had come from.

Peter knew what this meant: It would be hours until the runner returned with a new tire. Several of the other passengers had started a fire by the side of the road to keep warm in the dropping temperatures.

But Peter was too restless to sit. He paced, conjuring up in his mind alternatives to passively waiting.

The driver had an apologetic look on his face. "This may take some time," he said.

Peter waved the man's words away, "Forget it. I will camp near here." He had spotted a sign ahead that read "*The Great Zimbabwe Ruins.*"

The driver nodded and made a sign of blessing over Peter.

"The ride is free; may Allah watch over you."

Peter thanked him and started walking up the road with his backpack hanging on one shoulder.

At the ruins Peter followed signs to the site campground and set down his pack. There were several groups camped out, each with their own fire, but Peter kept to himself. Along with a change of clothes, a small cooking kit, some food and a sleeping bag, he also carried a compact tent. He set the tent up in the dark and then lit a small fire in a nearby pit.

From his backpack he produced a small pot and grabbed a can of soup from his supplies. After opening it he poured the contents into the small pot.

He added the fuel to the fire and waited for it to die down a bit. Then he placed the pan over the coals and watched the soup cook.

After he finished eating his soup he washed out the pan at a nearby tap, filled it with water, and placed it back on the fire. Once the water boiled he made coffee and sat there sipping it, half-listening to the conversation of other campers that floated around him like smoke, but he kept to himself.

While he sipped his coffee he opened the bundle that Christian had given him and pulled out a piece of smoked meat. Christian had not exaggerated when he had praised the meat. It was delicious—spicy—and satisfying. Peter chewed and stared at the fire, trying to calm his mind. The images of the people he'd encountered over the last few days merged with the mine cave-in and his nightmares.

In the distance some wild dogs howled.

After eating, he tried to shake his restlessness with a stroll toward the ruins. The glow from the growing moon was just enough to offer visibility. By the campground entrance he found a footpath that led to the ruins.

An erratic wind pushed the Acacia trees around the campground into a wild dance that set his nerves on edge. He knew that during the country's Iron Age in the 11th century this had been the capital of the Kingdom of Zimbabwe and more than eighteen thousand people had lived here.

He silently walked the path and seemed to feel the presence of their spirits as he moved across a small valley floor.

When Peter finally saw the ruins he took a deep breath. Massive walls appeared to rise out of the silver gloom and he felt like he was approaching a mythical place that didn't exist when the sun shined.

He knew from photos that the structure was shaped like a giant "C" with an enclosure inside, but he could only make out portions of the formation in the dim light.

The outer walls were well built and looked to be about forty feet high, but the smaller buildings that lay outside the protection of those walls had fallen to piles of rocks. Spreading across the valley floor, they looked like tombstones.

He felt utterly alone as he cautiously proceeded in the silent, moonlit night. When he entered the ruins he was soon funneled into a narrow passage that led to a place called the King's Enclosure.

Peter walked along the curved walls, which, as he noticed, had been built without mortar. The walls continued higher, blocking out the moon. The shadows thickened, and just as he began to fear there may be wild animals inside he heard a noise.

He stood still and listened. The air was stagnant and he felt deprived of oxygen.

Something moved directly in front of him and he heard a low growl.

He slowly backed away.

Outside he followed another path to a spot on the ridge that overlooked the site.

He sat down on a stone platform with a view of the valley below and the expanse of the ruins. Suddenly, his attention was drawn to odd flashes of light, sometimes colored, moving between the rocks.

They seemed as evasive as his strange dreams, and just like them escaped any attempt at rational explanation. He warily scanned the shadows.

Then a heavy wave of tiredness hit him. He leaned back against a wall and sleep whisked him away instantly.

In his dream he was back in Maasailand on the trip with his father, ten years ago. Young Peter and Lekai sat by a fire while a sky filled with stars burned overhead. In his hand Lekai held the *Eye of Enkai*.

He passed it to Peter so he could inspect it.

Lekai said, "This is the bag that Laibon uses to see the future."

Peter flushed with embarrassment as he said, "My dad says nobody can see the future."

A quick smile crossed Lekai's face at the boy's words.

Peter tested the weight of the bag and then handed it back to Lekai.

"The *Eye of Enkai* is in the mind, not the bag of stones," said Lekai. "First you look in your mind for the *eye*. When you have found it, you reach in and grab a handful of stones."

Lekai untied the bag, took out a handful of stones, and displayed them on a piece of leather – there were many small stones, but also seashells, bits of smooth glass, animal teeth, feathers and objects Peter couldn't identify.

"I do not know all of their names," continued Lekai. "In this bag are all the pieces that make up the life of Laibon. When you can tell the name with your finger, by touching, then the bag will want to help you."

As Lekai talked he ran his fingers through the stones.

He grabbed a fistful and let them fall, one by one.

Then he picked out a blue marble and held it to the light. Through the small hole in the middle he saw Peter.

"This one is you, Peter. I would have to jump very high to see the distances you will travel."

He fingered the blue marble again and then looked up sternly.

"Laibon will call you when it is time."

And then with a smile he added, "Do not worry, Peter."

Peter woke suddenly to find himself still surrounded by the ancient walls of stone. He looked around, slowly, to get his bearings; and with a start noticed the outline of a man standing just a few feet away.

He held his breath and slowly stood, desperately trying to not make a sound. He hadn't heard the intruder, and thought him to be a thief preying on the campers.

From his daypack he quietly retrieved a heavy flashlight and hefted it like a weapon. The man hadn't moved. Peter crept closer, and when he found the switch with his fingers he turned the light on.

Before him stood a Maasai scarecrow that swayed in the cool night breeze. Its red toga was worn and dirty, and the arms flapped as they draped over the horizontal spear.

Peter jumped back. The beam of light that lit up the red garment now betrayed how badly his hands were shaking.

He scanned the area but saw no one. Above him the stone walls rose up and connected to massive stones that the builders had worked into their designs.

Peter tried to control his breathing as he looked harder at one stone that appeared like a giant bird of prey looming out of the dark of night. With the adrenaline still coursing through his blood it looked to Peter as if the bird was leaning over him, observing.

He steadied himself and started back toward his tent, looking over his shoulder every few seconds. Earlier he had heard the sounds of insects and wild dogs, but all was silent now. Several times he thought he saw a man standing on the side of the trail, but each time it was a bush or small tree.

At the campground he hastily broke down his tent and poured some water over the glowing coals of his fire. It hissed back angrily.

Sunrise was still an hour away as he shouldered his pack and left the other sleeping campers.

Chapter Thirteen

Harare

*T*he day's first light found Peter on the side of the road, sitting on his pack, eating oranges while the bush along the road slowly came to life. He'd passed a vendor, a friendly old man with only a couple of teeth to hold up his wrinkled smile, who was just setting up his stall and held up a ripe orange as he walked by. Peter thought it a good omen for the day and bought a supply of the fruit.

The sky was golden and the earth soft with dew. Peter inhaled the rich air which was still cool at this hour. Behind him the trunk of a thorn tree lit up red in the first horizontal rays of sunshine that shot out from the horizon.

The trees were full of birds and their song carried clearly in this hour before the traffic started up. Peter chewed quietly as he listened to the bird calls. There came one that he was uncertain of and he promptly wondered whether his father would have known the bird.

The thought made him restless.

From a distance he heard a heavy truck approaching and he jumped to his feet, ready. He still had some distance to cover if he wanted to reach Harare, at least a half day's travel away. But at this hour most of the traffic was heading there, and if he got a ride now he would arrive in the afternoon.

The truck rounded a curve and came into view, and the driver slowed when he saw Peter pointing at the ground. He stopped and stared at the young man's bandages while Peter asked for a lift.

It turned out that he was indeed heading for Harare, and after Peter handed him a few notes the driver told him to climb in the back.

The metal truck bed with wooden sideboards was filled with about a dozen black men in worn work clothes.

He had to climb over a pile of shovels by the tailgate – a task made difficult as the truck sped up. The men huddled near the headboard and watched him climb toward them, their eyes shifting from the bandages on Peter's head to those on his arm.

The wind whipped sand from the bed of the truck everywhere, preventing conversation.

Peter felt worn. The sleep that had overtaken him at the ruins had not been restorative. It had been filled with memories of his father and with the nightmares surrounding Lekai.

Peter took out another orange and offered it to one of the men. He shuffled forward to grab it, but upon looking into Peter's eyes he smiled nervously and retreated before accepting the orange. They drove through the day, passing through the small town of Mvuma first, and about an hour later, Chivhu. Both were towns of under ten thousand people, but bustling with commotion.

They stopped once for gas in the oddly named New Featherstone, and made it to the outskirts of Harare around three o'clock.

Peter banged on the roof until the driver slowed and stopped.

Peter thanked him, shouldered his pack, and walked off, followed by the gazes of the men in the truck.
On the streets of Harare Peter stopped several travelers to inquire about a place to stay. Many of the overland trucks

finished in Harare, and their passengers often checked into one of the city's guest houses.

Peter hoped to connect with a ride going north, possibly to Malawi, and figured Harare was the best place to arrange it. The short rides from the previous day had made him edgy and now he just wanted to knock out some distance.

Harare — Zimbabwe's capital city — featured beautiful architecture, most of it colonial, and broad avenues lined with towering trees. The sidewalks were well kept, and on the shaded corners sat vendors with local crafts.

Peter casually walked past the traditional baskets and textiles, but he paused at a collection of stone carvings.

"You like the shona carvings?" asked a woman in her thirties. She had a pleasant smile and sat back, not pressuring him, while he looked over the pendants and small statues.

"I've seen this before," said Peter as he crouched down and pointed to a bird-like carving.

The woman slid forward.

"Then you have been to the Great Zimbabwe."

Peter thought back to his night at the ruins. Now he realized it was the carving of the giant bird, not an actual entity, which had hovered over him while he slept beneath the ancient walls.

He smiled at her as he stood to leave.

"How much will you give me for that piece?" she asked.

He shook his head.

"No, I am traveling and I don't have room for any trinkets."

She shrugged and explained that the stone came from her family's land while Peter set down his pack, opened it, and took out two oranges. He gave one to the woman. Then he shouldered his pack to leave.

"Wait," she said as she grabbed a smaller carving of the same image and placed it in his hand. "This is a gift."

Peter flushed slightly and thanked her.

With a tilting motion he slid out of his backpack again and set it on the ground. The woman watched him as he stuck his hand inside the pack and felt for the *Eye of Enkai*. When he located the bag he untied it just enough to squeeze the small carving inside.

When he stood to go a second time he realized he wasn't sure where he was going.

"Do you know of a good place to stay in Harare? Just for one night."

She thought for a moment.

"Many of the people stay at the Sable Lodge, and it is not far from here."

He nodded and she pointed down the road to the left.

"Just get on the local bus going that way. It is the fifth stop."

The Sable Lodge resembled a rabbit warren with numerous doors and hallways, and dorms full of worn but excited travelers. Zigzagging corridors opened to still more dormitories and smaller rooms; other doors lead to bathrooms or showers.

A young black man with a New York Yankee's T-shirt greeted Peter and escorted him through the maze to a courtyard on the side of the lodge. He moved fast, turning back at times to explain how busy they were.

Like the rest of the hotel staff, he wore a blue, button-up shirt and was clean shaved with a short haircut.

He flashed a white smile. "My name is Justice. If you need anything, anything at all, you just ask for Justice. Okay?"

Peter leaned against the wall to allow four blond, tall travelers to pass. Each one wore a large backpack, and carried a cooler.

"Ya. Thanks!" said the first one; and the others each muttered a respectful, "thank you" as they passed.

"We have been full every night but many people are leaving," said Justice hopefully.

Peter nodded and when they reached the courtyard he looked over the open area and noticed an empty swimming pool, and a lawn that was littered with a collection of collapsible chairs and tents. The pool hadn't been used in years it seemed, but the travelers that frequented the lodge had long ago decided that the courtyard was too cool to abandon—even if it meant lounging around a dead pool.

Peter marveled at being surrounded by travelers from across the globe. They sat around the porch, by the entrance, or out back near the pool. Some were writing letters, others were reading the notice board, a few sat listening to the African reggae music that blasted through the numerous speakers.

In the back stood a smaller building where a staff of young, enthusiastic black men and women organized everything from clean sheets to cooking burgers. Peter could see the pride and excitement they got from their jobs—and their proximity to the international crowd.

"Please wait until I find an available bed," said Justice.

Peter set his pack down by a lawn chair.

As Justice walked away he asked, "Can I order you something to eat?"

"Ya," said Peter, "I would like a cheeseburger and a Castle beer."

Justice said, "Have a seat, please, and I will be back soon."

It seemed to Peter that everyone had either just returned from an adventure or was about to set off on one. He watched a woman writing a letter, and the effort she put into her words was evident on her face—her eyes staring off at the wilderness landscape she had just left. She exhaled as she sealed the envelope and addressed it.

A Japanese man with long dreads methodically scanned the notice board; he then grabbed a letter off it and shouted. From across the courtyard a group responded in Japanese and he ran their way with the letter in his hand.

Peter lay back in the warm rays of the late afternoon sun. He realized he had not been warm since he'd left the hospital. The sun on his skin felt so good that everything else melted away, and when Justice returned with his food twenty minutes later he felt like mere seconds had passed.

He devoured the burger without looking up.

As he wiped his chin he glanced to his side and met the eyes of a young man with a shaved head. He nodded to him, and the man, a guy in his mid-twenties, grinned back. He had the muscular build of a soldier, and a pile of empty beer bottles by his side.

"This is life, yes?" said Q-tip. "I think yes! At home is different; at home I am in the army. In Israel everyone is in the army, and in the army is no life. No drinking, no smoking, and at times no ladies, this is no life."

Peter raised his beer and smiled, but remained silent.

"Oh, you are a quiet man, I see," said Q-tip as he cracked open another beer.

Q-tip grinned and looked over the crowd. There were about fifty people in the courtyard, and they all looked well-traveled. They all had a similar look, too. It appeared to Peter like the sun and wind had sculptured their features as much as the challenges and hardships of local transport and conditions.

These people, Peter thought, looked like they had come through something—an experience or an ordeal. Some looked happy—almost elated—and others seemed tired and worn out. But even the ones with exhaustion written all over their features still had a glow to them. They were living the biggest adventure of their lives and the look in their eyes spoke it.

As the Israeli took a swig of his beer he saw Peter observing the travelers.

He said, "You are in rough shape for someone who hasn't been on the road long."

"And how do you know how long I've been on the road?" asked Peter defensively.

The Israeli squinted slightly as he looked over Peter.

"Well, I can see enough of your hair to know when it was cut last; and your shirt may be dirty, but it is not worn; and you are still pale so I know you have not been under this hard sun for long."

Peter scoffed. "I have been traveling three days and two nights with no shower!"

Q-tip glanced at the bandages, and although he didn't say anything it made Peter self-conscious. He'd been told to keep them on for a week—and he was a few days short of that—but he figured he was close enough.

He began to unwind the bandage from his head.

"These are unnecessary now."

Q-tip motioned like he was patting the ground.

"Easy, friend," he said. "I am only curious. It is my nature."

Peter felt his head with his hand, searching for the scars that had been hidden by the bandages. "Really, I just kept them on so the wounds would stay clean on the road."

The Israeli nodded. "What brings you to Zimbabwe?"

Peter hesitated.

"I'm not really certain. I may just be passing through."

The Israeli guzzled his beer and cracked open another one. He downed half of it in one swig. Belching loudly, he said, "That's too bad. This is a good country. There's much to see."

Peter nodded. "Ya, I believe you. I guess I'm just drifting."

Q-tip laughed.

"From my experience, people either are running from something, or searching for something. They only drift for a short time."

Peter didn't reply.

"Don't worry," said Q-tip. "You will fit in here."

He gestured to the travelers around them and said, "These people, they come from all over Africa, some even drive from Europe. They think they relax, but they all run from something also."

The Israeli nodded his shiny white head in the direction of a group of Spaniards who had claimed a corner of the courtyard. They were sprawled out on a few of the rickety lawn chairs, and were passing around a jug while they sang a song.

"They just completed a drive from Morocco to here—through all of western Africa before somehow getting their vehicle across Zaire.

"And our German friends there have made an incredible journey as well," he added as he pointed to four tall men relaxing in finely carved Malawi chairs.

"They started in Cape Town and drove up through Namibia, and then crossed the Kalahari to reach the Okavango Delta. They started with two vehicles, but lost one in Chobe when the engine blew."

Peter looked over the two groups, and then noticed a middle-aged couple leaning against the wall. They seemed a little drunk by the way they swayed. They were giddy, but their faces were gaunt and worn.

"What about them?" he asked.

Q-tip gave a sad laugh.

"Those two are from England. They saved for five years to equip a vehicle for a big journey, and two weeks into it they were hijacked."

"What did the hijackers take?" asked Peter.

"They lost everything. Armed men stopped them and made them get out—and then they drove away with their rig."

Peter watched the couple. "They look pretty happy," he observed.

Q-tip nodded, "Yes, I think they just returned from a safari at Mana Pools. This place is on the Zambezi River, across from Zambia."

He gave a conspiratorial smile.

"It's a very romantic spot, and you can see the animals right from your tent if you camp by the river. I think they found the Africa they were searching for."

The Israeli rubbed his head.

"Two nights ago I am drunk and I have this German man shave my hair. The next day this head is white and I hide from the sun."

Reaching into his back pocket, Q-tip produced a small cap and placed it on his head. The hat had no visor and was circled by African designs.

"Everybody says my head is white like a Q-tip; so now that is what they call me. My name is David, but you can call me Q-tip."

Q-tip raised his beer to Peter and finished it, leaving foam on his lips. He wiped them with the back of his hand.

"I think you are South African. For me it is not a problem. I do not like politics. I am Israeli. Travel in Africa is sometimes difficult for me also."

Peter smiled and looked around, and Q-Tip reached for another beer.

"Do not let me offend you friend. I am helicopter test pilot. This job takes total concentration. I have ridden a stalled helicopter to the earth and survived. If you work hard, then you must play hard. This is true!"

Peter raised his glass and toasted Q-tip, but as the bald man lifted a newly opened bottle someone ran by and grabbed it, and then jumped down into the empty swimming pool.

"Deepend, you azhole!" shouted Q-tip.

Peter gasped, then got up and stepped forward to see that there was a mattress on the bottom of the pool—in the deep end—and the beer thief was sprawled on it dealing with a foaming beer, doing his best to suck up all of the foam before it spilled on the mattress.

Q-tip nodded at him.

"We call this man Deepend. We had to put this mattress under the diving board because he smokes too much on this diving board and always falls off."

Deepend looked about twenty-five, and had a wiry frame. His shoulder-length brown hair shook as he raised his beer at Q-tip in salute.

In an American accent he shouted, "Thanks for the brew, Q-tip. Feel like getting me another?"

Q-tip sternly shook his head and turned to Peter.

"He is crazy—this one—be careful. He sleeps in this swimming pool. If it rains at night he will drown for sure."

Deepend climbed out of the pool and loped over to them.

He said, "Yeah, well if I drown you'll be going to Vic Falls alone."

He punched Q-tip in the arm. "You gonna order us some beers or what? Fucking slacker."

Q-tip rubbed his arm.

"Easy, Deepend, or I'll start punching back."

The American danced around with his arms up like an old-time boxer, trying his best to annoy Q-tip.

"Come on, Q-tip. Show me some of those killer Jew army moves."

Q-tip ignored him.

Instead, he turned to Peter and said, "You should come to Victoria Falls with us. Everyone is heading that way for the lunar rainbow."

Justice was passing by and overheard the comment. "Yes, a silver rainbow cast by the full moon's glow. You must see this," he said.

Deepend looked at Justice's shirt and said, "Dude, the fucking Yankees suck. Take that shirt off."

A bit horrified, Justice hurried off.

Uncomfortable, Peter tried to back out of the invitation.

"I don't know, I may be heading further north, to Malawi."

Q-tip shook his head.

"No, you cannot miss the full moon. Anyway, you can always get a lift north at Victoria Falls, over the border in Zambia. We leave in the morning. I insist you join us."

Peter still hesitated. Then he said, "Okay. Sure, I'll go with you."

Justice returned, watching Deepend nervously out of the corner of his eye. "Mr. Peter, I have a bed for you."

Deepend picked right back up where he had left off. "The Yankees suck, dude. Seriously, take it off."

Peter grabbed his pack and left, following Justice, who was desperate to get away from Deepend.

Justice led him to a dorm where several people were already sleeping. Peter stowed his pack under an empty bed, took off his shoes and jacket, and lay back on the covers.

As he closed his eyes, Van Morrison's *Into the Mystic* drifted into the room from outside. The last three days were a blur in Peter's mind and soon exhaustion overtook him.

In minutes he slipped off into a dream.

He was once again inside Laibon's hut. It was evening and a dark breeze blew in from the entrance, but Laibon had lit candles, and their warm light offered some comfort.

Lekai crouched back on his haunches; the tall warrior looked surprisingly at home in the low hut.

Laibon sat opposite him. He sprinkled milk over Lekai's head and smiled.

A small calf was tied in the corner, but the place was tidy. The hard earth floor appeared to be clean swept.

Laibon said, "*Enkai* has told me of a danger coming for your animal brother."

Lekai wore a worried look. "If Kiboko is in danger, then I am his servant. I will go to him."

"There is a riddle surrounding your return," Laibon explained. "It is a thing that exists beyond my understanding."

Lekai stared at Laibon solemnly.

"I have no fear, great Laibon. May I watch the reading?"

Laibon nodded and reached into the *Eye of Enkai*. As the stones slipped through his fingers his gaze turn inward.

The candles flickered in the wind.

Laibon started to shake.

In a hoarse voice he said, "It is now the time of *Ol-maitai*, the ten years of bad fortune. This is bad for all of us."

As a particular stone passed between his fingers he paused.

"I see you on a journey," said Laibon. "To reach the spirit world you must fly far."

Again he hesitated, now holding another stone. Slower, he added, "You will return, my apprentice, but you will be different. Not everyone will see you."

Lekai watched him with a blank face.

As the last stone passed through his fingers Laibon smiled and exhaled. "The return of the *Eye of Enkai* comes also at this time."

Then the old seer sat back.

Lekai handed a long gourd decorated in seashells to Laibon, who drank his fill and handed it back.

Lekai said, "The *Eye of Enkai* is here, grandfather; it has not been lost."

The old man laughed and patted the shoulder of his innocent young apprentice.

Chapter Fourteen

Hwange

*P*eter woke from the dream with a sense of urgency. He sat up straight and looked around the dorm, but saw little in the dark other than seven sleeping forms. It was late and the music in the courtyard had been turned off.

He reached along the side of his bed, grabbed his pack, and fumbled inside until he found the small leather sack.

He took out the *Eye of Enkai.*

Apprehensively, he glanced at the sleeping men around him, and then he stuck his hand inside *the Eye* and grabbed a fistful of stones.

Slowly, he dropped all but one.

He opened his hand to reveal what looked like the tip of a horn. Etched into its side was the image of a Kudu.

Peter put away the *Eye* and looked out the window. In the east the sky was beginning to lighten, although sunrise was still a ways off. He would not be able to sleep anymore, so he quietly put on his shoes and prepared to leave.

One of his dormmates stirred and croaked with an Aussie accent, "That better not be you wankin' over there, Stewart."

"Sorry, it's only me leaving," explained Peter.

"No worries, mate," said the man with a yawn. "You travel well."

"Thank you," said Peter as he shouldered his backpack and headed for the door.

The morning chill forced Peter to wear his light jacket. He had taken a taxi to the edge of town and now stood on the side of the road with his finger pointed at the ground and waited.

He had asked Justice about the best way north. Peter wanted to go to Lusaka, in Zambia, but despite the fact that the most direct road went northwest, Justice had insisted that going west via Bulawayo and Victoria Falls would be the best way to get a ride there—especially if he hoped to get on an overland truck heading north.

He remembered Q-tip's invitation to go with them, but he felt better being in charge of his own momentum because he questioned their competency—especially Deepend's.

He regretted having left without saying goodbye, but he felt compelled to start moving and didn't want to wait until they rose.

A large truck pulled over and a man who appeared to be of Indian descent motioned for him to jump in up front. The back of the truck was piled high with corn husks that were tied down with a spider web of ropes.

As soon as he was seated they were cruising down a road lined with potholes big enough to swallow small cars. The driver avoided some of them but barreled through others with no method that Peter could decipher. The windows didn't shut, but they were high enough for the passengers to escape the dust that exploded out of the back when the truck hit a pothole.

The driver didn't want any money, just to talk to someone for a few hours, and he told Peter the story of his family's expulsion from Uganda during Idi Amin's bloody reign. Peter enjoyed listening to the man tell his story and not having to talk about himself.

They were now in the countryside, and as they passed by the simple villages that lined the road the sun slowly rose and lit up the faces of the people on the sidewalk. Peter knew that in villages like these most people got things done before the heat of the day. The driver was proud of his passenger, and when they passed groups of school children he hit his horn loudly and pointed at Peter.

Through it all the driver talked about Uganda, and slain family members, and the one other brother that did make it out, when he braked hard to avoid an old donkey crossing the road.

"Careful there!" he shouted at the donkey.

They'd been traveling for about two hours, and had passed through the town of Chagutu, when the driver pulled over at a road crossing where their ways parted.

Peter thanked him and waved as he drove off, then realized that a crowd of people had gathered around him, curious to see what he was up to. He started walking up the road to lose the crowd, but several young boys frustrated his efforts by following him.

"Hello, sir," said one of them. "What is your good country?"

Peter shared some oranges with them as he answered their questions, but in the back of his mind he was going over the distances he had covered, and those still ahead. He planned on leaving the Zimbabwe at the Victoria Falls border crossing, which was almost four hundred and fifty miles from Harare, and he'd only covered about a hundred miles so far.

He stood waiting for another vehicle as he watched the people around him going about their lives. A local bus swooped into the crowd and left just as quickly with another load. Peter saw the cloud of exhaust floating his way and decided it was time to start walking.

About a mile down the road he stopped again, set down his backpack, and pointed at the ground. Just as a pickup pulled over and the driver asked where he was going, screams erupted from further down the road. He turned and saw Q-Tip's shiny, white head hanging out of the window of an approaching Land Cruiser.

"Am I so scary that you cannot say good-bye to me?" Q-tip shouted.

He jumped out of the vehicle before it had stopped completely, ran over to Peter and grabbed him by his shoulders to steer him towards their Land Cruiser.

"Come, you ride with us. Is better."

Peter looked back at the driver of the pickup, but Q-tip was persuasive and didn't let go of him until they were standing by the Land Cruiser's door. The pick-up driver, whose patience had run out, pulled away.

Peter sighed. "I've decided to go directly north."

"Yes, of course," said Q-tip.

"No stopping. I'm serious," said Peter as he allowed Q-tip to open the door for him. Q-tip grabbed Peter's pack and pushed him in.

"Yes, of course, but everyone goes to Victoria Falls on the way—it is where the border crossing is. And first we see animals. Hwange Park is on way also."

Inside the Land Cruiser it was tight quarters. A pile of gear was strapped onto the roof rack, but a cooler and all of their supplies occupied the back seat. Q-tip shoved things aside to make some room next to the cooler, and then padded himself against it with a sleeping bag.

"It is better to have padding with this man driving."

Peter hopped in the front and looked over at Deepend in the driver's seat. Deepend was grinning like a boy with a big frog in his pocket as he started the engine and put the clutch in gear. He had a large joint hanging out of his mouth, and as he revved the engine he sucked on it and then exhaled a big, sweet tasting cloud.

A bunch of people had gathered around the vehicle, and some of the men were pointing at Deepend's joint.

"We should go," said Q-tip.

They had scarcely pulled into the road when Peter started to wonder how they had survived the past hundred miles. Deepend drove the Land Cruiser as if he was piloting a race car and his track encompassed both sides of the road.

Deepend offered his joint to Peter, who declined.

"No problem, dude," said Deepend, "more for me. You're welcome to come. . ."

Deepend jerked the wheel and shouted as a car cut in front of them, but the motion flicked ash into his eyes and for a moment he was blinded. He avoided a sure collision by turning hard left and driving on the footpath for twenty feet or so as he frantically wiped at his eyes.

The maneuver avoided an accident but sent a dozen people diving into the bushes.

Deepend and Q-Tip looked at each other.

"I fucking love driving on this side of the road," said Deepend. "Nice to have you with us, Peter, sure you won't smoke?"

He shook his hand which had been gripping the steering wheel and added, "Calms the nerves."

Peter looked at Q-tip and asked, "Are you sure he should be driving?"

Before Q-tip could reply a chicken ran into the road in front of them. It jumped up and flapped its wings to avoid the Land Cruiser, but Deepend hit the gas and tagged it with the grill.

The bird exploded into a burst of feathers.

Deepend howled, and then choked on a feather that blew in the window.

Q-tip slapped his back hard three times, grabbed a beer from the cooler and handed it to him, and then leaned in from the back to take hold of the wheel and steer.

Deepend guzzled the beer, his foot on the gas.

"This is insane." Peter said.

Q-tip laughed.

"I don't think you will find much sanity here. This one really is crazy. He chase the fire; he is not right in the head."

Deepend burped and reclaimed the wheel. His athletic frame was bouncing all over the front cab as he drove. He shook his fist and cursed passionately at drivers who got in his way.

"Don't they teach you fucking people how to drive?"

Q-tip sat back.

"Now I am easy with things, but when I was younger, I was crazy like this man. I would see a fire and I would run to it. Now I think first. I think, maybe the fire gets me and I no come out. So now I do not run to the fire."

Deepend flipped him off.

"Fuck you. You're so full of shit. You still like the fucking fire."

"Yes, is true," said Q-Tip. "But I chase the little fires. I chase the woman and the drink. When I am with you, I chase the big fire. Too much time with you and maybe the fire get us."

An hour later they passed by a small town named, Kwe Kwe, and Deepend started shouting.

"KWE KWE! KWE KWE!"

Q-tip said, "He sounds like a demented chicken."

Peter sat back and tried to think of a way to get on his own again. He knew they were heading in the direction he wanted to travel, and after the coming night in the game park they would reach Victoria Falls—from there he could set off by himself.

Luckily in Bulawayo Deepend tired of driving and Q-tip took over. They were about two thirds of the way from Harare to Hwange National Park, and the final stretch proved more relaxing with the Israeli at the wheel. They reached the gates in the late afternoon.

There were plenty of available spots at the park's campground because many of the travelers had already departed for the lunar rainbow. Q-tip found a site with a water tap that wasn't too far from the latrine and not too close to smell it. There was also a bricked fire pit with a grill.

The biggest trees surrounding the campground had been allowed to stay because of the shade they provided, but all the smaller brush had been cleared away.

Q-tip and Peter each had their own tents, Deepend had nothing. Because Peter's was a little larger he was going to share his tent with the American—a prospect that he dreaded.

While Peter and Deepend set up Q-tip got a fire going in a metal container held in place by three walls of bricks. It was about two feet off the ground and there was a solid metal grill that dropped over the fire when it was ready.

"We're gonna have a cookout?" asked Deepend.

"A cookout," sneered Q-tip. "How American."

"You are in southern African," said Peter. "When we grill, or barbeque, we call it a *brai*."

"Fine," said Deepend as he flipped off Q-tip. "Let's fucking brai."

Q-tip retrieved their kitchen supplies and a cooler full of steaks from the Land Cruiser and started sorting through them. He set the metal grill over the flames and soon the steaks were sizzling. To the edge of the grill Peter set a kettle to boil and when it was ready he offered everyone a cup of hot coffee.

"Fuck me," stated Deepend who was hugging himself. "I never imagined I'd be freezing my ass off when I came to Africa. What the fuck is up with that?" When the sun had set the temperature had started to drop, and they now stood close to the fire.

"In the southern hemisphere, the further south you are, the colder it gets." Peter said.

"Are you shitting me?" asked Deepend. "I left Kenya thinking it might be warmer down here. I even left my wheels behind."

"What exactly do they teach you in America?" asked Peter, but then he took one look at Deepend and let it go. "Forget it, go on."

"Me and some buddies bought an old Land Cruiser. They've all returned home so it's all mine. Not that I'll have time to use it. My flight departs Nairobi in two weeks."

"You might catch a ride with an overland truck in Zambia," said Peter. "Justice told me they run regularly between Lusaka and Nairobi."

"Really?" asked Deepend. "But isn't it like two thousand fuckin' miles?"

"It is," said Peter, "but those trucks cover some distance. My dad and I used to see them all the time on their way through South Africa and Botswana."

The thought of his father dampened Peter's mood, but when Deepend kept pressing him for information he continued. "The trucks take eight to ten weeks to drive to Harare from Nairobi, and they hit almost every game park on the way. Once they've dropped off their passengers they make the run back to Nairobi in less than a week to get another load."

"So why would they bother with hitch hikers?"

Peter topped off his coffee.

"Well, it's good money for the drivers. They have to make the drive anyway, and if each person in the back represents cash — and they do five or six runs a year — it's a good bonus."

Deepend cracked a beer.

"Not a bad idea, Peter."

Q-tip crawled out from his low military tent, wearing his African cap.

He dragged his sleeping bag with him and climbed into it. Then he settled down with a book and a flashlight. It was dark now.

Peter silently sipped his coffee and watched the fire.

Deepend looked restless and soon retrieved a flashlight from his belongings.

"I'm gonna see what game is running around tonight."

Q-tip waved. "I may never see you again, Mr. Deepend."

After a moment's hesitation Peter said, "I better go with you to make sure you don't get killed."

Deepend shrugged. "No need, dude. I'm a fucking ninja. I'm like one with the jungle."

Peter laughed. "That's what I'm afraid of."

The paths through the main camp were devoid of people, but plenty of creatures were moving about. Just beyond the reach of his flashlight Deepend watched a bat-eared fox fade out of view, and then something bigger hurried past.

"Holy shit!" said Deepend. "That was a fucking hyena."

"There are animals all around us," Peter said. "Look with your eyes, not the light. They come in close because they hope the big cats will stay away."

"What'd 'ya mean 'stay away'?"

"The campground is a pretty safe place for most animals. They know the lions and leopards don't like to be that close to humans so the hoofed animals come in hoping the proximity to people will keep the lions away. Every night the campgrounds are visited by more wildlife than you would ever imagine."

"Aw," Deepend said, "So we've got no chance of seeing a lion?"

"You might," answered Peter. "They mostly walk the perimeter, roaring, trying to scare the game away from the campers. More than likely if a lion does come through this camp it will be late in the night when you are sleeping."

Deepend looked over at Peter's tent.

"Thanks for letting me sleep in your tent. I'd lose my shit if I woke up staring at a lion."

As they walked through the quiet camp Peter saw the moon just beginning to rise on the horizon.

Deepend said, "Man, this is such a rush. It's like...like...it's fucking WILD, that's what it is."

Peter had not been on safari since the trip to Kenya with his father as a boy, and as they walked through the night his mind flooded with memories of animal encounters he'd had with his father, and his mother.

Once, in Kruger National Park, they'd been on a moonlight stroll when a bull elephant had walked right up to them. The elephant had approached slowly, almost soundlessly, and then stared at them for a full minute before ambling away.

On the outer reaches of the camp a lion roared and Deepend froze in his tracks.

"Fuck me."

Peter laughed.

"The moon is near full, there will be some killing tonight."

Deepend took a joint out of his pocket and lit it. While peering into the gloomy wood through which the trail led, he exhaled several dense clouds of smoke into the cool evening air. When they continued he extinguished the remainder of his joint with some saliva and stuck the roach in his shirt pocket.

Peter was walking through the bush quietly, as his father had taught him, Deepend stumbled along behind him noisily.

"Ouch!" he yelled, stubbing his toe, and in response a small herd of impala scampered away into the darkness.

Peter glared at him, and Deepend settled down.

Ahead the path led to a clearing, where a herd of antelope had assembled. The does were grazing while a proud male kept lookout. He stood about five feet tall at the shoulders and looked alert and fearless.

"I'd guess he has to be at least five hundred pounds," said Peter.

Peter gestured for Deepend to use the cover of a large tree to get closer.

"These are kudu," said Peter in a hushed voice. "They are one of the largest members of the antelope family. Isn't the male beautiful?"

Deepend nodded, but kept quiet. They were about twenty-five paces away, crouched low, and on Peter's signal they crept closer.

Suddenly the kudu buck snapped around to look in their direction. The moon was now overhead and flooded the clearing with silver light, but just as he looked toward them Peter pointed the flashlight directly at the male Kudu's soft brown eyes.

Quickly, Peter turned the light on, and then off.

The animal nervously blinked.

Peter took a step closer—pulling Deepend with him—and then he flashed the light at the kudu again.

In his quietest voice, Peter warned, "Be careful, they are great kickers."

Eventually they got up to the tree, within a few feet of the majestic animal.

The kudu stood stunned, blinking into the darkness. Its silhouette was clearly outlined in the moonlight and they watched the four foot spiral horns move in front of the stars. Peter remembered the piece of horn he pulled from the *Eye of Enkai* and the outline of the Kudu that had been carved into it.

Peter slid around the tree and extended his hand forward to touch the animal along its back. His fingers floated a few inches from the white vertical stripes that ran through the light gray hair.

As he touched the coarse hair on the kudu an image flashed across his mind. He saw an old man holding a large kudu horn. His red toga and elongated earlobes showed him to be Maasai. He raised the horn and blew hard, sending forth a long sad note.

Then the vision was gone.

Peter sucked his breath in loudly, and the animal jumped from his touch. He stepped back behind the tree.

He whispered coarsely, "Laibon?"

On their way back to the campsite Deepend babbled with excitement.

"That was fucking awesome."

Peter heard something moving and stepped aside, off the trail.

"Don't move," he warned.

Deepend froze, swaying slightly from side to side as the sound of pounding hooves on hard dirt came closer.

"'Sup?" he asked.

Peter grabbed him and pulled him off the path just as a kudu came charging by, barely missing them.

"Wow! Who the fuck was that?" asked Deepend as he picked himself off the ground. He looked up and down the trail to make sure there weren't more animals coming.

"Kudu," said Peter. "Something spooked it."

Chapter Fifteen

Elephants

Early the next morning Peter woke and took a walk. He felt refreshed in the cool air and walked casually to the edge of camp where it abutted a woodland. By the perimeter of the forest was a large termite mound, and a tribe of baboons had stopped there to feast on the fruit of a tree that shaded the area.

Peter sat about thirty feet away and watched the troop.

The pale yellow of the baboons' coats appeared to glow in the morning light. They flashed their large incisors at each other frequently, yet at the same time showed affection as they inspected each other's fur.

Every now and then one of them looked over at Peter, but they appeared to accept his presence.

He felt light-hearted as he watched them, and it wasn't until the entire circle of the sun was visible that Peter realized he hadn't had one of his nightmares the night before.

In the back of his mind he'd been wondering about the destination of this journey, and although he hadn't been ready to admit it to himself, he was sure he was going beyond Malawi.

He now knew that he was going all the way to Maasailand — beyond Tanzania and into Kenya. He was going there to explain his dreams and to admit to his role in Lekai's death.

Deepend sat up in the cab of the Land Cruiser, looking like a ragged dog with his hair sticking up in all directions. He looked around, suddenly remembering that Peter had kicked him out of his tent for shouting in his sleep.

He also remembered where they were. He jumped up and put on his boots.

"Guys, fuckin' get up! Please!" he pleaded.

He didn't know Peter was out walking, but he could hear Q-tip snoring.

He crushed up some paper and set it down on the ashes of the fire which had died down to coals. Then he dumped some kindling over that in a feeble attempt to revive the fire. "Get up guys, let's go!"

He blew on it, and sent ashes everywhere — including into his eyes.

He wiped his eyes and from behind his hands called: "What are you fuckin' waiting for? Get up guys. Get up, get up, get up!"

A traveler in a nearby tent shouted, "Shut up!"

Deepend instead raised his voice a notch. "Fuckitty, fuck, fuck, everybody get the fuck up!"

Finally, Q-tip stuck his head out of his tent.

"Deepend, be quiet," moaned Q-tip urgently.

The American took out his camera and polished the lens. With a crazy look in his eyes he said, "Hwange Park has thirty-fuckin'-thousand elephants; I'm getting a close shot today."

Q-tip crawled over to the fire pit with a blanket around his shoulders. He looked at Deepend's poor attempt at a fire and frowned in the cold air of the early morning.

"My American friend is ready to chase the fire," he mumbled as he moved some of the kindling aside and blew lightly on the coals. "And I am still numb from cold. Did you feel this temperature drop in the night?"

"I think it fell to almost freezing." This was Peter, just returning to camp.

"I do not sleep well at all," said the Israeli. "In army they make us tough, but I never like the cold."

"You poor fuckin' thing," said Deepend. "That's real tough for a soldier. What a fuckin' pussy!"

Q-tip eyed him seriously, "Easy friend, or you will get yours once I'm warm enough."

Once the fire was going, Q-tip retreated back into his sleeping bag. Peter filled a pot with water and set it to boil to make coffee.

They began to load their gear into the Land Cruiser and Peter noticed that Q-tip and Deepend were stowing the packs and sleeping bags in the back seat rather than up on the roof rack.

Q-tip walked over to Peter and dropped the keys into his hand.

He said, "You drive."

"Me?" asked Peter.

"Yes," said Q-tip loudly. "You can drive? Yes? I think yes. Ok?"

A bit defensively, Peter said, "Okay, okay."

With that, Q-tip climbed onto the roof of the vehicle with Deepend and set up two lawn chairs between the rails of a low luggage rack.

Skeptically, Peter said, "This looks dangerous."

With a shrug, Q-tip said, "What is the worst thing that could happen?"

Peter smiled, "Okay, I will drive. Look for the water holes. In the drought the animals will congregate there."

But when he started the Land Cruiser he was suddenly overcome with memories of his father and their time in the bush. As Peter stepped on the accelerator he had a flash of his bloodied feet, soaked red through the bandages as he drove through the night to get his father to the hospital.

But then Deepend started to howl like a dog and he was brought back to the present. Peter put the vehicle in gear and pulled out of the campground. Their plan was to drive through the park—a distance of close to one hundred miles—and then make their way to Victoria Falls which lay another hour down the road.

They had been underway for a while when Peter saw movement in the brush ahead and slowed to a stop. Suddenly something large emerged and almost ran into him.

He looked out of his side window at the kneecaps of a giraffe.

The animal had pulled itself up short and was attempting to turn around and lope off, but there wasn't much room for maneuvering and it was clearly frightened by the vehicle.

Deepend and Q-tip both shrieked as they found themselves face to face with the irritated creature.

"He's gonna fuckin' bite me!" screamed Deepend.

The giraffe finally turned and clumsily ran off, looking like some prehistoric throwback.

Q-tip stared at Deepend and said, "You is stupid. These animals do not bite."

"Well, you weren't acting all that brave for a fuckin' soldier. Let's hope the Palestinians don't attack riding giraffes."

Q-tip gave him another of his serious stares and shook his head slowly from side to side, but Deepend had already moved on.

"Put it in gear, Peter," he shouted. "Let's see some elephants. Get us closer!"

The sun was now high in the sky and animal sightings became scarce. Peter picked up the pace.

The Land Cruiser clung to the edge of a long dusty curve that skirted a patch of dry jungle, and Peter was leaning into it when he suddenly heard Deepend and Q-tip shouting. He slowed as the road straightened out. So caught up had he been in his own past that he'd almost forgotten his two passengers on the roof. "What the fuck, Peter?" yelled Deepend.

And then Peter gasped.

Their screams had attracted the attention of a massive bull elephant who stood just inside the jungle. The puttering sound of the Land Cruiser's exhaust annoyed the beast and when he heard the vehicle about to pass he decided to chase it off. In two quick steps he was at the edge of the road—Peter could make out vines and other pieces of the dry jungle that still clung to the huge animal's back. With his ears spread out and his trunk curled up he moved fast and appeared to be sailing with a cloud of dust billowing behind him.

Peter was startled. His focus was glued to the elephant's eyes, alert and wiry, as the huge animal came racing towards them.

A wall of gray now filled the passenger windows of the left side of the vehicle.

The bull blew a loud trumpet. Q-tip and Deepend screamed like girls, clutching at each other as they scrambled to the other side of the Land Cruiser's roof

Peter found a lower gear, popped the clutch and hit the gas.

The vehicle jerked forward and the two lawn chairs with Deepend and Q-tip in them lifted slightly, then folded in mid-air and collapsed backwards, taking the two travelers with them as they fell off the back.

Deepend managed to scream, "Fuck!" before he cratered into the soft dust. He struggled free from a mess of mangled lawn chair and sat up moaning. Q-tip lay dazed on his side.

For a few moments all was silent. The dust settled. Then there was a low growl, so deep that it made the Land Cruisers' windows rattle.

The angry bull stood and flared out his ears and shook his tusks aggressively.

From his eyes came a cold look of displeasure.

Q-tip shook off the fall, saw the elephant watching them and slowly stood.

He caught Deepend's eye and motioned for him to do the same.

Q-tip was a bit closer to the massive animal than Deepend, and when he took the smallest of steps backwards the elephant began to growl.

Q-tip froze and hoped Deepend was doing the same.

He took another, slow step backwards. This time the bull watched silently and it appeared that they might be allowed to leave.

Then a loud click broke the silence. Deepend lowered his camera and said, "Now that's a fucking photo!"

Peter had come to a stop and was craning his neck out the window to see what was going on behind him. From fifty feet away, Deepend and Q-Tip came running toward him, screaming.

Behind them the bull charged.

Peter threw the Land Cruiser into reverse. He wasn't sure he would get to his friends before the elephant did, but he kept the accelerator floored.

The men ran for their lives. The elephant was closing in. Deepend leapt toward the vehicle and slammed into the back plastic window with Peter still backing up.

The impact knocked Deepend out cold.

Peter hit the brakes. Q-tip grabbed Deepend by the shirt with one hand and the roof rack with the other, and held on for dear life as Peter put the Land Cruiser in gear and tore off. From the corner of his eye Peter glimpsed Q-Tip's hand losing its grip and slipping away and slammed on the brakes again.

The bull stood twenty feet away and stared at the men in the road.

It growled low and began to stomp the ground in an unmistakable challenge.

Q-tip, sprawled on the ground next to Deepend's limp body, looked back at the elephant, and was terrified.

The bull trumpeted and fanned out his ears. He took a step towards them.

Q-tip stood up, moaning and faced the elephant. The elephant took another step. Q-tip recoiled. He glanced at Deepend, who lay unconscious between him and the angry animal.

Peter pushed the Land Cruiser's door open. Its sharp creak drew everyone's attention. The men and the elephant stood transfixed.

Peter got out of the car and slowly walked toward the elephant to take a stand between the animal and Deepend. His movements seemed trance-like.

He stared at the elephant.

He raised his hand with the palm facing the elephant and spoke to it in words Q-tip couldn't understand.

The elephant rocked from side to side. Something about Peter's presence seemed to calm the animal. It slowly uncoiled its trunk and extended it to smell him.

Q-tip grabbed Deepend by the lapels and pulled him away. Then he hoisted his body into the vehicle. The bull stared at Peter, who was speaking to it softly.

The elephant emitted one last growl and then turned and disappeared into the jungle that lined the road.

Q-tip was buckling Deepend into the front seat. "Deepend," he said, "you are gonna get me killed some day."

Peter slowly returned to the vehicle. He had a look of confusion on his face like he'd just woken from a deep sleep.

Q-tip had the engine revving as Peter climbed into the back. The sound of the motor woke Deepend.

Deepend opened his eyes and looked around. Peter found a canteen and offered him some water.

Q-tip had driven for a few minutes when Deepend said, "Did you see that bull go ape-shit? That was fuckin' awesome."

Q-tip grumbled in disgust.

"Don't be a god-dammed candy-ass," said Deepend as he rubbed his forehead. "What're you sore about? I got the shot!"

Chapter Sixteen

Victoria Falls

They were all pretty rattled. Peter felt the adrenaline slowly subside while he drove toward the park exit. The elephant's deep rumble was still ringing in his ear, and the vibration of its stomp lingered in his bones.

Q-tip pasted a bandage to Deepend's forehead where his impact with the plastic window had split his scalp. Nobody said a word, not even Deepend. The scare seemed to have taken the wind right out of him.

They spent a few hours in silence on the highway to the town of Victoria Falls. Peter opened his windows and let the wind rush through his dusty hair. The afternoon was warm and the buffeting wind lulled them all.

Peter's mind drifted as he drove, and his thoughts returned to his father. It felt strangely unnatural that he was gone. He remembered driving out of the Maasai Mara with him, unconscious by his side.

As the minutes ticked by he contemplated the journey ahead. He was glad for the silence, and the wind.

They stopped at a small roadside shop to pick up a case of beer. Deepend and Q-tip sat silently sipping once they were moving again as they watched the countryside pass by.

It was just after sunset when a sign to the Victoria Falls Campground appeared and they took the exit.

The large camping area resembled a crowded festival ground. Hundreds of travelers were congregating to see the lunar rainbow which only appeared once a month.

Peter found a spot near the eastern end of the campground with a fire pit and a stack of split wood and kindling.

"Check it out," said Deepend. "They forgot to take their wood with them when they left."

He grinned. "Idiots — they must not know how tough it can be to find firewood at some of these sites."

Tents of every make filled the barren camping area; dripping clotheslines hung with hastily washed items were strung from scrawny trees and vehicle mirrors; sleeping bags patched with duct tape that dangled in tatters and all sorts of gear was piled on the ground.

Peter looked around. Crammed in among the tents were about fifty vehicles. Most of them were Land Cruisers, but there were also a few Mercedes. Near the back sat a row of overland trucks with a parade of small matching tents staked out in front of them.

The rectangular perimeter of the campground was lined with massive trees which framed the sky, and as Peter looked up he saw the first faint star of the evening. It was a clear night, so they decided to sleep in the open. Deepend plopped down on his worn sleeping bag and cracked open another beer.

"Fuckin' A! I'm tired."

Q-tip unloaded the two lawn chairs. One looked fine and he gave it to Peter who got them each a beer from the cooler before sitting.

The other appeared worthless, but Q-tip held it up and grinned. "This, I can fix."

After bending it back into shape Q-tip went to work on it with a roll of duct tape. Between deep guzzles off his beer he repeatedly wrapped the damaged sections with the gray tape.

"With this stuff you can fix anything."

"How about helicopters?" asked Deepend.

He shook his head, sternly. "No, not helicopters."

The road-smart veterans who populated the campground guarded their possessions closely, and as the darkness thickened Peter watched them repack much of the gear in the vehicles where it could be locked up safely. Although it wasn't often that one traveler stole from another, in Africa theft was always a problem and both baboons and unwanted hands might snatch anything not guarded or locked down securely.

Some campers were aided in their vigilance by their dogs, although the dogs seemed more interested in each other—this was, after all, a monthly event for many of them as their owners either lived in Zimbabwe or worked in tourism and made the monthly trip.

Under a canopy of stars several fires burned, each with a group of travelers sitting around it. Peter could pick out fragments of German, Spanish, and French floating in the moist evening air. Clips of African slang sounded from the outskirts of the site.

A couple of Brits were playing a drinking game that ended when one person stood and shouted, "M'Ding ding" and everyone replied, "Full Time!"

"What's up with that?" asked Deepend.

"M means great, and a ding ding is a party," explained Peter.

"Sweet," said Deepend as he grabbed another beer.

Along the back of the camping area a row of showers offered a much appreciated respite from the heat of the day. Peter headed there first and relaxed as the water slowly washed away the coat of dirt that covered his skin. Soap and water felt great as it rinsed off layer after layer of the grime that had built over the last two days. His muscles were sore from the long stint behind the wheel and he stretched out while the cool water pounded his back.

When he returned to the fire Deepend and Q-tip left for the showers and he began to prepare the evening meal. The fire pit consisted of a truck tire rim surrounded by large stones.

He built a fire thinking that he couldn't remember the last time he'd been this hungry. His stomach growled as he walked over to the Land Cruiser to scout out the food supplies. In the cooler he found a container of steaks.

He threw three steaks in a cast iron skillet and placed it over the fire. He peeled and cut up an onion and threw it in the skillet with a chunk of butter.

Deepend returned. He wore a fresh T-shirt advertising *The Rocks*, in Harare, Zimbabwe.

"Squeaky fucking clean," he said as he sat and stared at the cooking steaks. The aroma was overpowering. Q-tip joined them and the three looked at the meal impatiently.

"Should be ready soon," said Peter, but Deepend took his pocketknife out of his pocket, stabbed one of the steaks and sat back using an overturned Frisbee as a plate.

"That's fine for me," he said as he tore off a bloody chunk.

Peter was famished, and Q-tip appeared just as hungry, but as they watched Deepend dig in they could see that the meat was only partially cooked and they struggled to restrain themselves for a few more minutes.

They didn't last long.

Soon Peter was alternating fingers as he tried to get a bite of the hot steak in his mouth. By his side he could hear Q-tip curse as he burnt his lip.

Deepend grinned. "Fucking delicious, eh?"

Peter chewed a juicy bite and felt his body coming round.

"Ya, fucking delicious."

Q-tip raised his beer to the stars. "We live good tonight!"

Deepend and Q-tip had put a good dent into their case of beer on the drive, and by the time they lay back to relax by the fire it was almost empty.

Peter's gaze sank into the glow of their fire, his thoughts lost in the flickering of the flames just above the coals. The night was warm.

He looked to the horizon and saw the silver glow from the moon as it filtered through the trees.

In a few hours they would be heading to the falls, but it had been a long day and they were all wind-burned so for now they opted to rest. The fire had died down to coals when Peter placed a sleeping bag and roll mat by it.

Q-tip did the same on the other side, and then Deepend flopped down on a piece of cardboard in front of the fire — dangerously close to it. His sleeping bag had down filling; there were holes in it and whenever he'd shift around feathers would shoot into the air.

"Don't say a fuckin' word," he warned Q-tip the first time it happened.

The fire crackled and beyond it crickets and cicadas cried out. Soon they were asleep.

As they lay dreaming the moon peeked over the tree tops and slowly crept up into the night sky.

The full moon hung over the campsite impossibly large and bright; below it a great cloud of mist that rose off of the falls appeared to be reaching up, extending a thousand tentacles.

Two women passed by and one commented, "*Que linda!*"

Deepend sat up straight and fast as if the ground had shocked him.

"Fuck! Fuck! Fuck!"

Several dogs jumped to their feet and eyed him expectantly, but when nothing ensued they settled down again.

"What time is it? Shit!" he cursed as he looked in vain for something with a clock. "I'll bet it's late."

Q-tip said sleepily, "I think the park is closed now; we go tomorrow, eh?"

"Fuck you!" said Deepend. "I came here to see a lunar rainbow and I'm gonna see it."

He looked around. The campground appeared deserted. A few of the fires had one or two occupied sleeping bags, but it looked very different from the busy location it'd been earlier.

"This place is a ghost town — everyone's already at the falls. We can't just stay here; that would be fucking lame."

A conniving look passed over his face. "Did you see those Danish girls camping by the showers?"

"I saw them," answered Q-tip.

Deepend stumbled to his feet and started cramming his few possessions into his sleeping bag. Flip flops, the Frisbee—still greasy from the steak, a daypack and a shaving kit all went into the sleeping bag before he rolled it up with a burst of feathers.

"One of them was fucking hot, too. The one with the nose ring—did you see her?"

Q-tip moaned. "Please, Deepend, she has a big boyfriend."

"Whatever," said Deepend as he forced his foot into one of his boots and pulled the shoelaces so tightly it looked like he was strangling his foot.

He looked over at Q-tip. "Fucking pussy."

Q-tip sighed. "You have no chance with this woman."

The American gave him a sly look.

"Well, you'll never know; and without you there I'll have better odds."

Q-tip laughed. "With me there you would have no odds."

Deepend kicked Q-tip's sleeping bag hard enough to make him grunt. "Well, I wouldn't want to make you leave your little comfy bed."

Q-tip gave in.

"Okay, Deepend, relax, I go."

He stood and glared at Deepend, daring him to kick him again; then he turned to Peter and asked, "Do you come also?"

Peter sat up and looked up at the full moon.

"Ya, I won't sleep with this moon."

They locked their possessions inside the Land Cruiser and soon they were on their way.

The three men walked through the town of Victoria Falls. The streets were quiet, and the stalls were locked up tight.

They walked down the middle of the street, and soon other travelers returning from the falls came their way. They looked as if they'd been dunked underwater, but wore euphoric expressions as they talked about the magical lunar rainbow.

"This sucks so bad," lamented Deepend. "I bet there was a huge party and now we missed it."

Peter laughed. He didn't care how many people were there. He had come here because it was on his way north, but now the sheer power and energy of the falls were drawing him in.

In the trees on either side of the road the birds jumped between the dripping branches, sending down small bursts of silver drops. Drawn from their slumber by the intense African moon they pursued each other in the eerie light.

Peter watched them chasing each other from limb to limb and as his eyes scanned the area he noticed a pair of yellow eyes watching him.

In the distance Victoria Falls roared. A fine mist was coming down all around them, and the foliage here at the park entrance was lush and dense, as if it had never experienced a dry day.

The mist collected on the wide green leaves of the lush jungle around them. It pooled and puddled on the canopy, and then dripped down to soak the ground. The swaying, erratic motions of the leaves when they released their water made the jungle look alive, or better yet, made it appear like living things were moving through it.

"Hey, it's raining," said Deepend.

Q-tip scoffed, "You are an idiot. This is not rain, this is the mist from the waterfall and we are still a ways off. Now this is power!"

Q-tip shook the gate, which was locked, then shrugged and climbed over it with catlike ease.

Peter watched as a cloud of mist descended on the forest and obscured the eyes he'd been watching. For just a second Deepend saw them as well.

"What was that?" he asked.

Peter shrugged. "Some kind of cat."

"And we are waiting," Q-tip said impatiently from the far side of the fence.

Deepend looked around, and then followed Q-Tip over the fence. Peter climbed over last.

Ahead, a winding path led into the dense rainforest that thrived in the tropical vapor. The misty air glowed softly under the light of the moon. It felt like a unicorn might at any time step out of the mist.

They emerged onto a large, grassy plateau that greeted the falls head-on; about five hundred feet away the falls thundered into a three-hundred foot abyss with a deafening roar. A low safety fence ran along the perimeter of the plateau, apparently to prevent people from stumbling off the edge.

To the left of them the falls disappeared into a deep cylinder that extended all the way to the far side of the abyss where the water poured into it.

Q-tip shouted over the roar of the falls, spreading his arms to present to his peers one of the wonders of the natural world. "My friends, Victoria Falls! To your right we have Zambia, to your left, Zimbabwe."

Several islands sat in the middle of the river where it approached the falls, each with a tangle of trees and bushes. Many clung near the precipice, gripping the rocks while thriving off the steady flow of water. Small waterfalls punched through the vegetation and shot over the edge.

Two Australian men stood just beyond the low safety fence, watching the falls as Peter approached. They each held a can of beer, and one of them gripped the soggy remains of a six-pack holder with two beers left in it. He pointed to a group of low islands just above the foaming precipice and Peter overheard a few words.

"That's where Matt fell in, right there...when he was hopping across."

His mate shook his head sadly. "That's just tragic, getting taken out in a stupid accident."

His friend said. "I heard it wasn't an accident." The other man looked up. "What'd ya hear?"

"Well, I heard that when he was jumping he dropped his beer and he decided to go in after it."

He chuckled and cracked a fresh beer and raised it in a toast.

"That's when he got swept over the falls. Good on ya, Matt!"

Deepend was looking towards the deep and thunderous pool to their left where the plateau dropped away. It was partially obscured by mist, and from their vantage point it appeared that the world had ended and the falls just swirled into a bottomless pit.

"Fuckin' A! Look at that!

"That is the Devil's Cauldron," explained Q-tip. "It is very dangerous, we should not…"

Q-tip stopped because Deepend had walked off in the direction of the pool and was already out of earshot. His last words had been, "I gotta get closer."

Q-tip quickly pursued him, a protest of warning on his lips.

Reluctantly, Peter followed them.

They came to a sign that read *The Devil's Cauldron,* and next to it a solid, wooden staircase descended into the swirling mist below.

The mighty Zambezi River was now at eye-level. Right before them it plunged over the precipice and into the deep cauldron. The waters spiraled down the rocky cylinder, and three hundred feet below they splashed onto the rocks.

Q-Tip and Peter descended down the long set of steps to catch up with Deepend, who was charging ahead, and soon were dripping wet. Peter pulled out a handkerchief and wiped his eyes. He blinked and tried to focus on Q-tip in the mist below him.

The Israeli turned and shouted at Peter.

"From the bottom we can look up and see the lunar rainbow as it encircles the moon! Lower down you will have to feel your way!"

They continued down, gripping the railing tightly lest they slip on the wet boards.

Peter wondered how they expected to see anything at all through the thick, aquatic air, but at the bottom of the staircase they discovered they could make out at least part of the moon.

They gathered in the shelter of a dripping tree trunk. The noise was thunderous. Two hundred feet above, the water shot over the rim of the falls, a hundred feet below, it crashed onto the rocks.

"We're too late, the moon has moved!" Q-Tip yelled. "We can´t see it from here now!"

Deepend leaned over the cauldron, looking up, to improve his view. Then he gave a psychotic grin and climbed under the railing, onto the muddy, jungle-covered walls of the cauldron.

Peter screamed, "Deepend! What the hell are you doing!"

Even Q-tip protested, "No! This is too much! If you fall you is finished!"

Deepend just laughed. He was picking his way across to the near-vertical wall, his hands groping for the moss-covered tree trunks and slippery plants.

His feet scrambled in the mud to find firm ground, but the walls dropped almost straight down and he was forced to cling to roots and branches like a monkey as he made his way along the side of the cauldron. He found a stable position and turned to Q-tip and Peter.

"Candy ass!" he taunted.

The pounding of the falls had a grip on Peter and for reasons he couldn't really explain he found himself following Deepend.

"What the hell?" said Q-tip as he watched Peter duck under the railing.

He threw his hands up in the air and followed him. "Fuck it!"

The three of them were clinging to the side of the cauldron and watched the bright circle of the lunar rainbow as it circled the moon. A warm mist enveloped them and obscured much of the surrounding landscape, but the moon glowed strongly and the mist refracted its light and cast everything in an eerie glow.

It appeared as if the world no longer existed, only the silver swirling mist that caressed their faces and clung to their clothes. Even Deepend had stopped to appreciate the beauty of the silver glow as the moon rose.

The spirals of mist moved and danced like white birds as they rose up to the bright ring around the moon. Peter was captivated, and felt somewhere deep inside that if he could stay there long enough he might understand some of the mysteries that had taken over his life.

Upstream, on the mighty Zambezi River, a bloated hippo floated nonchalantly toward the falls´ edge. It bounced off a rock and spun around, revealing a gaping hole that a vulture had pecked into its side, and then a hyena had widened.

As the carcass approached the falls it picked up speed. It scraped against some rocks by the shore and briefly paused. Then it spun free and was carried over the edge.

The men were smiling at the moon and each other.

"Come on," Deepend called with a grin. "Tell me it wasn't worth it to climb out here. I dare ya."

Q-tip shifted his stare up to the edge of the falls, high above, and suddenly his face froze.

"What is this thing up there?" he asked.

For a moment the mist parted and they were allowed a quick glimpse. It was two hundred feet away, but the silhouette was unmistakable.

"It looks like a hippo," answered Deepend, "but it can't be crazy enough to . . ."

They screamed in horror as it cleared the edge and plummeted towards them. For a moment the giant mass of rotting flesh eclipsed the full moon.

Downward it plunged, whistling like a torpedo.

Peter yelled, "Against the wall!"

And then the hippo hurtled past them with a loud whoosh. A scent of decaying meat followed it, and Peter thought it smelled of death.

They screamed again as it cannon-balled into the cauldron below and disappeared from sight. There was a thud and Peter imagined the rotting mass hitting the rocks below and bursting.

Q-tip frantically clawed his way back to the platform. "I am through with you, Deepend! I think you always chase the fire!" he shouted.

The American laughed.

"Don't *huck* with the *fippos* — you know the rules."

Q-tip attempted to climb back onto the wooden platform. In his panic he almost fell twice, but luckily he'd been gripping a root tightly when his feet had slipped.

From the platform he shouted back at Deepend — who had been laughing hysterically as he watched his frantic retreat.

"Tomorrow I chase the fire no more! He comes too close! Thank you for the fire, but he is yours now!"

Deepend ignored him and looked up at the moon. "That was wicked," he said.

Peter carefully edged his way to the platform, and without looking back he climbed the slippery wooden steps up to the plateau's edge.

Q-tip and Deepend were arguing as he passed them at the top of the stairs.

"How can you call me a coward after this?" demanded Q-tip.

Deepend shrugged and ran his left hand through his wet hair. "Well, maybe you're not a coward — but you're definitely a pussy."

Peter had had enough of their bickering and walked on.

He stepped over the low safety fence that marked off the tourist pathway and walked along the wet grass until he reached the abyss. On the way he saw other groups of people, all hunkered down in the mist. Some had rain coats or ponchos;

other just accepted the conditions and looked drenched but happy. It was warm and many of the men were shirtless.

As the flow of the falls launched itself onto rocks far below, the force of the impact vaporized the water and shot it straight up the face of the plateau. It blasted right past the edge where Peter stood.

Above Peter's head the drops continued to float up, spiraling, until they collected and sank, only to rise up again. The moisture was silver in the glow of the full moon.

The roaring of the falls pulled Peter closer. The mist obscured his vision, and he felt his boots slip on the wet grass, but still he moved closer to the precipice.

He was only a few feet away now, and the blast of the wind produced by the falling water masses was so strong it stood his hair on end. He leaned forward, like a flower to the sun. In the back of his mind he heard a man call out the same word over and over, but the meaning of the word evaded him.

The pull was overpowering, and it affected him so deeply that an urge to let himself fall into the abyss surged up inside him. It would be an end to his nightmares and his anguish. But he resisted, and deep inside he knew that this was not where he would die. The grumbling in his stomach told him that he had unfinished business, and as he peered through the mist at the rocks far below he wondered what that could possibly be.

And then a voice from the tall grass behind him yanked him back into reality; its tone was deep and carried its own power. The voice was filled with confidence and authority, but also peace, and it somehow carried over the din of the falls.

"Africa is for the soul, *mon*. I see you can feel this."

Peter turned around and saw a large black man sitting in the silver glow. He looked about forty and was relaxing on a reed mat. Where Peter stood the wind roared, but just a few paces away where the black man was reclining, all seemed tranquil.

Peter took a few steps in his direction, away from the roar of the wind and the pounding of the falls. Instantly, it was quieter.

He looked at the man. He had long dreadlocks, a sparse beard, and he smiled when he spoke.

"My name is Henry. What would your good name be?"

The sleeves of his t-shirt had been torn off, exposing muscular arms which he had folded in front of him as he waited for Peter's reply.

"Peter."

Henry drew a deep breath as he raised his arms to the moon above them. He looked around, as if taking in the scene anew.

"The mystic is a powerful thing, Peter," said Henry, "but you should not fear it. It is the unknown, and you should embrace the unknown if you want to be free."

Peter tried to guess where Henry was from. He didn't look African, and he carried himself like someone who had been many places.

"Are you free?" asked Peter.

Henry smiled proudly. "Yes, *mon.*"

Peter's smile was grim. "And what do you think I should seek out—in the unknown?"

Henry laughed deeply; his dreads were speckled with dew that reflected the luminous glow. He tilted his head slightly and creased his brow, and then he said, "I think you should seek out a dog."

"Is it?" said Peter with a smile. "A dog?"

"Yes," answered Henry, "preferably a mongrel."

Peter laughed, and wondered how sane this man was. Henry must have read the expression on his face because he pointed to his reed mat and patted it.

"Sit, *mon.* Sit! And I will explain to you why you need a dog."

He looked Peter over as he sat on his reed mat with the tall grass behind him slumped over from all the moisture.

"You, my friend, are going to need help," said Henry.

He stared deep into Peter's eyes and added, "I do not know what your trouble is, but I think you will need help soon."

"And a mongrel is going to help me?" asked Peter with a raised eyebrow.

Henry laughed and slapped his knees.

"No *mon* walks through life alone."

Peter looked ready to leave as he asked, "And what kind of trouble will I need help from?"

Henry became serious. The falls pounded around them as the two men gazed into each other's eyes.

"You," began Henry, "have trouble all around you."

And then, before Peter could respond, he clapped his hands and added, "But not tonight! So let us thank *Jah!*"

Henry raised his arms and started quoting scripture.

Peter watched the man, not quite sure what to make of him.

Q-tip and Deepend found Peter sitting with Henry near the plateau's edge. They'd scored some beer and passed one over to Peter. Q-tip offered one to Henry, but he declined.

"I have no need for alcohol," said Henry as he tapped the wet ground.

"Sit, *mon*. Join us, and let us light a spliff and give praise to Haile Selassie."

Deepend shook his head.

"You're gonna have a fuck of a hard time rolling a joint out here."

Henry pulled a plastic baggy out of his jacket and took out a very fat-looking spliff. "In order to move through life in a godly way, one must plan ahead."

"I like this guy!" said Deepend.

Henry lit his spliff and blew a huge cloud of smoke into the silver mist. The mist kept the smoke low and it floated all around them like a spirit as the falls rumbled nearby.

"Let us share this spliff and give praise to Haile Selassie," said Henry as he raised his arms to the powerful forces around them.

He continued, "Great Selassie, who is descended from the line of Judah, the line of Kings, the line of David and Jesus. *Jah!*"

Chapter Seventeen

Conrad

Q-tip sat in the idling Land Cruiser, its nose pointed back to Harare; Deepend and Peter stood on the side of the road, their backpacks by their feet. Normally, Peter thought, partings are a sad thing that lingers, but this was different. He now felt impelled to go north, and Q-tip was almost as eager to get away from Deepend.

"I go back to the Sable Lodge," said Q-tip as he revved the engine. "Any more time with this man..." He pointed an accusing finger at Deepend, "... and I think I die."

He looked at Peter. "Hear my words, Peter, you take care if you continue to chase the fire with this man."

"Don't be a pussy," taunted Deepend, leaning toward the Land Cruiser.

Peter shoved Deepend away gently and extended his hand to Q-tip. "Thanks for the lift."

Q-tip asked, "Are you really going all the way to Nairobi with that crazy fool?"

"I'm not sure," replied Peter. "We will shoot for Lusaka today and take it from there. That's almost three hundred miles from here, who knows what will happen after that?"

They said goodbye and walked to a small customs office at the head of a bridge that spanned the Zambezi River just downstream from the mighty falls.

On the far side lay Zambia.

They passed through the small customs station without incident and slowly walked across the bridge. It spanned eight hundred feet and ran three hundred feet above the powerful Zambezi River. In the middle of the bridge they stopped and watched the water cascade over the edge of the mighty Victoria Falls located about a quarter mile upstream, smashing its way to the basin at the base.

Deepend looked down. "Right there one of the most intense stretches of whitewater in the world originates—I wish I had time to run it."

"Do it," replied Peter.

Deepend watched the white water below.

"No. And it's fucking killing me not to, but I've really gotta make my flight and you're my best chance of getting to Nairobi in time."

Peter grinned. "How very responsible of you."

Then he looked into Deepend's eyes.

"This might be the last peaceful moment you're going to have for a while—we've got a long way to go, and as you would say, 'I'm not going to be fucking around'."

Deepend grinned. "Bring it on."

They crossed the bridge and passed through Zambian customs. Deepend couldn't find his passport at first; when he finally located it in the bottom of his backpack the Zambian guards charged him extra for his visa because he was American. Deepend bitched so much the guards exchanged glances of relief when Deepend and Peter finally left and Peter wondered if it was a wise move to travel with the American.

On the street they scanned the crowds for means of transit, but all they encountered were tourist coming to see the falls and vendors setting up for the day.

They had hoped to find an overland truck, or at least some local traffic heading north, but nobody here appeared to be in a rush to go anywhere. It was still early in the day, but Peter now feared it might be difficult to get to Lusaka at all.

Then he noticed a tall, rugged, white man with an overgrown military haircut. The man smiled as he met his gaze, but something about this character alarmed him. He was trying too hard to look casual.

He looked about fifty, and hardened—even from fifty paces away he stood out like bad news. Peter didn't like it one bit.

"Let's just start walking," said Peter. "Maybe our luck will improve at the edge of town."

They began to walk away from the commotion of the tourists and vendors, but no sooner had they left the crowds behind them that the unnerving man Peter had noticed earlier pulled up alongside them in a battered red truck. It belched noisily as it approached and backfired loudly. The vehicle was in such rough shape that even Deepend did a double-take.

His brakes screeched as he came to a stop; a dust cloud floated past them like a ghost while they stared at the truck.

It sat well above the ground, and looked like it had been rammed by a rhino. The tailgate was peppered with dents from shotgun pellets; the back left window had been broken; and several long, spidery cracks stretched across the windshield.

"Dude, this thing looks like it's been through a war," said Deepend.

The man almost choked on his laugh before he said, "Not quite, but very close I assure you."

He extended his hand to Deepend.

"My name is Conrad," said the man as he tilted his head to the side and spat. He kept pulling on a red bandana that was tied around his neck. It seemed the bandanna was too tight.

Deepend turned to watch an attractive young woman walk by. She wore a colorful dress with tribal patterns on it, and smiled at him playfully as she passed. Conrad watched Deepend's face closely the entire time.

Peter noticed several scars on his face and forearms, and he didn't like the sneer that was taking over his unshaved face as he observed Deepend flirting with the black woman.

His heavy eyelids obscured some of his sly glances, but whenever Peter turned away he felt his eyes on him as well.

Conrad turned from watching Deepend to shake Peter's hand, but found he had already moved on. Peter's stomach did a flip when he heard Deepend ask, "Hey Conrad, are you heading toward Lusaka?"

Conrad smiled wide, showing a mouth full of yellow teeth.

"You know, actually I am."

"I couldn't help notice you seemed to be heading in the same direction as I am," Conrad said, "and I was actually stopping to see if you wanted a lift—it's a long way to drive alone."

Deepend yelled over to Peter.

"Hey, hold on! I got us a lift."

Peter knew Conrad's type all too well and didn't want to ride with him, but he needed the lift so he reluctantly came back.

He nodded at Conrad, threw his pack in the bed of the truck, and started to climb in with it.

"Hold on there, boy!" shouted Conrad, "You two are riding up front with me!"

Peter eyeballed Conrad for a brief moment before he lowered himself back down. There was something wrong, he knew it, and it went beyond Conrad most likely being a racist or a drunk.

"We won't arrive in Lusaka until after dark, but if you'd like I've got a bunkroom there that you are welcome to use."

Deepend energetically jumped into the middle seat, Peter followed him with measured movements. He shut the door and stared out the side window.

"We can't stay long," said Peter. "I want to be on the road north at first light."

Conrad put the truck in gear and they began to move. "Early birds, eh?"

Conrad put on his best smile for Peter. "I can hear in your accent that you are from Southern Africa."

Peter nodded. "South Africa."

"Then we are neighbors! I've lived in Zambia for a few years now, working to preserve the old ways of life."

Deepend gave him a questioning look and Conrad slowly shook his head. "Once, all of southern Africa made up a great country called Rhodesia, but it's all gone to hell since then. I remember how glorious it was back when there was order."

They drove along in silence. Conrad kept throwing glances at his passengers; Peter was looking out the side window absorbed in thought, and Deepend was happily smiling at the fact that they had scored a ride.

When the American finally met his stare, Conrad said, "I hate not having my own transportation. What would you do if you didn't get a ride?"

Deepend thought for a minute. "I guess I'd just rough it and camp for the night."

"Camp in the bush?" asked Conrad, incredulously. "Are you not afraid of the snakes? We have mambas here in Africa, black mambas."

He shifted into a higher gear and soon they were bombing down the road at what had to be the vehicle's top speed.

"The Black Mamba—I tell you I've seen them well over twice the length of your body. Get between them and their den they will come at you, and *yes* they are fast!"

"I fucking hate snakes," said Deepend.

Conrad slowly shook his head from side to side. "If you are already running, then maybe you will live. But to start from standing, the mamba will have you every time. You will be dead before you hit the ground."

He grinned. "The mamba is a quick killer."

Around mid-day Conrad stopped for gas and picked up a case of beer, but things took longer than expected. The woman behind the counter, an old lady who was missing her two front teeth, didn't have enough change for the note he handed her, and Conrad started an angry argument.

"You shouldn't be allowed to run a business if you can't do it properly!" he spat out.

She shrugged.

"Well," he nodded. "Just give me three cases of beer then."

She smiled, lifting her soft brown cheeks.

"I'm so sorry; sir, but this here is the only case of beer I have."

"So you're telling me I have to pay three times the value if I want the case?"

When she nodded he spat on the floor. He then dropped his note on the counter, lifted his case and started walking to the door.

She followed him, cursing his back as he exited the store with the case under his arm.

When he got back in the truck his face was beet red, and back on the road he emptied can after can of beer. He crushed the cans with one hand and threw them out the window.

Deepend gladly shared Conrad's beers when he offered, but Peter only took one and nursed it.

"Drink up!" toasted Conrad as he tried to get Peter to loosen up; Peter's hesitation seemed to bother him.

"I am celebrating a successful mission. You should drink with me."

Peter faked a smile and took another beer.

Through the long afternoon they continued.

The road was lined with scrub brush and some acacia and thorn trees and clusters of baobabs here and there. A few monkeys and baboons were searching for food along the side of the road.

Occasionally they passed by simple villages, and Conrad made a game of chasing the donkeys in the road.

He clipped one animal and covered his mouth like a guilty child.

"Oops," he said as he grabbed another beer.

It was hot and Deepend had fallen asleep with his head on Peter's shoulder — Peter eventually pushed him away when he began to drool. Conrad also had begun to fade; his buzz had worn off and he was pale and sweaty.

For an hour he drove without saying a word.

But as soon as the sun touched the horizon he stopped to buy another case of beer, and within an hour he was drunk again. They'd been traveling for over ten hours when they reached the southern outskirts of Lusaka; here they left the bush behind and drove among simple houses with corrugated roofs.

Suddenly, Conrad had to pull his truck hard to the right to avoid hitting an old black man who was walking in the middle of the road. This jerked Conrad out of his drunken stupor and angered him mightily.

He slammed on the brakes and backed up to confront the old man.

"Hey, stupid old fool, why are you walking in the middle of the road, eh?"

The man smiled, showing only three teeth.

"There is no traffic," he said.

"There's plenty of traffic, you idiot! You better stay out of my way if you know what's good for you!"

The old man eyed Conrad warily, but then said defiantly.

"This is my country and I will walk where I want."

Conrad's eyes bulged in his head. The old man had turned his back on him and started to walk away, and Conrad threw his beer at him and hit him in the shoulder.

"Bloody kaffirs!" shouted Conrad.

The old man stopped and stared at him, then stepped off the road and into the shadows. Deepend looked at Peter, and for the first time he seemed to share Peter´s uneasiness with the situation.

An hour after nightfall they reached Conrad's place on the outskirts of Lusaka. There were no neighbors, and an eerie silence surrounded the yard. Conrad opened the truck´s door and a barrage of empty beer cans clattered to the ground. He stumbled over them into the darkness to turn on the lights in his small house.

Peter and Deepend listened to him curse when he bumped into something, and then burp loudly. Suddenly, the lights in the house flicked on, and then a spotlight lit a dark building near the back of the property.

Conrad returned to the truck. He grabbed their packs with one hand and led them to his bunk room. He disappeared into a back room and came back with a glass kerosene lamp and a six-pack. He handed two beers to Peter and Deepend, then opened one for himself and went to ignite the lantern.

151

He fiddled drunkenly with the lighter, then cursed it and threw it against the wall. Deepend handed him his own lighter, and after a few more attempts the lantern was lit. Conrad's angry scowl turned to a happy smile.

"See, that's better," he slurred. He swayed as he spread his arms and spun in a circle to show off the bunk room. Then he hung the lantern from a pole in the middle of the room and turned the light up. It cast long shadows of the three men on the walls behind them.

Peter was surprised to find himself in a large room with ten new cots. The walls were made from new, rough-cut boards and there were two windows on each side, each framed by a frilly curtain. It smelled of sawdust, and in a corner sat a pile of planks, waiting to be cut and nailed to the far wall which was unfinished.

Conrad placed the six-pack on the only other piece of furniture, an old dresser under the lamp.

"Nice place, dude," said Deepend and Conrad grunted.

"You must be glad to be home. Did you spend much time away, in Zimbabwe?"

Conrad's face turned into a squinty smile.

"What would you like to know" he sneered, "Just now? Or in the past?"

Deepend rolled his eyes.

"Whatever, dude, I'm just making conversation."

Conrad croaked out a loud laugh.

"Okay then, my Yankee friend. Yes, I did some work in Zimbabwe, back when it was still Rhodesia, showing the kaffirs the true price of independence."

He made an evil grin, and scratched his neck under the bandana.

"What kind of price can you put on Independence?" asked Deepend.

Conrad chuckled and motioned to the room. "Do you like this? I just built it."

"Nice," said Peter as he looked at a calendar hanging next to the door with a woman wearing nothing but an AK-47 machine gun.

Deepend asked, "Is this some kind of guest house?

Conrad looked at him with a sneer.

"No, it's not a guest house, although you might think so with those frilly curtains. I wanted to have one thing that was homey for those who stay here. Business has been slow lately, but I have a feeling it's about to pick up."

Deepend looked at Conrad, then at Peter with a blank face. "I don't get it."

Conrad downed the rest of his beer.

"Let's just call it a barracks, eh? Would that work for you?"

"Like for the army?"

Conrad crushed his beer can in his hand and glared at Deepend.

"No more games, eh?"

He measured his guests with a penetrating stare, like a big cat summing up its prey.

"I was what you might call a travel agent. I sent those kaffirs straight to their father, to Lucifer, the father of all kaffirs."

Conrad opened another beer and downed half of it.

He laughed at himself in his choking way, and twisted his neck, pulling at his bandana.

"But I was a good travel agent. I tell you, I did my job quick and with skill. When they saw me coming they knew fear."

He grinned proudly as he added, "I even gave them a fire permit so they could make fires down there."

"Down where?" asked Deepend.

Conrad yelled, "In hell you stupid fool!"

"I don't get it," said Deepend and Peter leaned over and quickly said, "He was a mercenary."

Conrad's laughter died and he fixed his stare on Peter, who dropped his gaze to the floor.

Conrad snarled, "Everything I did for a government: the Rhodesian war, the South African bush war, Angola, Mozambique. I am a patriot!"

Peter continued to focus on the new floorboards.

Deepend looked horrified.

"And now they will not even let me enter South Africa. For my last job I had to sneak over — like a thief in the night."

153

He grinned. "Maybe they knew I had a score to settle, eh?"

He untied his bandana to show a long, horrible scar across his neck, and then, as if the thought of the horrible looking skin left a bad taste in his mouth, he spat on his new floor.

"You see this?" asked Conrad in a hateful tone and craned his neck to the side to expose the scar. "A man did this to me, but he didn't finish the job. He just left me there to die. What honor is there in that?"

He rubbed the scar. "That's how I treat animals."

Peter stepped away from the lamp light, into the shadows.

Conrad adjusted one of the frilly curtains and said over his shoulder. "Maybe you don't mind what I did, only the fact that you know I enjoyed it. Eh, brother?"

When Peter stepped out of the shadows there was a new look about him. It was angry and defiant and when Conrad turned to face them again Peter raised his head and matched Conrad's stare. The man threw his half-full beer at the wall and glared at Peter.

Something in the young man's eyes unnerved him.

"You look familiar, boy—have we met?" he snarled.

Peter continued to look at him, silently.

"And you better stop staring at me that way, boy! I won't have you judge me! I was defending whites in southern Africa before you were born!"

He started to pace the room, "Those kaffirs are animals, anyway! Have you ever seen how they live?"

He pointed to the scar on his neck.

"The man who cut me did it because I killed a black—can you believe that?"

Incredulously, he looked up at the ceiling as if an answer might be there.

"Who really cares if another black dies? They breed like rabbits— like rats is more like it!" He spat again, "At least I killed the right man; the one I shot was the young Seer and when he died the tribe fell apart."

Conrad wiped the sweat from his forehead and grinned.

"Got a whole flock of birds with one stone."

He laughed rambunctiously.

154

Then he pointed at his scar again and said, "The man who gave me this finally got what was coming to him, too."

He nodded, satisfied, and added, "It might have taken me awhile, but I got him."

Peter's stare had turned icy. Conrad bent to straighten the covers on one of the cots.

"These days," began Conrad again, "nothing gives me more satisfaction than seeing those same Maasai begging and stealing on the streets of Nairobi."

When Conrad stood he turned to say something else but Peter swung and landed a solid punch to his face. The blow snapped his head back, and for a second the big man reeled. But he remained standing and shook his head angrily.

"Holy shit!" exclaimed Deepend.

Conrad twisted his neck and opened and shut his jaw.

A trickle of blood was running to his chin.

He tasted it.

Then he opened the top draw of the dresser and pulled out a large knife. He looked at Peter with a frown. He touched the tip of the knife, and then felt along its edge making sure it was sharp. Peter took a step back.

"You'll pay for that, boy," Conrad said. He shook his head slowly as he reached for Peter, asking, "This is how you repay my hospitality?"

Deepend grabbed one of the heavy planks and swung it at Conrad, but he hit the lamp first. The glass shattered and the lamp burst into flame, sending a shower of glass and burning fuel over Conrad.

In an instant Conrad was aflame, along with the walls and floor near him

Peter jumped back and Deepend pulled him toward the open door of the bunkhouse. Conrad was screaming and stumbling into the curtains and setting them on fire.

Peter snatched their packs from the doorway as they scrambled out of the burning bunkhouse. They were twenty paces away before they turned and looked back.

The entire shack was now in flames which cast an eerie glow on the surrounding trees. Suddenly, Conrad burst through the doorway. His hair had burnt off in patches and his shirt was reduced to burning rags that barely covered a charred upper body.

He screamed at them, but his words were incomprehensible.

They ran for his truck.

Conrad fell to his knees in agony, slapping at the flames.

"Go ahead, run!"

Peter threw the packs in the truckbed and yanked the door open.

"I will find you!" screamed Conrad as he sank backwards. He moaned and reeled.

Peter saw that the keys were still in the ignition.

"Get in. Now!" he commanded as he turned the key and revved the engine. Deepend jumped in. Peter tore out of the driveway and from the corner of his eye caught a glimpse of Conrad lying on his back by the entrance. He turned his burnt face to watch them, and for a moment, Peter met his hateful gaze.

"What the fuck have we done?" whispered Deepend.

Peter was panting as he pulled away.

"I think that might be a man they call Red Beret. If he is, and he lives through the fire, he'll come after us. And he won't stop until we're dead."

Chapter Eighteen

The Mongrel

On the road north, about two hours from Lusaka, they walked away from the pickup, which they'd driven into a gully off the side of the road. The morning was still gloomy and with the thick brush around it Peter hoped it might be some time before the truck was discovered.

"Hope we didn't ditch the truck too soon," said Deepend as he looked back at where it lay concealed in the thicket. "We could still put another five hundred miles between us and that fucker."

"Conrad will be after us very soon and we have to shake him. He'll catch up with the truck eventually so I think our best hope is to flag down somebody quickly; besides, we could never drive it across a border without the proper paperwork."

To Deepend's dismay Peter threw the keys deep into the forest which was just now beginning to stir, and then walked to the edge of the road.

"Maybe we should blow it up," he offered as he followed Peter.

Peter looked back at him for a moment, but then decided to focus on what was important.

"I want to get out of Zambia and into Tanzania," said Peter. "We need to cover about five hundred miles as fast as possible."

"So how we gonna do it?" asked Deepend.

Peter shrugged. "A trucker with a load might take us, but ideally we'll find an overland truck."

"What's the difference?"

"Overland trucks carry passengers across Africa. Most of the other trucks aren't as big, won't always pick up hitch hikers, and don't cross international borders. At the Sable Lodge Justice told me this road is the main route north for overland trucks returning to Kenya."

Deepend exhaled. "Let's hope so."

They then stood on the side of the road, impatiently waiting for a ride. Deepend began jumping in place, and then started a series of upper body twists.

"We need some luck...and right fucking now," he said.

Peter restlessly stared at the sun which now peered at them through the thorn trees, hovering just over the horizon. The tree bark was blazing red in the early morning light.

The silence around them weighed on Deepend. He picked up a few small rocks and tried to hit a sign across the road. When he finally hit it, the clang was shockingly loud.

Peter glared at him.

He dropped his remaining rocks and asked, "So you met that crazy bastard before—Conrad?"

Peter was silent. The birds were singing around them. He thought of the trip to Kenya with his dad and their encounter with Red Beret; he also thought of the previous evening, but his recollection of the events in Conrad's bunkhouse was patchy and not at all clear—as if he'd been drunk. The missing memories puzzled him. Why couldn't he remember clearly?

"I only saw him from a distance and I never had a good look at his face," answered Peter. "And it was ten years ago," he added.

Deepend nodded. "And what about that job he said he'd just finished? The one in South Africa."

Peter's face turned pale. He said nothing and stared at the ground. Deepend thought he wasn't going to get an answer, so he went back to pacing and eying the road nervously. He was taken completely by surprise when Peter replied.

"I think that may have been my father."

The sun was now peeking over the tops of the trees, preparing to float freely in the sky. It was less than an hour since Peter had ditched the truck, but he knew Conrad couldn't be far behind. The dread he felt was tangible and he had trouble swallowing. From his pack he retrieved some water and forced it down.

They had ditched the truck at the top of a long hill, because Peter figured that vehicles coming their way would slow down as they ascended. About a quarter mile down the hill the road hid behind a sharp curve, but they could hear approaching vehicles for some time before they came into view.

Peter picked up the sound of a distant engine.

Deepend heard it too and they looked at each other nervously.

Breathlessly, they listened to it get closer.

For several minutes the sound hovered in the air.

"What the fuck!" cursed Deepend as he stared, unable to take his eyes off the curve.

Suddenly, a small white car came around the corner, ascended up the hill and sped past them. An old white woman with a wide-brimmed hat was driving. She looked the other way when Peter extended his arm and pointed at the ground the way hitchhikers do in southern Africa.

Deepend glared at the back of her car. "Bitch. We didn't want a ride in that piece of shit Toyota anyway."

He turned and looked down the hill again.

Peter exhaled. He'd been hoping for a ride, but he was just as relieved that it hadn't been Conrad.

"Did you see how fucked up Conrad was when we left?" said Deepend. "I bet he'll have to go to a hospital first to get fixed up."

The serious look Peter gave him should have been enough of an answer, but it wasn't. "Come on, dude," said Deepend, "you're telling me he'll come after us with burns all over his body?"

Peter nodded. "He's had military training and Special Forces in southern Africa are trained to move beyond the pain—and he's bent on revenge and that can drive a man a long way too. Either way, it's not gonna take him long to find another vehicle so somebody better pick us up or we're gonna have to get off this road."

Before either of them said another word they heard a truck engine.

"Fuck me," said Deepend. "This is it."

They listened. Peter said, "That sounds bigger than a passenger vehicle. We may be in luck."

"If it's Conrad, I'm fucking running and you're on your own," said Deepend. "That dude scares me."

A big, blue overland truck rounded the curve.

It had ten large wheels, four in the back on each side and two up front, and the doors featured a painting of a bulldog with a spiked collar. The words *The Mongrel* were painted underneath.

Peter smiled. The Rastafarian, Henry, was proving to be a bit of a seer. Had he somehow known?

He was pulled out of his reverie when he realized that the truck appeared to have no intention of stopping. Peter reached into his pocket, pulled out a wad of bills, and waved it at the driver.

Brakes screeched in response. The truck was pulling over.

The front of the truck had a canvas top with plastic windows. The windshield was hinged so it could be laid on the hood for unobstructed views in the game parks; and the back of the vehicle sat well above the ground so the passengers had great visibility of the landscapes they passed through.

Deepend and Peter had to run to catch up with the *Mongrel*. The driver was unzipping the plastic window and as it flapped open it created a small cloud of dust.

In the cab sat two men in their mid-thirties. Their sunglasses were caked with dust. One sported a visor and the hair on the top of his head stood straight up, the other had a face full of stubble and had his hair buzzed short.

"*Oy,*" said the man with the visor in a thick Australian accent. "What can I do for you fine gentlemen?"

Deepend went to speak but Peter cut him off.

"We need a lift north, as far as you're going," said Peter.

The man nodded. "We're heading north—all the way to Nairobi."

His co-pilot leaned forward and said, "But nobody rides free here, you know how it goes—ass, grass or gas—and we're not pooftas."

Peter nodded, "I have cash."

The driver grinned. "It's a long way, mate...Mbeya...Dar es Salaam...Arusha."

"I know how far it is," said Peter.

"Good," said the driver. "I'll take ya, but it's gonna cost one hundred U.S. each, and you gotta take care of your own food. All I do is drive."

Deepend went to protest, but Peter punched his arm and silenced him.

Another vehicle was approaching below the curve. With a sense of anxiety Peter could hear the sound of the engine growing louder.

Peter looked toward the curve apprehensively.

"Okay, that's fine. Can we go now?"

The driver noticed the look and sat back a little.

"You look like you got some trouble. Is it with the local police or the military?"

Peter hesitated. In his ears the sound of the approaching vehicle was growing unbearably loud.

"It's neither."

The driver laughed.

"Then get in. It ain't my problem. I'm Doc, and this here is Reggie."

Peter introduced himself and Deepend.

Doc said, "It'll take a few days to get to Nairobi, and we've got some horrible roads ahead of us, but we drive day and night and should be at the Tanz border tomorrow."

Then Doc nodded to a reflection in his side mirror; above him, in the back, there had been a third person watching—a backup if necessary. The face of the man was obscured by the shadows inside the truck, but a hand appeared to flip the lock on a metal gate that sat above a solid ladder bolted to the side of the truck.

The door swung open.

The bed of the *Mongrel* sat about eight feet above the ground and Peter wasted no time climbing the ladder. Deepend followed as Doc revved the engine.

Doc turned his head back and said, "I know it makes things more comfortable to lower and raise the side panels when the weather is nice, but if you fall off my truck while you're adjusting them you're on your own."

"What a nice guy," said Deepend as he paused in the doorway, looking down at the bend to see the approaching vehicle.

Doc heard him. "I'm just warning you; I'm not gonna lose my job because I got delayed taking you to the hospital. You fall off, I'm not even stopping."

Reggie shouted, "So hang on!"and Doc popped the clutch. The momentum forced Deepend to dive for the floor of the truckbed to prevent being thrown out the side door.

Inside the *Mongrel* everything was covered with a fine layer of dust. The truck bed was enclosed by an overhead canvas canopy with metal ribs; long canvas flaps with two plastic windows each hung over the sides. The back of the bed contained eight double seats arranged in two rows of four with an isle down the middle. They each had cushions and arm rests, and faced forward.

As Deepend staggered towards a bench he felt two long, black arms embrace him. From just behind his ear came the voice of Henry, the Rastafarian.

"Rasta!" roared Henry, "My good friends, Peter and Deepend, nice of you to join us!"

Peter watched as his long arms encircled the American and held him tightly. Even away from the powerful waterfall where they first met the black man exuded a special energy. Peter wondered again if it was the confidence in his eyes, the sheer physical size of him, or if it was something more.

When Henry had finished hugging Deepend he turned to Peter. The South African smiled. "I´m in need of a mongrel, huh?" he asked.

Henry laughed. "Well, I knew the *Mongrel* would be passing through Lusaka, but we were a long way from there and I didn't know if *Jah* would allow me to travel fast enough to get there in time."

Doc shifted up another gear and Peter grabbed the side of the truck for support.

"Hold tight, *mon*!" shouted Henry as he stepped into the aisle and gripped the backs of two of the seats while firmly planting his feet. "Like this."

Henry glanced at the cab and added, "Watch out! Or that bad man up front will kill you with his driving."

Peter quickly took stock of the vehicle they would likely call home for the next few days. The far back of the bed had a plywood partition and Peter suspected that it hid a storage area for tents and other supplies for safaris.

He figured the structure would keep out a fair amount of wind and rain. Typically, on safari, ten to twenty young adults would populate these seats during the day, and spend the nights at game park campsites.

Two of the side benches were piled high with sleeping bags and Peter spotted a leg sticking out of one of them and realized there were two other hitch hikers on board.

At the front end of the truck bed two cushioned benches faced inward, away from the sides with a wooden table bolted between them. Up against the cab stood a bookcase filled with well-worn novels, magazines and several rolls of toilet paper wrapped in plastic. A cassette player was bolted to the top along with several speakers held in place by metal brackets. The bookcase was bolted down as well and netting had been stapled in front of each shelf to prevent the contents from spilling out on rough roads.

Doc shifted to the *Mongrel's* highest gear and the entire back end began to vibrate and jump around. Henry cautiously climbed through the side benches and reached for one of the front benches. Peter followed, and when they were firmly seated Henry smiled at him. "You, my friend, I knew would make Lusaka in time."

Peter looked him in the eye. The front bench was out of the wind and Peter found they could talk there without always shouting. "And why's that?"

Henry shrugged, and then unabashedly stared deeply into Peter's eyes. "Because you looked driven."

Deepend claimed one of the double seats that faced forward and stared out the plastic window.

"*Mkushi Boma!*" he shouted out as they passed a sign as if it was a landmark of great importance. Minutes later he added, "*Mkushi River!*" when they approached a bridge with another sign.

A swirl of dust chased them down the road and Doc drove fast enough to leave most of it behind them. They left the small towns and the empty plains stretched off around them. From time to time they passed large outcroppings of rock that looked like they had been exposed to the harsh elements since time began.

Soon pot holes and eroded sections jolted the passengers into the air, and Doc had to slow the truck. There was not much room for maneuvering; the road dropped off sharply at the edge of the pavement.

"Well, I feel like I should thank you," said Peter.

Henry held up his hands, palms forward. "No, for this ride I will take no thanks."

Peter noticed his backpack on the floor and stood to carry it to the back of the truck.

"I have ridden these trucks before," said Henry. "You will be lucky to get off without a broken bone. I have ridden with men covered with blood and others who cradled broken limbs."

Deepend spotted a jug of water in the bookcase netting and walked over and grabbed it. "Cool it, man, it's like surfing."

Henry shook his head. "He should not take this casually."

Henry moved to the aisle again, crouched, and grabbed the back of a seat on each side. "This is how you should ride on the bad roads."

"How's this?" asked Deepend as he stood on a bench with his arms out.

Peter stared at him. "Stop fuckin' around."

"What?" asked Deepend as he stood and guzzled half of the water while not holding onto the chair in front of him.

Doc hit the horn and suddenly the *Mongrel* was forced off by an oncoming truck and the vehicle dropped through the air.

Deepend screamed. "Hold on! This is it!"

The *Mongrel* slammed into the ground, and the front end bounced two feet in the air. Everyone in the back bounced through the truckbed like pingpong balls. Deepend had been standing in the back and when the back four tires hit and bounced he was catapulted up into the canopy ribbing and then dropped harshly into the alley. Peter was thrown into the side flap, and if it hadn't been tied down he would have been ejected right out of the vehicle. Henry stood in the center aisle and gripped two of the chairs so tightly it looked like he'd rip them right out of the floor.

"RASTA!!" he screamed.

The pile of sleeping bags rose in the air, shifted slightly, and the leg that had been exposed was pulled deeper, out of sight. Peter wondered how the sleepers could have possibly slept through the accident.

In the cab they could hear Doc cursing as he slowly maneuvered the truck back onto the road.

Painfully, Peter and Deepend picked themselves up and made their way back to a seat. Peter tried to look ahead to see what else lay in store, but the side flaps were lashed down tightly and prevented him. Deepend stared at him with panic filled eyes.

"What have we gotten ourselves into?" he asked as he rubbed a welt on his forehead.

"Just settle yourself into one of those seats and sit tight."

"This is not good, *mon,*" said Henry, "but I did warn you."

Deepend plopped into a side bench and Peter found one for himself. He faced forward and found the motion of the vehicle a bit easier to deal with.

An hour later they passed over another smooth section of road and Peter reached through a slit in the bookshelf netting and grabbed a *National Geographic* magazine. It was going to be a long ride and he hoped reading might help pass the time, but soon the bumps and vibrating cranked up again made it almost impossible. It took him five minutes to read the first paragraph and he gave up.

The banging of the back suspension, the flapping of the canopy, and the whine of the engine all combined to make such an obnoxious racket that Peter plugged his ears with a piece of toilet paper.

Peter sat on one of the side benches. On the bench in front of him he noticed Deepend looking out the window with his mouth wide open.

He leaned forward and shouted, "What are you doing?"

Deepend yelled back, "I'm afraid I'm gonna smash my teeth or bite my tongue off on one of these bumps! Do people really pay to experience Africa like this?"

Peter shook his head.

"No. Like I told you, we're just catching a ride back with the driver on his way to get another group."

Peter leaned forward to talk to Deepend and looked at the two sleeping passengers taking up another row of benches. He doubted very much that they were actually sleeping and figured it was probably the safest way to ride. Each had a sleeping bag wrapped around their upper body, and another around their head. He marveled that the last accident hadn't dislodged them, but saw that they'd wedged themselves securely into the benches.

With all the jostling, Peter understood why they had padded their heads; it would be a miracle if any of them completed the journey without serious injury. They must have been like that for awhile too, thought Peter, as the sleeping bags they hid in were covered in dust like the rest of the truckbed.

Deepend was realizing just how rough the ride to Nairobi was going to be and frowned. He climbed out of the side bench and moved to the front bench in the vague hope of finding a smoother spot near the front.

Peter joined him and watched as Deepend grabbed an African guidebook from the bookshelf. He flipped through the pages.

"Think there's a map that might show distances in miles — not fuckin' kilometers?"

Before Peter could answer they hit a deep pothole and the book shot right out of his hands and landed in the back between two of the side seats.

"How many miles did you say it was to Nairobi?" Deepend yelled with a wobbly voice.

Peter calculated in his head.

"I would guess about one thousand five hundred miles."

Deepend threw his head back impatiently, "Fuck me!"

167

The truck hit another bad pothole and the jolt threw them all off their seats and onto the floor by the front benches. Peter smashed his elbow on one of the benches and got up rubbing it.

"We got trouble, *mon*," said Henry when he had righted himself, "Because it's going to feel like ten thousand miles back here."

Henry looked out the window, a touch of sadness on his face.

"You know, *mon*, I like to walk places. I like to see how the land is connected."

Deepend watched the countryside bounce by.

"Well, you're seeing a lot of it like this—and fast."

Henry gripped his seat tightly to steady his large frame.

"I fear that may be a problem."

When the sun was high enough to gleam through the scratched plastic windows the other two travelers crawled to the forward benches. Doc had just found a nice stretch of pavement when they stirred; a stocky man in his late twenties sat up first, followed several minutes later by a young woman with most of her face obscured by scarves.

Both looked like they'd just crossed some major desert as they sat up to the table.

Neither spoke, and it was obvious they'd had a rough night.

Henry had been sitting at the table with Peter when they appeared.

"Peter, this is Andy and Pilar."

They nodded.

"That's Deepend back there," said Peter as he gestured with his chin to the back where the American sat.

"Sup?" shouted Deepend.

Andy wore cut-off jean shorts and a faded green t-shirt advertising the white water stretch of the Zambezi, just downstream from Victoria Falls. His legs, arms and neck were muscular and well tanned, and he looked like he'd spent a lot of time outdoors.

His tired eyes still held confidence and Peter imagined he'd be competent in the bush. There was an ugly bruise on his forehead that Peter thought he'd probably sustained on the ride. He wore a blue bandana over his hair; his unshaven face and his forehead were caked with dust even though he'd had his head covered by the sleeping bag.

Pilar mumbled, *"hola"* as she took a pair of sunglasses out of a plastic case and Peter caught a glimpse of warm brown eyes just before the sunglasses eclipsed them. She now looked like a Bedouin about to brave a sandstorm. Despite the erratic motion of the truck, she moved slowly and cautiously, like a chameleon.

Peter quickly took out his earplugs. "Hi."

As Peter watched her staring at the table in front of her he sensed she would give anything for a nice cup of coffee — not that she'd be able to drink it. The road may have been smoother, but they were still in the back of a moving truck.

The ride in the *Mongrel* had taken an obvious toll on them. Andy had numerous bruises and scrapes on his head and arms, and Pilar looked exhausted even though she'd just risen.

Peter remained silent and watched the countryside pass by until they'd woken enough to talk.

"Finally a decent road," said Andy with a New Zealand accent. "We did ten hours on dirt roads yesterday — what a long haul."

Pilar added, "Yes, and then in Lusaka there is no water when we stop."

Something about her voice caught Peter's attention.

"We have not had the best roads today, either," said Henry.

Andy laughed. "Oh, I know. I've been awake for hours but I've been waiting for a good road to sit up. I'm just too tired to hold on anymore."

"Oh, for a warm bath," said Pilar, and Peter's heart quivered as he listened to the soft tone of her voice.

Andy grabbed a cloth sack that hung from a hook on the bookcase and emptied the contents on the table. The others sat forward and extended their arms so nothing fell off the table.

"You're lucky, we restocked our supplies in Lusaka last night."

He had avocados, bananas, fresh loaves of bread, pineapples and cookies.

"It's a bit of an eclectic meal, but you'll find that you have to grab what you can here."

Andy tossed an avocado to Peter.

"There'll be plenty of time for a real meal when we reach Nairobi."

The cache also contained several rolls of toilet paper, a pack of rolling papers, toothpaste and a plastic bottle of sunscreen. Henry opened a roll of toilet paper and blew his nose loudly, and then pocketed the rolling papers, giving a grateful nod to Andy.

Pilar picked up the sunscreen and placed the tube in her lap. She then took the toilet paper and added it to several other rolls already in the bookcase; she made sure the plastic wrapping was closed tightly before putting it away. She set the pineapples on their sides in the bookcase as well.

Andy took the items that remained on the table and put them back in the bag, and then hung it back on the peg. "Grab what you want if you get hungry."

Pilar took the sun screen and started to apply it. She had to undue one of her scarves and take off her eyeglasses to do her face and Peter secretly stole a few glances and glimpsed her deep-set eyes.

Her skin was a lovely olive that hadn't been burnt by the African sun. Her nose was finely chiseled and slightly upturned, and Peter thought her lips were perfect the way they curved slightly and pouted when she paused.

He watched them longingly when she spoke.

"You go also to Nairobi?"

He nodded. "If this ride doesn't kill me first."

"It really is a horrible ride."

Deepend opened one of the side flaps to glimpse the road ahead and a burst of dust swept through the back. Pilar quickly stowed the lotion and wrapped herself in her scarves again.

Peter angrily glanced at Deepend after he'd watched Pilar's lovely face disappear.

The sun pierced the window of the side flap. It was strong already. The wind whistled loudly through the canopy.

Deepend came forward, grabbing the chair backrests for support.

"Hey, how long have you guys been riding back here?"

Andy considered, then said, "I got on in Botswana three days ago, but it certainly feels like it's been longer."

Pilar added, "I found them one day later."

Deepend turned to Peter and asked, "How long will it take us to get to Nairobi?"

Peter shrugged and looked at Andy.

"That depends," said Andy.

Frustrated, Deepend asked, "What the fuck does it depend on?"

The Kiwi laughed. "It depends on how good the roads are and how long the *Mongrel* holds out!"

Andy stood on the bench and grabbed one of the canopy's metal ribs for support. In the partition in front of him—just below the ceiling—there was a small plastic window that allowed him to look over the cab and glimpse the road ahead of the *Mongrel*.

Chilonga 2km, said a sign on the side of the road, and Andy smiled and pointed at the flaps that lined both sides of the truck.

"Hey, we're gonna hit Chilonga in five minutes. The sun is shining and the road is smooth—we should roll the side flaps up when we pass through town."

He looked at Deepend and added, "We take advantage of the fact that Doc has to slow when driving through the towns."

The flaps were tied to the base of four supports. Andy untied them all and made his way to the end near the cab. A low railing ran horizontally between the supports and he sat on it while the long canvas flapped in the wind.

He placed one leg on the outside of the railing, straddling the metal siding, and stuck his head outside. A puff of dust erupted and flew off behind them.

"That's the closest I've had to a shower in a few days!" shouted Andy.

He looked at Deepend. "Hook your foot under one of the seats so you have some support!"

Deepend nodded, and Andy added, "You go to the other end and do the same thing I'm doing here."

Deepend watched as Andy grabbed the flap and began rolling it up, then staggered to the other end of the truck and worked on the second flap.

Andy yelled over. "I've got to warn you, it's a little dangerous!"

Deepend grinned.

Pilar stayed inside and went to the middle of the roll and assisted from the inside, while Andy and Deepend hung out the side and rolled up the ends.

Even on the stretch of what Andy had called smooth road a pothole appeared every so often and they each worked with one hand read to grab for life. They had reached the edge of town but the traffic hadn't slowed them yet.

A goat drifted in their way and Doc cut the wheel sharply.

The *Mongrel* veered and Deepend went swinging out over the street. Somehow he managed to keep his grip and a second later he paused on the railing while gripping the support. "Fuck'n A!"

Reggie had relieved Doc up front, and when he saw Deepend's legs dangling in the rear view mirror he chuckled and accelerated, sending pedestrians scattering.

"What a prick," said Andy.

"He is a bad man," said Henry.

Another obnoxious bump almost dislodged Deepend from his position, but Peter grabbed him at the last second.

"Fuck me!" shouted Deepend. His eyes were sparkling with excitement.

Once he regained control he leaned out and screamed the town's name as if greeting its inhabitants. "*Chilonga! Chilonga!*"

The kids on the street shouted back and pointed at the man clinging to the side of the overland truck. "*Wazungu! Wazungu!*" they called. (White man! White man!)

When they had passed through the town, Deepend sank back onto his seat. Judging from his wide grin, risking his life had clearly been worth it; with the sides now open, the travelers sat back and watched the countryside pass by. They were at top speed again. The wind felt good—just a little cool—and the swiftness of their ride seemed to speed up time.

Pilar grabbed a few small blankets from under one of the side seats and shook them out, then passed them around; and Andy put a cassette into the player on the bookcase. Soon *Cat Stevens* was warbling through the four speakers.

"What I'd give to hear some *Cold Chisel*," he said. "But this'll do for now."

Zambia appeared less developed than Zimbabwe, but also more fertile. The dry red dust of Zimbabwe turned into a moist brown-red here.

From the back of the truck Peter watched large baobabs towering over the acacia trees and scrub; villages dotted with smiling faces and children waving at them; rolling hills and valleys, cluttered with rocks and dry brush.

In the distance the horizon was lined with faded blue mountains.

Peter felt a sense of trepidation. He was on a journey to explain his dreams, and the mud huts on neatly swept courtyards seemed to hint that he was getting closer to its source; even though he knew they weren't Maasai dwellings. South Africa had felt a long way from Maasailand, but these simple villages looked similar.

173

An old woman sitting with a baby smiled at him as they flashed past.

In late afternoon they passed through another small town. Far to the east the Muchinga Escarpment rose up and caught the sun's rays that were now stretching long over the Miombo plains on their left.

In this light everything softened, and even Doc appeared to have mellowed as he drove along through the last hours of daylight.

They still had a long road ahead of them, and Doc and Reggie had no intention of stopping. At night there would be little warning for potholes or bumps, but at least Doc had to drive slower.

As the light faded and the sky turned from purple to black, they untied the flaps, rolled them down, and secured them. Without the roar of the wind the ride seemed suddenly quieter.

The *Mongrel* was passing through a large town, and had slowed to a speed that allowed normal conversation. Everyone but Deepend moved to the forward benches where they faced each other and got comfortable.

Henry looked at Andy, and then at the top spy flap.

"Any idea what town this is, *mon*?"

Andy stood on the bench and looked out the front window flap, "I'd guess, Mpika."

Pilar sighed. "Only Mpika?"

Henry reached into the bookcase and retrieved a chess set and turned to Peter.

"Do you play chess, *mon*? I have a magnetic board."

A stinging memory of playing chess with his father on safari hit Peter, but he forced it away and nodded yes. He put on his light jacket while Henry set up the board.

Then Henry hesitated.

"First I must make power," he said as he produced a bag of ganja. When he opened it the skunky smell filled the truck and Deepend's head popped up from one of the back seats.

"Hey, I'm in on that," he said as he climbed over the backpacks and sacks that had tumbled into the aisle between the rows of seats.

He dropped down next to Peter.

"We hooked up good, didn't we?"

"Ya, we did good," answered Peter. He looked at Deepend's curly black locks. "Hope they don't give you a haircut in Tanzania."

Deepend was in shock.

"What d'ya mean?" he asked.

Peter shrugged. "Some countries in Africa don't like hippies and they make you cut your hair before entering."

Deepend looked at everyone and defensively said, "I didn't go to fuckin' Malawi 'cause they were gonna cut my hair!"

Henry lifted his dreadlocks.

"Yes, *mon*," he said. "I don't go to Malawi also. My dreadlocks are a covenant with *Jah* and the Ancients."

Henry paused and tried to sense if a pothole was approaching in the darkness ahead; then he took a pinch of ganja and placed it in a rolling paper, licked the adhesive and rolled it into a cone.

They had left the town behind and Doc now had the *Mongrel* going as fast as he dared at night. There were no streetlamps and the tired light cast by the dirty headlights didn't extend far ahead of them. There was no moon either so Doc had little warning before dropping into a pothole.

At night Doc just gripped the wheel tightly, pointed her straight, and let the *Mongrel* take the hit when it had to, which meant the bumps would come fast and hard for the passengers riding in the back.

Everyone was impressed with Henry's skills as they watched him twist the top and then tap the cone into shape.

Henry considered making a smoke to be an art, and he knew he was being watched.

He finished his work, and then looked up.

He said, "This Malawi official who wanted to cut my hair, he made me very angry."

He looked around, a bewildered expression on his face, and shook his dreads. "Who are they to cut my hair?"

Deepend grabbed his mane. "Nobody's touching my fuckin' hair."

"In Tanzania I have no problems," said Henry. "They treat me only in a godly way, but in Malawi they will not listen to reason. They say the haircutting is mandatory. I talk to the *mon*, and he tells me to cut it. I say that I will not—that it is my hair and not for him to say."

Henry took a piece of cardboard from an empty cigarette pack and rolled it up into a filter. After inserting it into the narrow end of the spliff he continued.

"I tell him it is not a problem to me if he grows his hair long."

He smiled, but then shook his head. "But in the end they still say cut, so I don't go to Malawi. It is not a godly place, *mon*."

He looked up to the heavens, as if he could see someone up there looking down, raised a lighter to his smoke and inhaled deeply.

He exhaled and the smoke lazily filled the back of the truck for about thirty seconds before it was sucked away by the breeze that snuck past the flaps.

"So you think they'll be cool about my hair in Tanzania?" asked Deepend.

The black man shook his head.

"You should have no problems in Tanzania; I have been there many times."

Henry extended his arms out to both sides in a wide gesture. "Africa is paradise, *mon*." He shook his finger dramatically, which made the spliff jump all over the place. He laughed when he saw Deepend's eyes following every movement of the joint like a dog watching a steak. He then noticed everyone else looking at him, too.

He apologized, "For me, a spliff is a *mon's* business. A spliff is for one *mon*."

Deepend looked crestfallen, but Henry motioned for Deepend to take the joint. "But because it is difficult to roll, I share this one with you, brother Deepend. *Jah*, Africa is paradise, *mon*!"

Deepend smiled so wide the joint almost dropped out of his mouth as Henry lit it.

On his first inhale he took too big of a hit, tried to hold it too long and coughed until his eyes bulged. He offered it to Pilar who declined.

Peter declined also and nodded at the chessboard as he said, "If you keep smoking, I will beat you easy."

Henry's laugh was almost a roar. He said, "When I make power, then I play strong chess, *mon*. In chess I am a warrior."

Several hours before dawn, Doc drove the *Mongrel* up a long hill. Reggie was digging through a box of cassette tapes when something in the side mirror got his attention.

When he looked back he saw Deepend hanging off the side of the truck. Deepend was yelling and waving his arms until Doc slowed down a little.

"I gotta have a crap, Doc!" shouted Deepend. "I've been banging on the cab for twenty minutes. I can't do it off the side."

"What's your problem, yank?" asked Doc. "You got a nice smooth road — and I'm not going fast either."

As crazy as Deepend was, this he couldn't do. He had actually tried for about thirty seconds, and then had to admit to himself that he couldn't pull it off.

"What kind of crazy bastard are you?" asked Deepend. "Do you really expect me to drop a number two off the back of this thing while you're driving?"

"Sorry, Mate," said Doc, "we're making time. Do it or hold it in. We'll be at the Tanz border by first light. It's dark, nobody will see ya."

He turned and grinned at Reggie.

Ahead, a sign read, *Isok 5 km*, and Reggie had an idea.

"Hey," he hollered to the back, "Doc's bound to slow down when he goes through Isok, just do it then."

"You're sick," said Deepend. "I'd like to see either of you do it."

"Oh, Doc could do it all right," said Reggie. "How do you think he got his name, eh?'

Deepend looked confused.

"Well, I thought you were a doctor," he said.

Both men burst out laughing at the pathetic image of Deepend in the side mirror.

Reggie said, "Doc here won the farting contest at the Oktoberfest in Germany."

Doc nodded proudly.

"Yes, I did!" he said, "And that is why they call me Doctor Poo."

Reggie said, "Well, that's one of the reasons."

At this they both burst out laughing again, and then Reggie shouted, "Just hold tight! We'll be at the Tunduma border post in an hour."

The *Mongrel* crept to the top of a hill and then began coasting down the far side. A few minutes later Conrad's faded red pickup appeared in its wake. His upper body was covered with open burns that oozed and throbbed. The pain was almost unbearable and he couldn't even tolerate the touch of a T-shirt on it; the only thing that kept him going was his rage.

Luckily he had a first aid kit in his truck. He had put some salve on the burns, but he hadn't received proper medical treatment yet, and wouldn't until he found the men who did this to him.

Finding his vehicle had been a good break; he located it about two hours out of Lusaka where Peter had ditched it. He would have driven right past the old truck had he not caught a flicker of the sun's reflection off a side mirror, and when he looked had glimpsed a flash of red in the bush.

A friend had driven him up to that point, and they pulled Conrad's old pickup out of the bush with his truck. The driver door was dented but it opened fine.

A sinister smile lit up Conrad's face as he opened a side panel and retrieved his spare key; and he was thrilled to find that his heavy pistol was still there as well. After checking to make sure it was loaded he stuck it in his belt.

His friend wasn't the most ethical person around, but Conrad still wasn't sure he wanted witnesses on this journey. Once they got his truck back on the road and running he thanked his friend and sent him home. The man looked ready to flee anyway; and the way he kept staring at Conrad's burns was annoying.

Ahead, he caught a glimpse of the *Mongrel*, and he sped up behind it and then skirted over to the side. When a side flap blew open he caught a quick look at Deepend sleeping in one of the side benches.

"There you are, boy," he said in a hateful whisper. He slowed and let the *Mongrel* coast ahead. "You've gotta stop somewhere, and I'll be there."

Now that he had sighted his target he could slow and tend to his wounds.

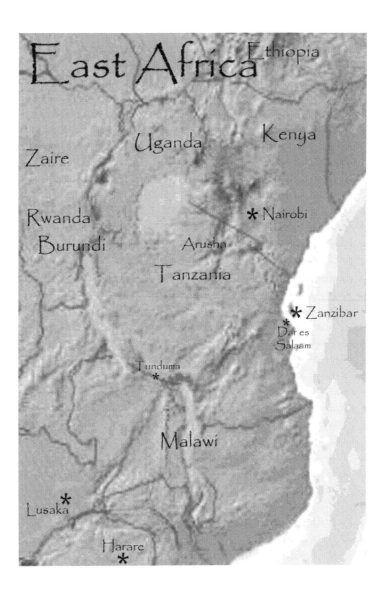

Chapter Nineteen

Tanzania

*T*he day's first light found the *Mongrel* parked by the Zambian customs office, waiting for it to open. They had covered a lot of road since Lusaka and everyone was bruised and sore. The engine still groaned and pinged from the long haul, and the travelers had been trying to get a few hours of sleep without the constant lurching and jarring of the truck.

Deepend sat up and rubbed his temples and said, "My fuckin' head is killin' me."

Someone else grunted from the back but the blanket around their head muffled their words. The long night had taken its toll on the passengers and the living quarters were in disarray.

Several massive potholes had dislodged the backpacks that had been stacked on the double seats, and then the wind had confused the scene even more by depositing a layer of fine dust over the entire vehicle bed.

As the birds came to life in the trees around them they all slowly woke up. Andy did his best to straighten out the area around the two front benches; Pilar tried to collect some of her things that had fallen behind one of the side seats. Peter swept the dust off the carpeted area around the front benches with a broom—even Deepend helped by organizing the items in the bookcase.

Henry sat at the front bench and went to light the remnants of a spliff. Andy stopped cleaning and stared at him. "Mate, we're parked outside of customs."

Henry shrugged and put the joint away, inserting it deep into his dreadlocks.

"No problem, *mon*."

Pilar handed Peter a damp rag, and while she cleaned the front table, he wiped all the seats down.

By the time the Tunduma border post opened they were all organized. They climbed down the metal ladder and filed through the door to the customs building. None of them had set a foot on solid ground since Lusaka—twenty-four hours before.

They stumbled more than walked into the building.

A bored custom guard lazily flipped through the pages of peter's passport. He exhaled, slowly, as if what he saw was tiring him.

Suddenly, he shut the book and stared at the South African seal on the cover.

He looked up at Peter and said, "In South Africa you do not treat the black man well—maybe I will not let you enter my country."

Peter held his hands up, defensively. "Apartheid is finished now."

"Perhaps," said the guard, "but in Africa we have long memories."

He looked up into Peter's eyes and something there made him back away from the bribe he was leading up to. He thought briefly of just locking up the South African, but decided he really wanted him far from the station—and the sooner the better.

He smacked his large stamp violently on the passport page and said, "Guard your back, my friend—and pray you won't have to pay for the sins of your fathers."

Behind him Deepend stood with his hair pulled back behind his head; his shirt was yanked up high to cover it. He smiled wide as he approached the guard.

"Hello, officer."

The man looked through his passport.

"American, is it?"

"That's right."

"We like Americans in Tanzania—but you still have to pay more for visa."

Deepend's face turned dark red. He lowered his head and stared at the floor, trying to calm himself, and his hair spilled out of his shirt collar.

"You have nice hair. It is like a girl's."

Deepend looked at him with wide eyes. "How much for the visa?" he asked.

An hour later the *Mongrel* was heading northeast, toward Mbeya. To the northwest lay Lake Tanganika and southwest of them was Lake Malawi. The road skirted the Kipengere Range to the south, on their right hand side.

Early in the day they passed through Mbeya and then their luck held with a long stretch of smooth road. Peter reckoned that it was almost five hundred miles to Dar es Salaam from the border, and they had covered at least a third of the way when they entered the town of Iringa.

It was early in the afternoon when they cruised down the dusty streets of the small Tanzanian town.

Iringa seemed deserted. Only the marketplace, a large dirt lot filled with tables of vegetables and fruit, was bustling with people and activity. Vendors were shouting prices, shoppers were hollering greetings, and pungent smells of produce and earth were drifting through the air.

When the overland truck approached, the commotion took a new direction: the vendors gathered some of their wares in their arms and rushed toward it, eager to sell their goods at a higher price. They were assuming that the truck had a fresh batch of overland passengers, not seasoned travelers anxious to get home, and some vendors were holding out their traditional baskets, woven from local reeds. Andy waved them away, gesturing that what they needed was food.

Doc turned around and yelled at everyone in the back.

"You've got ten minutes—and believe me—I'll leave without ya!"

Andy stood up and took control.

"Henry, you mind watching the truck with Deepend while we shop?"

"It would be a pleasure, *mon*."

The Rastafarian climbed down the ladder, jumped past the last rung, and started walking around the truck. He smiled at the crowd who looked upon him as something wild. He hadn't showered in days and looked like a werewolf with a growing beard and his dreads shooting off in all directions..

As the kids stepped closer to get a better look at him he suddenly rushed forward with his big arms outstretched and a scary scowl. "Boo!" he yelled, and they screamed and ran. He circled the vehicle and made sure no thieves were trying to get their hands on their stuff while he was distracted by the children.

Peter, Andy and Pilar had disappeared into the market. Doc and Reggie had also stepped away on their own business. Only Deepend remained in the bed of the *Mongrel*.

"Henry, you got this under control?" he called. "I've got special business, if you know what I mean."

Henry raised one of his bushy eyebrows, and Deepend leaned over the side and explained in a low voice: "Andy made me throw out the weed you gave me, in Zambia, before we hit customs."

Henry laughed. "Andy is paranoid."

He reached into a pocket and pulled out a few shillings.

"Put this toward your purchase, *mon*."

As Deepend trotted away he added, "The leaves of the tree of life were for the healing of the nation, Revelation 22:2, *mon*. These things are in the bible for all good men to read."

"I don't read much, brother," called Deepend. "But I do know how to score. I'll be back in a few minutes."

"Good luck, brother Deepend!" shouted Henry as Deepend disappeared into the crowd.

In the marketplace Peter, Andy and Pilar were quickly absorbed by the crowds. They grabbed whatever fruit or snack looked healthy and edible and paid for it with a mix of South African rand, Zambian kwacha, and Zimbabwe and U.S. dollars.

If a vendor was not fast, or quoted an unusually high price, they moved on leaving a wake of vendors who shouted after them with lower prices. A dozen vendors accosted them with curios: baskets, bracelets, batiks and wooden carvings. They had to fight their way through the crowd to get their shopping done.

Andy yelled out: "Please, no baskets! No carvings! We only want food."

Half of the vendors turned away then, although they watched from a distance. The rest surged forward holding up fruit and vegetables.

"Hey, this guy's got avocados, but he won't take kwacha!" shouted Andy.

"Try dollars," said Pilar as she handed him some.

Peter asked, "How much toilet paper do we need?"

Andy looked over the stack of toilet paper rolls in front of him. "About twice that."

They stuffed their purchases into their bags and made their way back to the truck.

Doc was revving the engine and looking into the rear mirror for a thumbs-up. But Peter extended a halting hand instead. He looked around and frowned.

"Where's Deepend?" he asked.

As if on cue, a big commotion was boiling up in the market. Peter saw a tent collapse, and then Deepend scrambling over a cart of bananas with several men in pursuit.

Andy yelled, "Doc, we got a problem!"

Reggie pointed to Deepend, who was sprinting toward the truck, and Doc hit the gas to meet him. Other men appeared from side alleys and joined the angry mob that was now closing in on Deepend.

Reggie shouted, "Move your ass, Deepend!"

"Faster, *mon!*" yelled Henry.

Deepend dodged a guy who almost headed him off, then accidentally tackled a small donkey that stood in his way. He jumped back to his feet, shook off another man who was reaching for his shoulders, and picked up his pace.

Doc had pulled the *Mongrel* around hard and alongside Deepend, who reached and jumped onto the back ladder all in one move.

The men were only a few paces behind.

Doc accelerated and dusted the pursuers to the cheers of the locals who had watched the entire show and were laughing hysterically.

Deepend was panting hard through a wide grin. He handed a rolled-up newspaper to Henry, grabbed Peter's outstretched arm and swung up into the truck. Then he turned and flipped off the men who were now standing in the middle of the road cursing him.

He turned to Peter. "I wish Q-tip had seen that!"

Henry unrolled the newspaper and revealed a bundle of ganja.

"*Jah!*" said Henry.

As the *Mongrel* sped away from the town, its passengers settled down to examine their purchases. Food was one of the few distractions from the monotony of the journey, and rummaging through a fresh bag of supplies was exciting for everyone.

Pilar spread out a small blanket and they each emptied their purchases on it: several loaves of coarse bread, avocados, pineapples, oranges, watermelons, bananas, cucumbers, peanuts, cookies, and butter.

Deepend held up some chocolate and Pilar's face took on a mesmerized look.

Reverently, she said, "Without food I can go for some time, but no chocolate and I die."

Deepend handed it to her; she took a small bite and then folded up the rest.

"Maybe I put some away for later," said Pilar.

Peter watched her and thought: Next time we stop all I'm shopping for is chocolate.

As they reached the open grasslands a shower of banana peels and watermelon rinds flew out of the open side flaps and into the bush. All organic garbage was jettisoned.

The road had turned to dirt and its surface was covered with about six inches of soft, powdery earth. The *Mongrel's* tires kicked up a dense cloud of dust that rose up almost fifty feet above them and extended in a long wake behind.

Driving through what looked like a dust storm, Conrad had sweat pouring off him in the stifling heat. He'd started out with the windows cracked slightly, but the dust was so thick and fast that twice he'd driven off the road while trying to wipe his eyes.

Now his windows were shut tightly, but a fine mist of dust was seeping in, turning his sweat muddy.

Suddenly a large watermelon rind landed on his front window and he jumped in the air and cursed. Then a banana peel flopped onto the hood and slid up the cracked glass. He tried the wipers, but they had died long ago.

He saw the back end of the *Mongrel* come into view through the dust ahead.

He slammed on the brakes and let the truck pull further away.

"You can run, but you can't hide," he said through clenched teeth.

In the back of the *Mongrel* Henry tried patiently to roll another spliff. Cautiously, he held the thin rolling paper between his fingers and focused his entire body on keeping them steady. A sudden bump made him rip the paper and spill half of the weed on the table.

"*Jah*, help me in my time of need," he prayed as he started over.

Peter lay back on a bench near the rear of the *Mongrel*. He stuck his backpack behind him to cushion himself from the side of the truck and his boots solidly planted on the back of the next seat for support.

He reached backwards into his pack and took out the *Eye of Enkai*.

He glanced around to make sure nobody watched, then stuck his hand inside the *Eye* and grabbed a handful of stones.

As he let each one pass through his fingers he tried to identify it and flash through what that item represented. Even after ten years of practice he only recognized some of the stones, and the message was always patchy and confusing.

Still, he felt the *Eye* held an answer to the chaotic world he lived in.

He let go of all but one stone, but before he could focus on it the *Mongrel* swerved hard and dropped off the edge of the road. The move launched him into the air, and he heard Doc cursing up front while he fought for control.

Reflexively, he held the bag tightly against his side as he was lifted; luckily he came down on his backpack instead of the armrest. Deepend was thrown a good three feet in the air, and Peter grimaced as he saw the American land on the backrest for the bench ahead of him.

Peter righted himself and made sure none of the contents of the bag had spilled out, and then put it away.

He watched Deepend climb to his feet, amazed he hadn't broken a bone.

This section of road had proven unforgivable, and all the travelers had worn and tired expressions that stated they were approaching their limits.

Andy sat at the front bench. He shook his head when Peter joined him. "I'm about ready to start walking. Even when we stop I feel like I'm bouncing all over the place."

Several hours later the road passed through Mikumi National Park and Andy gave a sigh of relief. "This section isn't bad, and Doc can't go too fast because of the animals."

They rolled up the side flaps. The sun was now above them so all the benches were in the shade. The alluvial plain around them appeared to elongate with the distant horizon shimmering in the heat.

Among the baobabs and acacia trees scattered throughout the plain they glimpsed the occasional palm tree. At one point Deepend claimed he saw a lion sitting in a tree, but nobody else could confirmed this.

Andy at least defended him.

"Actually, they do have tree-climbing lions here."

Through the hot hours of the afternoon they kept going. Giraffes, impalas, eland and kudus appeared on the plains to the left and right of the road, but Doc wouldn't slow for photographs. Only once did he brake when a bull elephant stepped on to the road — eyeballing Doc defiantly.

As the day wore on some of them dozed a little. It had been a long night. Peter slept with a blanket around his head, twisting in a dream that was oblivious to the dangers around his physical form from the motion of the truck.

In the dream an officer with a red beret was sitting by a fire at night. There was a noise to his right and he reached for his pistol.

As he turned a long knife came at him from the left. The knife found the officer's throat and cut into it while he struggled with his gun.

He fired two shots at the stars, and just before he slumped he squeezed the trigger once more—this time nicking his assailant.

Then he collapsed into the arms of the figure behind him, and as he dropped Peter saw his father standing there. His face was flush with anger and adrenaline and Peter almost didn't recognize him.

His father lowered the knife and let the body sink to the ground. Red Beret's eyes were still open as his blood oozed into the sand. He tried to talk but couldn't. Then he dropped his head.

Simon stood looking at him for a full minute before he walked away.

Chapter Twenty

Breakdown

*P*eter was yanked from his dream by a loud clanking sound. It seemed to be coming from the front suspension, and the others were sitting up with worried faces; although their mode of transportation had proven torturous, the thought of being stranded held its own horrors.

Doc pulled over to diagnose the trouble and his passengers spilled out of the back and hurried straight for the bushes to deal with more immediate problems first. Deepend almost fell as he tried to pull his pants down while he was still moving.

Only Henry got out in a leisurely way, swaying like a sailor just getting off a long stint on a ship. He slowly strolled over to Reggie's side where he waited for Doc's verdict.

Henry said, "I think this is where I go my own way, *mon*."

The tall black man stared at the *Mongrel*. "This truck is a good ride, but she moves too fast for me."

He scratched his scruffy beard. "I think a Godly man should not travel so fast."

Reggie nodded politely, not really understanding Henry's spiritual pursuits, and then asked Doc how bad it was.

"We just blew out a shock, that's all," said Doc. "*Oy* think *oy* can fix it in 'bout an hour."

Doc stood and straightened up, and then went rummaging around behind the driver's seat looking for a spare shock.

Reggie turned to Henry.

"In case you hadn't noticed, we're in the middle of the bloody Mikumi National Park—why don't you catch another ride once we´re out of here?"

Henry laughed loudly and pointed to the road.

"There is a road, and I have my feet! Should I fear walking through Eden?"

The Mongrel was parked at the top of a steep bank, below a clear stream flowed by. Andy had just returned from the bushes and was eyeing it.

"Don't know about you guys, but I'm washing up."

Peter, Andy and Pilar lumbered down the embankment to find a beautiful pool of water sparkling in the sunlight.

"Listen up!" warned Andy. "We're still in the national park, and they have hippos here—and crocs—so let's make sure this is safe before we jump in."

The crystal clear stream did look inviting, and there were no predators in sight. Yet no one wanted to be the first in the water after Andy had so drastically illustrated the dangers. Peter stared into the deep pool in front of them and noted that it did appear to have something dark on the bottom.

"I can't tell whether it's a croc or an old log," said Andy.

And then Deepend stumbled down the embankment.

"What's the holdup?" he asked.

Andy nodded at the stream.

"We're just checking the water."

Deepend scowled and looked at Peter.

"There's nothing down there," he said.

Pilar began to skirt the bank as she stepped toward a shallower section.

"Then you go first," dared Andy.

"You guys are fuckin' pussies, too," he said and cannon-balled into the middle of the clear pool. He stayed under for about thirty seconds, exploring the bottom of the pool before he resurfaced with a rotten piece of wood in his hands."

He shook his head like a dog.

Peter frowned. "You are so lucky."

Andy added, "Stupid is more like it...but thank you."

He whooped loudly as he jumped in and Peter wasn't long behind him.

Pilar returned and quickly discarded her scarves and all but her shorts and a bra; then she made a shallow dive near where Deepend had jumped. She surfaced with her face to the sky and her eyes closed, her hair slicked back as a silky band of dripping water flowed onto her neck and shoulders.

When she opened her eyes she caught the gaze of peter´s blue eyes. They were sparkling with the reflection of the water and he looked at her unabashedly.

"I almost don't recognize you without your scarves," said Peter, dumbfounded by her beauty. He had been tantalized by the glances he had stolen at her, but now that he saw her smile in the sunshine, water dripping off of her skin, his knees weakened.

She squeezed the water from her hair and said, "You have a strange look in your eyes. Is it that you have not seen a woman for a long time, or maybe not one from Spain?"

Peter blushed. "My mother was from Spain."

At the top of the steep bank Doc could see them clearly as he crouched by the hood with Henry standing by his side. Reggie was on his back working on the repair. Andy shouted up to him. "Hey Doc, take a break and join us!"

"Some of us have work to do!" yelled Doc as he crawled under the vehicle to help Reggie.

Henry was handing them whatever tools they needed. He was singing an old Reggae tune and was surprised when he looked up to see a red pickup that had coasted up right next to him.

Deepend glanced up and saw the pickup. He tackled Peter, forcing him underwater. Peter angrily resurfaced, ready to smack the American who pointed up the hill at a red pickup.

"Shit, dude, is that Conrad's pickup? How the fuck did that get here?"

Peter saw the red truck and a figure in its window. Quickly, he moved with Deepend to a spot near the back where they were sheltered by the foliage.

In the driver's seat was an angry man—Conrad—with ugly burns that were hap-hazzardly covered in gauze which obviously hadn't been changed in days. Flies buzzed around them and Henry stepped back, revolted.

Conrad smiled like a crocodile, attempting to look lighthearted, but he was fooling nobody.

"I'm looking for two young men: an American and a South African—any chance you've seen them?"

Doc slid out from under the *Mongrel* and looked at Henry.

"No, *mon*," answered Henry. "We got nobody like that here. Only a few spoiled English."

A faint splashing sound made Conrad try to look past Henry, at the creek down the hill, but the black man blocked his way.

"I answered your question," said Henry. "Maybe you should move on now."

Conrad looked miserable in his dirty truck. There was a bad odor coming from it and his wounds looked infected. The whole thing smelled of death.

He turned and spat, "Maybe I'll decide when I move on."

Reggie and Doc were now standing behind Henry. They had each picked up a large wrench and Conrad scowled as he watched the solid tools swinging lazily in their hands.

"You can all rot in hell," he said as he turned and drove away.

Minutes later the others appeared.

Henry looked at Deepend and Peter and said, "It's none of my business, *mon*, but if that man is looking for you I suggest laying low."

Peter nodded somberly.

"Ya, we know. We just want to get to Nairobi."

He looked at Doc. "We don't want trouble."

Doc laughed, "As they say, *hakuna matata* — this is the final stretch."

Deepend felt his head, assessing a bruised spot, and asked, "How much further do we have?"

"Well, we got about a hundred and fifty miles to Dar," said Doc, "and then four hundred and fifty to Nairobi."

"Fuck me," lamented Deepend, "six hundred more miles of this."

Henry told the others that he was staying behind. He grabbed his gear from the truck, and then hopped down to say goodbye.

Reggie had just put the tools away. He wiped his hands and then shook Henry's.

Deepend and Peter went to shake hands with Henry but he embraced them both with a big bear hug.

"You are welcome to take Deepend with you if you want," offered Peter with a grin as he stepped away.

Henry laughed heartily, shaking his dreadlocks.

"My good friend, Deepend, has the courage of a lion," declared Henry. "*Jah!* Do not underestimate him."

Deepend nodded.

"Yeah, and I'm as loyal as a dog."

Henry placed a hand on Deepend's shoulder and looked into his eyes. "Go with God, Deepend."

He held up a finger of caution. "And watch out for that bad man."

Doc climbed into the cab and muttered, "If we hadn't had that spare shock we would'a been fucked, that's for sure."

Five minutes later the *Mongrel* was on the move again.

For the remainder of the day they kept ticking away the miles, and sometime later that night they passed Dar es Salaam. Memories of a life not in constant motion seemed far and unattainable as they each envisioned what they would do when they finally reached Nairobi.

Peter thought of the long road he had been on, and tried to figure out how far he'd come. He ran the numbers through his head until he thought he had a good estimate. Three thousand miles on mostly primitive roads and in rough vehicles, he thought; no wonder his body hurt.

The train from Orkney to Beitbridge felt like a journey from another lifetime, but it had been a good start to knock out the first five hundred miles. He'd hitched from Beitbridge to the Great Zimbabwe ruins and from there to Harare, then on to Victoria Falls. That amounted to roughly seven hundred miles, plus another three hundred more on the ride from Victoria Falls to Lusaka with Conrad.

From Mbeya to Dar es Salaam was well over a thousand miles as close as he could figure, and then it was another five hundred to Nairobi from there.

In the early morning Peter was watching the orange sun rise over wild and untamed land. Much of the terrain they'd driven through had been protected, but here the eye could see not just empty plains, but areas rich with vegetation and herds of animals. In the night they had passed the Usambara Mountains and they were now on the Maasai steppe—to the north lay Tsavo National Park, and to the northwest was the Serengeti.

They also saw more animals in the villages through which they passed. Several times the *Mongrel* had to slow as a tribesman led his cattle across the road, or a vendor with an overloaded donkey traveled in the middle of the street. Camels were part of the village stock here, and in the early morning Peter had witnessed a few tribesmen near the coast directing a herd of them to water.

They left the villages quickly and returned to the plains where impala burst out of the high grass like popcorn. Giraffe lumbered close, cropping trees that lined the road; Doc actually slowed down at one point as they passed a herd of eighteen. Jackals and hyenas lifted their noses from whatever road kill they'd found when the overland truck passed in the hope that someone might throw some food at them.

Peter dug into his pack, retrieved the biltong that Christian had given him and passed some around. As they chewed the spicy meat they all looked to the north where Mt. Kilimanjaro rose up, its icy peak battling with a dark group of clouds.

Deepend crawled to the bench and sat beside Peter.

He nodded. "I really wanted to take down that peak, but I couldn't afford it."

In the late afternoon Peter stared out at a village in the distance; a thick wall of brush surrounded the dwellings, and over the top of the thorn enclosure he glimpsed mud huts and red togas.

The land here was reeling from a ruthless drought. The *Mongrel* carried a tank with enough water to last them a week, but in the dry air their lips cracked and no amount of lip balm would stop it.

Peter's eyes were sore and his thirst unquenchable. His stomach had continued to growl through the journey, regardless of how much he ate; but that morning when he woke it seemed to have quieted a little.

When he first looked upon the children with the red togas it mysteriously disappeared altogether.

"Are those Zulus?" asked Deepend.

Peter suppressed a smile.

"No, they are Maasai."

He took a deep breath. "We have crossed into Maasailand."

The *Mongrel* slowly continued on its way and Peter watched the villages they passed. All of this felt strangely familiar. He had dreamt of these villages for ten years and part of him seemed to be coming home.

He saw a clean-swept courtyard with a calf tied in the corner and children running, naked except for a red toga draped over the right shoulder; another flash of red betrayed a young boy hiding in the dry, yellow grass, watching the truck as it passed.

He felt excited and nervous, and almost comfortable watching the Maasai children until he saw a tall warrior stepping out of the high grass.

That sight left him frozen inside. It was too close to his dreams of the Maasai warriors. He didn't recognize the warrior, but it made his head spin and he lay back on a bench and wrapped a blanket around his head.

At sunset they passed Arusha, with the outline of Mt. Meru starkly lit by the sun setting behind it. Doc warned that they would hit customs at night, and they started to organize their gear while it was still light out.

Only Deepend lazily lounged on a bench until Andy pressured him into getting his things together. Now all four backpacks were in a pile by the ladder. If needed they could each be unloaded in seconds.

The sky was overcast and filled with thunder and lightning, but no rain. Reggie had found a radio station when they passed Dar es Saalam and related that because of the ten-year drought most of the hotels in Nairobi didn't have running water.

The news hit everyone hard but Andy was optimistic as always.

"I don't care if I have to buy bottled water and heat it myself to take a sponge bath—I'm washing up."

Pilar sighed, resigned that their ordeal would never end.

As the darkness settled in Andy and Deepend crawled into their sleeping bags. The road wasn't too bad, and before long they were both asleep on one of the side benches.

Peter had sat next to Pilar for most of the last twenty-four hours, and although the roar of the wind and the snapping of the canvas flaps made conversation difficult, Peter now felt they now shared a silent pact.

The *Mongrel* slowly crawled up a long hill and with the reduced momentum they could talk without shouting. Pilar looked at Peter and said, "So, your mother was from Spain, eh? Are you saying I remind you of her?"

Peter flushed red. "I'm sorry, but you do."

The two sat on a side bench, facing forward.

Pilar turned to face Peter and looked into his eyes.

She kissed him.

She asked, "Does that remind you of her?"

Peter blushed again. "No."

"Good," said Pilar as she snuggled up to him.

The glow from a sharp-horned moon cast them in a soft blue light. They embraced and kissed again. Peter was lost in the touch of her lips, and the slight perfumed scent that still clung to her skin despite what they'd been through. Their kisses were soft and fleeting as they both knew to linger too long was to risk losing teeth if the *Mongrel* hit a bump.

Suddenly Peter tensed and sat up.

He turned to look out the window.

Pilar looked at Peter, puzzled, and followed his gaze out to the passing countryside. The *Mongrel* had reached the top of the hill and coasted over the summit before descending down the other side.

An old Maasai man sitting on a rock appeared in the moonlight, watching them roll past at eye level. The man looked sad and tired, but upon seeing Peter he smiled and his spirits seem to lift.

Peter sucked in his breath.

"Laibon?" he said as he turned his head, his gaze fixed on the disappearing man.

He fumbled free the rope that held down the flap and stuck his head out the window to see the man again, but was forced back inside as fat raindrops pelted his dusty face — the first rain to hit Maasailand in ten years.

Pilar looked at him. Peter's expression was one of complete disbelief.

"Laibon, could that really have been you?" he whispered

A strong breeze hit the *Mongrel*, and the rain began to pour down hard.

Pilar smiled, "The end of the drought, *gracias, Dios.*"

Doc slowed down.

Pilar stuck her face out the window, and into the hard rain, and yelled with joy.

Chapter Twenty-One

Nairobi

Doc stopped the *Mongrel* on a busy street, blocking traffic; instantly horns blared and curses were shouted all around them. They echoed off the tall buildings, an alien noise after the quiet of the wilderness.

Doc revved the engine nervously and honked back three times, each time longer as if to announce that he wasn't intimidated.

Peter stood in the back with his backpack on. He checked the buckle and cinched the straps tight; the three other hitchhikers were also checking their equipment as they lined up by the doorway above the metal ladder.

Aside from their backpacks they were also carrying daypacks loaded with extra gear. Deepend and Pilar had strapped theirs to their chests, Peter held his in his left hand, and Andy had his sitting on a bench and was frantically searching through it for his guidebook.

He pulled the book out, zipped his pack shut and stuck his passport holder deep down into his shirt.

"Welcome to Nairobi," he announced.

Peter promptly checked his own pouch underneath the waist belt of his backpack.

Pilar scanned the pedestrians overrunning the sidewalk, many of whom were craning their necks to see inside the vehicle as they passed by. Deepend was inhaling and exhaling deeply, preparing himself for the landing on Nairobi's hectic streets.

More horns sounded, followed by angry shouts in what Peter took to be Swahili.

"Get your asses out of my truck!" yelled Doc over the commotion.

There was a note of exhaustion in his voice, and his eyes were rimmed with red as he glared at them through the side mirror. The travelers in the back had had a rough ride, but Doc and Reggie, too, had been on the go since Botswana.

Reggie leaned out the window.

"Don't mind him, he's just cranky."

Andy backed out through the narrow doorway, backpack first, and began to descend. The bottom rung was several feet above the ground and when he jumped the weight of his backpack made him stumble backward into the crowd.

A space in the crowd opened near the base of the ladder.

Peter followed.

"Thanks for the lift," Peter said to Reggie and Doc.

Reggie nodded. "Watch your ass on these streets," he said.

Deepend came down next and for once he was serious. "I know about these streets, Reggie. Don't worry about us."

Doc leaned out the window, over Reggie.

"*Oy!*" he shouted.

Deepend paused briefly in his descent until Doc grinned and added, "Fuck off."

Pilar was the last to get off. She stopped to show Doc the back of her clenched fist, and then she extended the middle finger.

"Nicely done," said Andy as he helped her down.

Reggie waved, and then with a burst of smokey exhaust they were gone.

The four travelers found themselves abandoned on a busy city street with cars and people all around them. It was morning and the shops that lined the street were still locked up tight with heavy metal grates, but there was no shortage of pedestrians.

As a group they moved off the street, watching each other's backs as they proceeded to the sidewalk. The crowd moved fast and people nudged them as they passed.

Peter backed against the metal grate of a shop and again cinched up his straps tighter. A young man stumbled into Andy and as he righted himself his hands explored the New Zealander's back pocket for a wallet.

Andy turned, eyed him angrily and pushed him away.

"Fuck off, mate."

Andy looked a bit alarmed.

"This is bad. We've got to get out of here. Does anybody know where to get a cheap room?"

Deepend snapped awake. "I'll get you a room, but we've got bigger problems. If we don't stand together right now we're gonna lose everything."

Deepend nodded at a group of four large men heading in their direction. Their leader was a tall, black man with a long scar on his right cheek and he glared at them as he approached. His intensions were obvious — he wanted their belongings.

"Move in there," said Deepend and motioned to a shop with a recessed doorway.

The others did as he said, and followed his lead as he took off his backpack and placed it behind him. Instinctively, the three men stood in front of Pilar who sat protectively on the packs.

The four Kenyans were only about ten feet away, but they seemed to realize that the travelers were onto them and they would have a fight on their hands. Peter, Deepend and Andy stood in front of their packs, their hands free and ready to defend themselves.

The man with the scar scowled and the four turned into a side street, leaving the travelers alone.

"I may be a dumbass when it comes to southern Africa," said Deepend, "but I know this city and if you don't watch your ass here you will lose everything fast. Why do you think they call it Nairobbery?"

Peter nodded. "Ya, I hear it is like Jo-burg."

Andy turned to put on his pack again but Deepend stopped him.

"We're not out of it yet."

He nodded across the street.

"Look at the sidewalks and watch the people who pass, after a while you'll pick out a pattern."

The others stared silently as the minutes ticked by, and sure enough it seemed that the same people were just moving back and forth. None appeared to pay any particular attention to the travelers, but they felt they were being watched.

Deepend smiled. "What tripped me up when I first came here was I was always on the lookout for the seedy-looking cats — you know, the ones that looked desperate with worn clothes. But after a while you realize that these guys are all working together."

Peter watched a tall businessman with a briefcase walk by and said casually, "I've seen him three times now."

Andy added, "Yeah, and that little chap over there."

Everyone looked at a small man in ripped pants that was crossing the street.

He walked to the corner and nodded at the man in the business suit. They each gave a slight glance at the travelers, but when they saw they were being observed they disappeared around the corner.

"You have to be careful who you trust," continued Deepend. "And hide your money deep, and in a few different places."

Peter and Andy exchanged smiles; everyone had been so used to seeing Deepend stumble through life that it came as a surprise to see him on his game.

"So, what's a good hotel, Deepend?" asked Andy.

"For you, I'd say the *Iqbal*. You don't smoke weed, and as long as you don't do laundry in your room they're pretty cool."

He looked at Peter and added, "You should go there too, it's central and they've usually got water."

"Oh, what I would give for a cool shower!" said Pilar from behind them. "And then to sleep in a soft bed."

Her words made them suddenly feel their tiredness and sore joints. Peter's eyes were crusty with dust, and he had bruises all over his body. He looked over his companions and saw the same assortment of battle scars from their time in the *Mongrel*.

The bruise on Andy's forehead had turned from purple to yellow, and he'd gotten himself a black eye the night before while trying to pee off the side of the moving truck. Deepend's arms and legs were covered with scrapes and bruises and he had a fat lip. Pilar still hid behind her scarves, but her eyes showed she was exhausted.

"What about you, Deepend?" asked Peter.

He'd gotten used to the American and thought at this point he might actually miss him.

"Oh, I'll be around," he laughed. "I've got to go to Mama Rosch's Guest House and sort out my wheels. The place is a bit rougher but it's the closest thing to a home I've had for a few months."

A silent nervousness was rising up in Peter as he looked at Pilar. He had been dreading the moment of their goodbye for days.

The night before they'd talked about their future together and Peter felt empty as he reflected on their conversation. Inside he was empty and he didn't want to lose her.

He sensed she yearned for more of him as well.

"I will stay at the *Jambo* Guest House, near the Spanish Embassy," she'd informed him. "If I can extend my visa then I won't have to leave Kenya."

She would also need to change her flight, but she felt that this wouldn't be a problem.

"And what will you do then?" Peter had asked, his heart racing as he waited for her reply.

Her soft brown eyes had held him in a trance.

"*Pienso que*...sorry, I think I go to the island of Lamu. It is beautiful there."

He had looked at her, unable to speak while he waited for her to continue, and Pilar had stared into his eyes looking for answers of her own.

"Peter," she had begun. "There is something troubling you, I can see it."

He had nodded.

She had taken a deep breath. "If you can find it in your heart to break free of this thing that troubles you then you should come with me."

His heart had quickened at the prospect.

"But if you continue to be burdened by it then you should stay and resolve it."

Reluctantly, he had agreed.

Now, as they stood on the sidewalk he felt his throat closing. Pilar shouldered her backpack and took a step toward the street. Peter reached for her arm and turned her around.

"I will visit you tomorrow night at the *Iqbal* hotel," she said in a tone that expressed both hope and a warning. "If you can find room in your heart to love then you should come with me to Lamu."

Andy had sighted a taxi and flagged it over.

Peter kissed her quickly and the three men escorted her to the cab.

She got in and smiled at Peter from the back seat. "I will see you soon."

He nodded and closed the door. As the taxi drove off he continued to watch it.

Andy signaled to another taxi and when one pulled over Peter and Andy got in.

Deepend looked at the driver.

"*Iqbal* Hotel, down by River Road."

The driver grinned. "I know it."

"What about you?" asked Andy.

Deepend had been the one to warn them about the dangers of the city, but now he would be on his own.

He smiled confidently and put on his sunglasses.

"I'm not afraid of this fuckin' place."

He threw his arms up toward the sky.

"I love it here!"

Deepend didn't look like a resident of the city: his hair still stood straight up and his face was caked with dust, but there was a bounce to his step that suggested familiarity and confidence.

Then Andy and Peter saw that the man in the suit started to follow Deepend. The short man in ripped pants crossed the street and walked a few paces behind both of them.

"We need to help him!" said Andy.

Peter laughed. "They're the ones that are going to need help if they mess with Deepend."

Chapter Twenty-Two

Jacob

*D*eepend was walking along the busy city sidewalk, excitedly taking in the scene. He had walked two blocks when he noticed that he was being followed. At first he spotted the man in the business suit, and then the short man with ripped pants; both knew he was now alone and paid little attention to looking inconspicuous.

He stopped by the entrance to a bank and stood by the armed guard while the two walked by. He eyeballed them and said, "Yeah, I fuckin' see you."

They glanced back awkwardly, then turned left at the next intersection. Deepend quickly walked across the street, turned into an alley on the right and lost them.

But a block further he had picked up another tail.

This time it was a young black man wearing a faded sports-jacket. Deepend stopped in front of a curio shop that offered wood carvings and watched the man in the reflection; he looked to be in his early twenties, and had a worn, haggard look about him.

Deepend continued down the street, turned a corner and stopped abruptly. He surprised the young man when he appeared.

"What'd'ya want? Eh? Why the fuck are you following me?"

The young man answered defensively. "My name is Jacob and I only want to make business with you. If you want something, I can get it for you no problem."

Deepend scowled as the man continued.

"You want to go on a safari? I can organize it—I am Maasai."

"You´re fuckin' with me, aren't you?" challenged Deepend as he pushed the other's shoulder. The young man looked shocked and offended.

"I would not dare," answered Jacob.

Deepend began walking down the street, moving quickly in the hope that he would lose Jacob, but the young man was not to be put off that easily. He loped along, about a half pace behind the American.

Deepend looked back at him. "Well, I know the Maasai have those fucked-up earlobes and yours are fine."

He reached back to flick Jacob's earlobe but the young man pulled his head away, giving the American a hurtful stare.

"And I know the Maasai still embrace the traditional ways and here you are hustling me."

Jacob watched Deepend, eagerly, as he continued to pursue him. A section of sidewalk had been torn up, and the pedestrians were bunching up while waiting for a break in the traffic so they could circumvent the construction site.

Deepend glanced over his shoulder and saw Jacob standing right behind him.

Deepend held up his palms in frustration. "Okay, I give up. What's your fuckin' story?"

Jacob lifted his head and looked at Deepend. His eyes were tired, and sad, and looked like they should have belonged to someone older.

The crowd moved into the street and Deepend followed with Jacob close behind.

He began, "I was born Maasai, but they are a silly, superstitious people, and I walked away from them before

Enuto." He paused as a pedestrian moved between them, but seconds later he was back. "I was not there for the ceremony which would have opened my earlobes."

"Boo-fucking-hoo," said Deepend. "Jacob's not a Maasai name either."

The American stopped and took in the appearance of the street hustler again. Then he nodded, as if confirming something he'd already guessed.

He said, "You're sketchy, get away from me."

Deepend was about to walk off when an old man in traditional dress ran up to Jacob and started shouting. He wore a Maasai toga, blood red and faded from years of wear, and his neck and long earlobes were adorned with beaded jewelry. He also carried a staff, and around his waist were tied several small bags.

The old man's skin was covered with a layer of ash. His face appeared ancient. Lines of worry circled his penetrating eyes, but he was excited as he shouted at Jacob in a language that the American assumed was *Ol Maa,* the language of the Maasai.

People walking by gawked at the old man and avoided him.

He grabbed Jacob's forearm and tried desperately to pull him away; but Jacob resisted and wrestled himself free.

Deepend watched, amused.

"You see why I left the tribal life?" Jacob called to Deepend with exaggerated gestures of resistance.

"This one I have not seen for years; now he tries to bring me home."

Jacob laughed scornfully at the old man and pushed him away.

"You see how they are?"

The old man realized he was getting nowhere and stepped back. Now that he was no longer shouting the pedestrians were moving on and the circle of space around them was collapsing.

He looked at Jacob.

"Lekai comes," he said solemnly, in English.

211

Then the old man turned and left. Deepend could see him look over his shoulder several times before he was lost in the crowd.

Jacob appeared shaken.

"He is Laibon," explained Jacob. "He was the Seer for the tribe that I left."

Jacob looked pale as he leaned against a street sign to support himself.

He tried to catch his breath.

Jacob raised his head. His sad eyes appeared to be looking back in time as he said. "He is crazy and always has been."

With a forlorn look he glanced at Deepend, desperation written on his face.

"I have left the tribal ways, but still he talks of prophecies."

A teenager in a Boston Celtics t-shirt bumped into Deepend and he felt the youths hands search his pockets before he elbowed him away. Jacob suddenly recovered and shouted after the young man and although Deepend didn't know the words he could tell they were a threat.

The American looked up and down the street and tried to orient himself. His evasive zig-zag through the streets had gotten him lost. Jacob said, "If I do not live the tribal life then my only hope is to make money with the tourist, but you will not even talk with me because you believe I am *sketchy*."

Deepend frowned.

"Okay, fuck it," he said. "I'll give you one US dollar just to shut the fuck up."

"Really?" said Jacob.

"No, loser," said Deepend. "I didn't spend that dollar on a taxi because I'm trying to save what I got."

"Oh, I see," said Jacob. "But where were you trying to go for a dollar?"

Deepend scratched his dirty head, stirring up a dust cloud.

"Well, I was heading to Mama Rosch's Guest House, but I seem to have gotten turned around."

Jacob smiled and pointed back the way they'd come.

"Yes, you have. Mama Rosch's is back that way," he said.

Deepend stared at him.

"If you're fuckin' with me I'll cut your balls off."

Again, Jacob was defensive. "I would not dare."

"Okay," said Deepend as he began walking. "You get me there and I'll pay you the money I would've given the taxi driver."

"Very good, sir," said Jacob, gratefully, as he fell into step behind Deepend. "A taxi would cost about two US dollars."

Deepend stopped in his tracks and Jacob crashed into him.

"Look at me, Jacob. Do you think I could talk the driver down to one US dollar?"

Reluctantly, Jacob conceded. "Yes, I believe you could."

"Good, then start earning your dollar."

Jacob followed Deepend as he opened the metal gate that lead into the guest house compound. The gate was the only opening of a tall cement wall lined with sharp pieces of glass on top.

He stopped short when he heard dogs inside.

"These dogs do not like the black man. When you need me, I will be outside."

A loud howl sounded from somewhere deep in the compound. Jacob froze.

"Beware of the crazy dog," he said and backed out through the gate. "I have heard many stories about him."

Deepend laughed. "I'm not afraid of a fuckin' dog—besides, that dog knows me."

Once he was inside the gate Deepend crossed a courtyard about forty feet wide by one hundred and fifty long. Land cruisers, overland trucks, cross-country motorcycles—even a converted passenger van called a *matatu* – were parked to the left and the right of the gate. Some that sat tucked against the walls appeared not to have run for some time.

A few campers stood between the vehicles and as he made his way through the compound he passed tents and scattered fires surrounded by groups of people. Scraps of German,

Spanish, and English were floating through the air. Every inch of the courtyard seemed occupied and he began to wonder if he would find a place to camp.

The travelers Deepend passed were lean and tanned — a few looked too skinny. Many sported tattoos and long, unkempt hair. Their clothes were faded and frayed, and few wore pants that hadn't been patched at least once.

Instinctively, he touched his money belt to make sure it was securely in place.

In the middle of the compound sat Mama Rosch's small house. The cottage looked transported from Europe with its flowerboxes and shutters, and it seemed out of place surrounded by all the makeshift travel gear.

An attempt had been made to plant grass around the house but very little of it saw the sunlight because of all the tents that covered it. Close to the house a garden was being weeded by a young African man.

Along the back wall of the courtyard stood two long buildings that acted as dorms, a porch in front was occupied by at least thirty travelers who were smoking and talking. Some were cooking food on small camping stoves. The smell of ganja floated in the air and Deepend inhaled deeply.

The American smiled. "Home at last."

The sound of the dogs barking had grown louder, and as he walked toward the porch a large, black German shepherd trotted at him with several smaller dogs in tow. The shepherd's eyes were tinged with a crazy look. It growled at him. The fur on its back stood straight up.

Deepend grinned. He extended his hand and said, "Hey Wolfie," but pulled it away quickly when the dog snapped at him.

"What's up with you, Wolfie?" asked Deepend as he stared at the dog. Wolfie's lips curled back in a way that he found unnerving. The dog growled again and slowly advanced.

Deepend hopped up on the porch and stood next to a few of the travelers but the dog kept coming. The other dogs lined up near the steps and watched. Wolfie seemed concentrated on biting Deepend who looked about ready to shit himself.

Suddenly a large woman in her sixties—Mama Rosch—stormed onto the porch and yelled at the dog. Mama shouted, "*Volfie*, no! *Volfie!*"

She held a notebook in her hand and threatened to hit the dog with it. He continued to advance and she had to yank him back by the collar.

The dog finally relented. It glanced at Mama for a split second, lowered its eyes, and continued toward the back wall.

She glanced at Deepend and warned. "It is better you don't touch him."

Deepend nodded vigorously in agreement. "Sorry, Mama, I thought he would remember me."

Mama shook her head. "You must be careful with *Volfie*. He is sometimes a little crazy. His father was a nice dog, but the mother is from the street and she gave this craziness to *Volfie*."

"Don't you remember me, Mama?" asked Deepend. "I was here about three months ago before I went south."

Mama stared at him, but there was no recognition.

Deepend added, "My friend, Ian, left our Land Cruiser in your care when he went home about a month ago."

The old woman thought for a moment, and then her face lit up in a smile.

"I love your friend, Ian!" she said. "Such a nice boy."

Deepend felt a bit let down that she didn't remember him.

"But you don't remember me? I stayed here for almost two months."

Mama eyed him, working her brain to run through the many travelers who had passed through over the last few months.

She took a step closer to him and squinted. Finally she cracked a smile. "Francis!"

Deepend blushed. "Actually, I go by Deepend now."

She shook her head. "Not for me, Francis."

She patted his dusty head. "Yes, I remember you now—you smoked too much and fell off the porch."

A bit embarrassed, Deepend grinned.

"Yup, that was me."

She added, "Ya, and when you stayed here we were very full and the only place you could put your mosquito net was under the mango tree."

Deepend nodded. "And it was mango season and every night I'd wake up when one of the fruits dropped and tagged me."

She laughed.

"So good of you to come back. What can I do for you?"

"Well, I need a tent spot, but if there are none I can sleep on the porch."

Mama nodded and looked around.

"Maybe the porch is better for tonight."

She then handed him the notebook.

"Sign my book; you can pay in the morning."

Deepend entered his information and signed.

When he handed it back Wolfie growled again. Mama yelled at the dog again and it turned and crept away; the other dogs followed and they disappeared in the direction of the front gate.

"You will be fine now," she said. "The dogs won't bother you anymore."

"I also need to get my Land Cruiser; I believe Ian paid for the storage fee."

Mama flipped through her book and found the entry. She frowned. "Ian only paid until last month. You owe me five hundred shillings for this month."

Deepend sighed.

"I'm almost out of money, mama, and I fly out in a few days."

They stood in uncomfortable silence.

"I'll tell you what," Deepend finally said. "You let me use the vehicle for a couple days and when I leave I'll give it to you."

She cocked her head, then stuck out her hand to close the deal.

Deepend hesitated, "And I'm broke, Mama. Can you include meals and a tent spot until I fly out?"

Mama creased her brow.

"And when is your flight?"

He grinned. "It's in five days."

"Good," she laughed. "Not in five months."

He smiled warmly. "I wouldn't do that to you, Mama."

He tried to run his hand through his dirty hair but could barely get past the roots.

"So we got a deal or what, Mama? I gotta take a shower."

"Ya! Agreed," said Mama. "I will get your keys in a minute."

She waved her hand in front of her nose.

"Goodness, Francis, you stink."

She sat down on the porch, gesturing for Deepend to join her.

"The water will come on in two hours so you might as well rest."

A traveler with long dreads came over and handed her a mug of tea.

"Relax, mama," he said.

Wolfie trotted by to investigate a noise by the back wall. He paused and gave Deepend a psychotic look.

Mama's gaze followed the shepherd. "I am sorry, but I need these dogs. Maybe it's good sometimes that *Volfie* is crazy. If he liked everybody, then the Africans come and take everything. Then no more travelers and I will be finished with Africa too!"

Chapter Twenty-Three

On the Street

Peter stepped out of the Iqbal Hotel and squinted into the bright sunshine. He turned left and walked down the street, ignoring the calls of a beggar on the corner.

From his bloodshot eyes and tired expression it was obvious he hadn't slept despite getting a clean bed. The shower had offered only a trickle of water, but at least he was clean, he thought, as he proceeded down the busy street.

Horns from buses and cars blared in every direction; their exhaust fumes filled the narrow streets. The sides of the street were lined with shops whose wares spilled out onto the sidewalk. Vendors were hollering, offering their goods or greeting their neighbors and competitors.

Hundreds of people moved around him and while he walked through the crowd he realized he was the only white man in sight. He remembered the gang that had zeroed in on them when they first stepped off the *Mongrel*, and he was sure there were bad men closing in on him, but he couldn't possibly watch everyone.

He'd stored his valuables in the hotel safe and only had a few notes on him so he wasn't really afraid of being robbed.

He had more important things to deal with than worrying about thieves. He had finally reached Nairobi and he knew the key to his nightmares was within reach. He could feel an explanation lay just around the corner.

The sun was beating down on him relentlessly. He turned a corner and saw that the far end of the street disappeared into a wall of dust. The evening before it had rained, and he'd watched the drops trickle and roll down the dusty windowpane in his room, but the relentless heat had dried any traces of it, and now the wind was whipping the dust around like it had a score to settle. The memory of rain and the smell of moisture in the air had departed with the rising sun, just like a dream.

He passed dried-out flowerbeds and dead shrubs planted along the sidewalk. The street trees looked like they were barely holding on, and their leaves were brittle to the touch. The dry, lifeless wind that blew through the city streets sucked away all humidity.

Peter wove his way through the crowd of pedestrians on the pothole-ridden sidewalk, shuffling left and right to avoid collisions and pits. Black faces flashed in front of him, then moved on. Peter wondered if they could tell he held no more than a few shillings in his pocket. But there was something else in their looks, a strange recognition. It was the same look he had seen in the eyes of the miners in South Africa. Here, more than three thousand miles away, it puzzled him again.

After the long, jarring truck ride he had thought life would now feel stable, but it didn't. The ground felt shaky beneath his feet and he half feared half expected the sidewalk would fall away at any moment. The sky spun above the city streets like a great blue bowl on a potter's wheel and he had to lean against a signpost to steady himself.

From the end of the street came a loud commotion.

He heard shouting, and then a cheer, as if there was a sporting event just out of sight. Around him there was suddenly a tension, and he felt like everyone but him knew what was about to happen.

Just beyond the crowd on the street Peter watched a woman grab her two young children and quickly lead them into a narrow alley. To his side he noticed that the vendors were bringing items back inside their stalls, and he spotted a few people reaching down and picking up whatever rocks or stones lay on the ground in front of their feet.

They whispered to each other in a language he didn't know.

Suddenly, there was another roar of the crowd, and then a man emerged from the cloud of dust at the end of the street. He was running and stumbling, desperate, and at the end of his strength.

A few seconds later an angry mob followed. Some of the pursuers were throwing rocks at the running man.

Someone stepped out of the crowd that lined the sidewalk and as the man ran past kicked him, and he almost fell. The crowd roared in response. People on the sidewalks were now also throwing stones at him.

The eyes of his pursuers were filled with anger and adrenaline.

As he got closer Peter could see the man was Maasai.

His black skin shone under a layer of sweat, and he labored to get a fresh breath of air into his depleted lungs.

He stumbled forward, on the verge of complete exhaustion. He was bleeding from several wounds, and as Peter watched a rock hit him in the left shoulder and he screamed in pain.

His hands were empty, and Peter wondered what crime he might have committed.

As he approached, Peter sensed the air around him thicken. He felt like he could not move, and in some strange way he sensed he was as helpless as the running man.

And then, as the man passed, he looked directly at Peter.

There was a look of recognition in his face that was so strong it made him actually slow and stare, but then a rock flew past his head and he seemed to remember his peril. He resumed his escape, then looked back at Peter one more time, and finally stumbled into a side alley where only one at a time could follow.

Peter's face had gone pale.

"Sendeyo, I recognize you," he whispered.

He looked around, as if he were seeing Nairobi for the first time.

"What happened when Lekai didn't return?"

He remembered Lekai's men watching him drive by in the dark, his father lying against him, bleeding and unconscious.

Within a few minutes the crowd had dispersed and things went back to normal on the busy street.

Peter stayed where he was and thought about the man he'd seen. There were no answers waiting for him back in his room, but now the thought of walking the streets of Nairobi filled him with fear.

Sendeyo appeared to have aged more than ten years. In the dreams the young warriors all looked on the cusp of their twenties, but the man he'd just seen had lost that youthful appearance. His eyes had been devoid of hope, as if the chase had been inevitable.

Peter continued down the street, watching the faces of the pedestrians in the hope that one might contain a clue. The wind and dust battered his eyes, but he could not look away.

The sun burned high in the sky.

He paused when he spotted two Maasai women purchasing some fruit from a vendor. As if pulled by a string, the two women looked up and directly into his eyes. He didn't recognize them, but something in his appearance disturbed them. With a dismissive gesture they set the fruit down and quickly disappeared into the crowd.

He drifted through the streets like he was stuck in a bad dream, unable to wake or change the outcome.

Again, he remembered Deepend's warning about walking the streets of Nairobi but now it had become irrelevant; he didn't care about the robbers. What he was searching for here was also what he feared most. It was as if a current pulled him along and like a bit of flotsam all he could do was go with it.

Two hours later his nerves were shot. He looked around and realized he didn't know where he was. Tall trees lined the wide road and in the shade of one a group of about fifteen men huddled. In their middle sat a man at a card table.

"Ben is best!" shouted the seated man.

His voice was deep and carried authority as it boomed from across the street. Peter thought of Henry, his Rastafarian friend from the *Mongrel*. He walked closer and saw that Ben was a large black man with a knit hat in the rainbow colors of reggae. On the card table he was laying out a game of chance with three cards.

The men around Ben jostled in a tight circle, all competing for the best view as he moved a queen and two aces with lightning speed. He would flip all three cards over and shuffle them about, but after a moment he'd flip one card — and always it was the queen.

Ben paused and a man dropped a note on the table and pointed at one of the three cards. Ben flipped over the card to show it was an ace, snatched up his money, and continued with his game, shouting, "Ben is best!"

Over and over he shuffled the three cards, face down, and then flipped one over. Each time the exposed card was the queen of hearts. He made it look easy, and even laughed and pointed at the Queen when she appeared. He then flipped the other two cards to show the aces.

Then he shuffled the cards and started over, challenging people to determine where the queen was. "Find the lady!" shouted Ben as he moved the cards. "Find the queen. Play the game!"

It looked easy enough, but again and again, the men who put their money down pointed to a card that turned out to be an ace. Peter suddenly found himself hovering over the table, watching Ben move the cards. He wondered for a second how easily he had moved through the crowd, as if the men had casually parted for him to let him in.

Then his attention returned to Ben´s hands. Peter found his movements predictable. He saw how Ben was deceiving the crowd, but he felt he knew where the queen really was.

"Ben is best. Play the game."

Ben looked up at Peter, assessing him.

"I think I am too fast for you," said Ben in a challenging voice. "I think the lady is too quick."

Peter shook his head from side to side. "I see where she goes, but I do not play these games."

"Of course you do not," said Ben slyly. "Just show me a note so I know you have money to wager if you are so eagle-sighted. Just show it! Play the game. If you are right, maybe you bet next time."

Peter hesitated, and Ben teased him again in a soothing voice.

"What do you have to lose? Just show me a note, you can bet next time if you want."

In the back of his mind Peter registered that it had suddenly gotten quiet around him. Reluctantly, he held up a note and watched the queen dance across the table. He knew with certainty where she was.

Ben finished.

"Play the game. Ben is best. You think you know where she lies?"

"I know she is there."

He pointed reluctantly. "But as I said, I do not gamble."

Ben reached over and flipped the card.

To Peter's surprise the ace of spades stared up at him.

Quickly Ben snatched the note from Peter's hand.

"Play the game. Ben is best."

Peter stepped forward, directly in front of Ben, preventing him from continuing.

"I did not play. I said this. I did not bet. Give me the money back."

Ben stood, knocked the card table aside and pushed his chest against Peter.

"You pointed."

Suddenly the crowd grew hostile and Peter realized that most of them worked for Ben.

Peter was determined to stand for his money. He cursed himself for his stupidity and he became angry.

He stood tall, and a transformation took place.

He stood tall like a warrior.

He seemed to move in a trance, and as the men looked into his eyes they saw a light burning there that spoke of strength and confidence; something that had not been there moments before.

Peter saw an image of Lekai grinning confidently, and then he felt himself fading away.

Peter stared at the crowd, slowly moving his eyes from one to the next. With a strong voice he said, "You are all weak and soft."

He smiled at them.

"You think your numbers will protect you, but you will remember my passing if you do not return what is mine."

He glared at Ben who involuntarily stepped back from the strange, powerful energy emitted by the white man.

He grunted and tossed Peter's bill on the table.

Without another word, the crowd parted to let Peter return to the street. Peter took his money and walked away.

Hours later he stumbled into the Iqbal Hotel.

Had someone asked where he'd been, he couldn't have answered. In his mind he just saw the faces of Lekai and his men. They flashed by one at a time, leaving him fearful and confused.

He went to his room and locked the door.

Chapter Twenty-Four

Pilar's Proposal

*P*eter lay on his bunk, an open window by his head. It was dark out and close by was the sound of traffic, but in the distance he could hear drums and countless crickets. Slowly those sounds took over.

With his eyes closed he listened to the drums as their rhythm worked its way into him. But it soon started to bother him. He tried to ignore the heavy beat and drift off to sleep, but instead he found himself thinking about Lekai and the Maasai he'd seen in the streets that day.

He almost missed the light knock at his door.

He sat up, walked to the door and opened it to find Pilar standing in the hallway, smiling.

Peter smiled back, and tried to look light-hearted as he invited her in.

She'd showered and changed into clean clothes and no longer hid behind her scarves. A white blouse hung on her shoulders and Peter felt his burdens lighten as he leaned forward to kiss her cheek.

She smelled deliciously of soap and perfume, and as she hugged him he felt a new vitality in her. She looked well rested.

She glanced at the single bed.

"You are not sharing a room with Andy?"

"He should already be at the airport by now. He called it close arriving yesterday, and was lucky the *Mongrel* didn't break down more than once."

Through the long journey north Peter and Pilar had stolen moments together—and quick kisses—but now that they were alone it felt like there was a wall between them. Peter longed to hold her, and lose himself in her warm embrace. But he still had his own life to sort out.

She looked up into his blue eyes and read the anguish that lived in his soul.

"What is it that troubles you?"

He stared out the window and into the dark night.

"It wouldn't make sense if I tried to explain it."

"Try me," she said, her voice as soothing as warm chocolate.

For a minute Peter considered spilling everything, but he couldn't. Not yet. She'd think he was crazy.

"Tell me about Lamu. How do you get there?"

"Oh, Lamu...to be there again!"

Gently, Pilar led Peter to the bed and lay him back, then she nestled herself next to him.

"To get to Lamu you must take the overnight train to Mombasa on the coast," she whispered softly. From there you ride the bus to Malindi. It's about a three hour ride and the road is pretty good."

"Doesn't sound so difficult," said Peter.

She laughed and the laughter echoed in Peter's mind. How good it sounded, he thought, and how nice it would be to have her in his life.

If only he weren't plagued by the nightmares.

"That part is easy, for sure. From Malindi you must take a local bus and the road is very bad. The last time I made the journey it took six hours and I had to stand the entire time."

Peter forced himself to smile. "We've done some bad roads."

"*Si, es verdad*. And at the end of the bus ride you have to catch a ferry to the island — sometime the tide is not right and you must wait."

Peter nodded and she looked at him expectantly.

"I just need a little more time."

Sadly, she looked him in the eye.

"How much time do you need, Peter?"

"I will try to sort everything out tomorrow."

She stood and slowly smoothed out her blouse.

"Then I will see you tomorrow evening."

Gracefully she crossed the room and closed the door. Peter sat up, and then walked to his backpack leaning against the wall. With reluctance, he opened his pack and took out the *Eye of Enkai*.

For several minutes he just stared at it, afraid of what it might reveal. Holding it up, he examined the outside of the *Eye*. It didn't appear special, just a leather bag with a leather string to pull it shut.

He toyed with the leather thong, but he found his fingers slowly untying it, and with a sigh he opened the bag.

With trepidation, as if he were about to stick his hand into burning hot coals, he reached into the bag and grabbed a handful of stones.

One by one he let them pass through his fingers, and tried to identify them. Some he knew, but he felt unconnected to most. He suddenly thought that the *Eye of Enkai* had never spoken clearly to him.

When he was down to the last stone, he held his hand tightly, afraid to look, or even feel what it might be. He raised his clenched fingers out of the bag and looked at it.

"Why was it so certain Lekai would return?" he asked.

The curtains fluttered.

He was gripping the stone so tightly that his knuckles had turned white. He stared at the *Eye* as if expecting it to answer.

"What am I supposed to do with this?" he said as he raised his fist.

"Did Red Beret screw everything up? Or was it me?"

For just a second the lights flickered.

Peter looked around nervously.

"Show me the way," he begged.

Suddenly someone banged on the door loudly.

Startled, he dropped the stone he'd held on the bed.

The door flew open and Deepend entered. He was covered in sweat and looked agitated.

"The fucking taxi drivers here are worse than in Zimbabwe," he said.

He took a six pack of Tusker beer from his daypack, opened one, and tossed another to Peter.

"It's piss warm," Deepend, "but it's Tusker!"

He toasted. "I fucking love this beer."

Peter looked on his bedspread and was surprised to see not a small stone, but a bullet casing.

"How can you not like a beer with a big fuckin' elephant on the label?"

Peter picked up the shell and examined it. It was old and had lost its shine, and appeared to be from a large caliber rifle.

Deepend watched him.

He grinned as he said, "You got some fucked up shit going on in your head, don't you?"

Peter looked him in the eye and nodded.

"I thought so," said Deepend. "That's why we're gonna find some fire tonight. Let's…"

Peter began shaking his head and Deepend put up his hands defensively. "Okay, we don't look for fire, but let's at least get a drink."

With a sigh, Peter agreed.

Deepend was already half out the door when Peter placed the bullet shell back in the *Eye of Enkai.*

He took a few shillings and stuffed them in a front pocket of his jeans; then he tucked his pack under the bed and shut the door and locked it tightly. Then he headed after Deepend for the lobby.

Chapter Twenty-Five

The Modern Green Bar

*D*eepend and Peter walked through the sweltering night. Deepend led Peter to Latima Road where he cracked a beer and began to down it. It was late and the traffic was low, and for once they weren't instantly buffeted by the dusty wind. In fact, the night was so still Peter yearned for a breeze. They walked to the end of the block and then turned onto River Road.

Here the city narrowed and the street was lined with shops — all locked and barred up tightly. They had to look where they stepped because the sidewalks were treacherous for their potholes in the dark. All was quiet, almost peaceful, until they approached the Modern Green Bar.

The bar had the look of a place where people finished their evenings. There was nothing appealing about it — it was just open late, and therefore a line had formed outside the open door, a bunch of men swaying like sleeping elephants. Through the open door Peter could see a dense cloud of people, shouting and laughing and drinking.

As far as he could make out, there were no white people inside.

"Maybe we should just go to a tourist bar," said Peter.

Deepend shook his black mane, which he had finally managed to wash.

"They're all fuckin' closed at this hour."

"Besides," he added, "My taxi driver said this place has been rockin' lately."

With a second swig he finished the beer.

On a wooden stool by the entrance sat a large black man. He wore a skin-tight black T-shirt that stretched tautly around his impressively muscular chest and biceps. He looked mean as he eyeballed each person in line, letting none pass for the moment. Peter thought he seemed to be past his prime, but not too old to hold his own in a brawl. He also noticed the guy was gripping a thick stick.

"I bet he's kicked some ass," declared Deepend as he examined the bouncer.

Peter eyed the drunks in line around them.

"Ya, and I think this crowd needs watching."

The bouncer turned and stared at the two white men. His eyebrows touched over his nose as he glared at them, sizing them up and assessing how much trouble they might be.

Deepend squirmed under his gaze.

Finally, the bouncer nodded for them to go ahead into the bar, ahead of the others waiting.

"Thanks, dude," said Deepend as he extended his hand, but the man only looked at it and then back into Deepend's eyes.

A murmur arose in the line as Peter and Deepend stepped in front of a few of the locals, but a stern look from the bouncer silenced the protests.

The bar was a rectangular room with chipped, avocado-green paint and windblown spider webs in the corners. All the tables were occupied and the majority of the customers were standing on the cement floor that was sticky with spilled beer.

The bartender sat in a wire mesh cage at the back wall and exchanged warm beer for money through a small window in front of him.

A large ceiling fan provided the only circulation in the place; cobwebs clung to it and twirled. Even at this time of night the heat persisted. The smell of sticky sweat mixed with that of beer and urine.

An African song with a wild beat pounded through cracked speakers; the patrons smiled drunkenly and swayed with the musical rhythms of the metal drums.

A toothless old man with a white cap stood and danced in place to the cheers of his inebriated friends. He moved his hips rudely and slapped his ass with his hat, like he was riding a horse, until one of his friends stopped him by handing him a fresh beer.

Near the back wall stood a few prostitutes in short skirts. They looked bored and resigned that the remainder of the night held little promise.

Most of the bar patrons were recklessly drunk.

Peter made his way through the crowd and approached the cage. "Get me two cold ones."

The man grunted in response. Peter handed him a couple of notes and he turned away to get two beers from a little fridge behind him.

While they waited they looked over the bar. In the far corner a couple of people were pounding on the back of a man who was choking on something. To their left two men started a scuffle, grabbing at each other's collars.

The bouncer had taken up position on a stool by the door. When he saw the men fighting he slammed the base of his staff on the cement floor and the vibration stopped the two fighters instantly.

Deepend said, "I just love this bar."

Peter looked at him.

"No, really," said Deepend. "Where else can you get a show like this?"

He nodded at the toothless old man with the white cap, who was now looking quite drunk. He kept pushing himself upright in his chair, attempting to appear dignified.

The bartender handed over two cool Tuskers and Peter tipped him.

Peter placed the cold bottle against his temple, which felt like it was burning up. Deepend raised his and downed half of it in one focused attack. "Just watch that dude," said Deepend. "He's up to no good."

Peter looked over at the old drunk in the white cap and watched him stare at the enormous behind of a huge woman who was moving between two tables.

When she passed him the drunk leaned a little closer; his cap tilted precariously on his head and he looked poised to fall off his seat. He lifted his beer and downed it, and then grinned. The woman had hesitated in front of him and he reached out and grabbed a fistful of her behind.

The large woman looked back at him, smirked a little as if she appreciated the gesture, and then backhanded him. He flew right out of his seat and onto the sticky floor.

His hat had slid off in the tumble and he howled in despair as he searched the floor for it. Then he found it, and with hat in hand he sat on the wet floor and carefully examined a smudge on it while he absentmindedly rubbed his cheek. He pointed at the hat for all to see, as if smudging it were a bigger offense than the slap in the face.

With an accusing finger he then pointed at the large woman.

The bouncer just smiled and wagged a thick finger at him.

While they were watching the pair a beautiful Kikuyu woman had maneuvered her way to Deepend's side. She wore a loose top and a dangerously short miniskirt and she leaned into him, pushing her breast against his elbow.

She smiled, apologetically. "This is not a polite crowd."

Deepend looked to Peter for assistance and whispered, "Dude, I'm bad on the will power thing so make sure I go home with you when we leave."

The crowd was surging in their direction as a drunk man fell over and the woman used the momentum to slide up against Deepend. She placed her head on his shoulder, sniffing his neck.

He turned to Peter again and added, "I've got twenty US left to my name and I need it for the airport departure tax so I can't spend it or I'll be fucked. So make sure I go home alone."

This time she heard him. She looked offended.

"You think I am working?" she asked angrily.

He stammered to respond as she added, "You think I want money?"

Peter looked across the bar at the blur of faces, wishing he were back in his room; and then he saw a man he recognized about twenty-five feet away. With a jolt he realized the man was another Maasai from his dreams.

The man's name was Kulet and he was one of the warriors who'd tried to talk Lekai out of going on his journey alone. Peter couldn't believe his eyes, but sure as the African sky is blue he was standing there. Like Sendeyo, he appeared worn and down on his luck.

Since that fateful trip to Kenya ten years ago Peter had dreamt about his encounter with Lekai and the violent events that had followed in the Maasai Mara, but once he began his journey north his dreams had evolved and shifted. Now they increasingly revolved around events he had not witnessed and their mysterious meaning scared him.

By his side the Kikuyu woman was hollering at Deepend who had not managed to gracefully detach himself, but Peter's attention was riveted on Kulet who was now looking back at him, his expression a mix of fear and wonder. He appeared on the verge of fleeing, but couldn't seem to look away.

Could he possibly recognize me from the one time he'd seen me at night in the Land Cruiser? Peter thought. He didn't think so. Then why else would he stare like that? Peter could feel his pulse racing; his breath was shallow and rapid as he tried to take a step in Kulet's direction, but it was as if unknown forces were holding him in place.

He felt the air around him thicken, like it had when he saw Sendeyo running through the streets.

Finally he shook his head to break the spell and tried to force his way through the crowd in Kulet's direction. With fear in his eyes Kulet began to back away, knocking over a table as he retreated.

His movements were followed by curses from the patrons who'd been sitting at the table. One stood and pointed at a stain on his trousers. He began to shout at Kulet who was still backing away in the direction of the door, his gaze fixed on Peter.

The bouncer noticed the new commotion and raised his stick.

"No fighting," he said, but as he noted Kulet's fearful gaze he turned and looked at the South African with a new curiosity.

The bouncer stared at Peter and then hesitated as he caught a glimpse of his eyes. He saw confusion, and behind it a darker confidence that puzzled him.

He could tell something was different with the tall white man, but what exactly evaded him. He continued to watch him.

Peter nervously glanced from Kulet to the bouncer, and then saw a white man slyly slip past the bouncer and into the bar.

It was Conrad. He leaned against the far wall in a dark corner opposite from the bar and searched the room, scanning the faces methodically.

He had re-bandaged some of his burns with fresh gauze, and changed his shirt, but he didn't look rested. Around him a circle of space formed as even the drunks instinctively knew to keep their distance.

Peter glared at him—the man who had killed his father and he wanted to set him on fire again.

Conrad's bloodshot eyes scanned the crowd, and with a slight smile of recognition his glare finally settled on Peter.

Peter had momentarily forgotten Kulet who stood frozen about halfway to where Conrad leaned. A new wave of panic had taken over Kulet when he'd seen Conrad and Peter watched as he struggled frantically to get to the door.

The bouncer threw a disapproving glance at Peter as Kulet burst past.

Deepend was still arguing with the Kikuyu woman. She was calling some men for help and yelling insults at him when He looked up and noticed Peter and Conrad staring at each other.

"Oh, fuck!" he shouted.

Conrad made his way across the bar, calmly eyeing Peter.

He seemed to be enjoying himself, and wasn't in a rush. Peter imagined a black mamba approaching its prey.

He reached Peter and stood in front of him with his hands on his hips, "Now I remember you, boy. It's been some time, eh?"

Peter tensed and seemed ready to pounce.

A twisted smile spread over Conrad's face, "Small world, eh? That I pick you up at the border just after I killed your father. What are the odds...?"

In an explosion of rage Peter jumped at him and clutched his neck with his fingers. But Conrad was not your ordinary invalid. He'd been in many fights and knew how to handle himself even when he was wounded. He knocked Peter's hands away with a sweep of his arm and then punched him in the stomach.

Peter doubled over in pain but his rage wasn't spent. He went at Conrad again, this time trying to trip him.

A circle formed around them as the other patrons watched the show.

The bouncer stood and came in their direction. He raised his stick and was about to strike Peter when Deepend attempted to tackle him. The bouncer was much larger and when he saw Deepend coming he let go of the staff with one hand, backhanded the American, and sent him ricocheting off him ineffectively.

The bouncer eyed him. "I will knock you out."

Deepend had momentarily saved Peter from the bouncer's wrath, but now Conrad was choking the life out of him.

And the bouncer now blocking his way, pointed the menacing staff at him and said, "Stay."

Deepend froze and looked at Peter and Conrad with panic-filled eyes. Only Peter's rage kept him from being pummeled, but he was losing. As Deepend watched Conrad grabbed Peter and roughly threw him to the pavement and then jumped on him.

The bouncer turned and brought the staff down hard on Conrad's back. He let go of Peter, pivoted, and glared at him. Peter struggled free from under Conrad and threw another punch.

Peter had just managed to get to his feet when the bouncer brought the staff down on his head and everything went black.

Conrad stood over Peter, grinning, just as a prostitute screamed, "Police! Raid!"

A door suddenly opened out of the back of the bar, and someone yelled, "Run!" In a flash the entire crowd charged that way.

The bouncer was pulled away by the escaping crowd and Conrad tried to hold his ground next to Peter by gripping his shirt, but then Deepend, who had cut around the bouncer, hit him in the face. The blow surprised Conrad and he fell back into the panicked crowd. He flailed his arms but by the time he regained his footing, he had been pushed fifteen feet away.

He glared at Peter and Deepend, but then he saw the police enter the bar and turned to disappear.

"I'm not done with you, boy," he hissed as he made for the back door.

The bouncer was pushing his way back toward Deepend, and the American put up his hands in submission.

"I will not tolerate fighting!"

Deepend nodded meekly and knelt by Peter. "Hey, I'm just looking after my friend."

Suddenly the bar was empty, save for Deepend, the Bouncer and Peter on the floor. He appeared unconscious, but he was having another one of his dreams.

Lekai was stepping out of Laibon's hut and into the dark night. The sky burned with bright stars and he stopped and looked up at them for a moment.

Around him, the Maasai warriors of his Moran waited attentively.

Sendeyo stood proudly with his weapons ready; the others looked to him with expressions of concern.

Lekai addressed them.

"Laibon has seen my return, so it will be. We are not to question it."

He smiled confidently.

Sendeyo said, "But if you do not return, then we will be left without guidance against our enemies. You are our Seer. You are our eyes into the future. What shall befall us if Lekai does not return?"

Kulet added, "If we cannot trust the great Laibon with the safety of Lekai, how can we trust him with the safety of the brotherhood?"

Lekai replied, "Laibon says I will return. Yet there is a riddle surrounding it. You must watch for the light behind blue circles. When you see the light you will know I have returned."

The men reluctantly nodded in acceptance.

Sendeyo gave Lekai a long spear for extra protection, and a few of the others left him with talismans for luck. One by one they embraced him, and then Lekai walked out of the thorn enclosure and into the night.

Peter opened his blue eyes and blinked into the bare overhead lights. He was looking at the ceiling of the bar, dreamily, his gaze floating to a cobweb that danced on the fan; and then his world came into focus and he saw Deepend grinning at him from above.

He slowly sat up on the dirty floor and felt the aching welt on his head.

"That dude tagged you," said Deepend.

The bouncer nodded.

"I am sorry, but I will not tolerate fighting here."

Peter stood slowly; with a start he remembered Conrad and jerked his head around apprehensively.

"Don't worry, he's gone," Deepend said. "I checked the street too. He must really not like police."

Peter nodded and had Deepend help him hobble out of the bar. Deepend had to support him on the way back to the Iqbal hotel.

By the hotel door Peter paused.

"I'm going to spend a few days in Maasailand looking for a certain village," he said.

"I'm up for that," replied Deepend. "I've got time before my flight."

He looked up and down the street nervously.

"I don't really think I should be hanging around Nairobi with Conrad here. Can I go with you?"

Peter gave him a skeptical glance, then said, "You can come, but I'm leaving in the morning. At first light, I do not have time to play."

Deepend laughed. "You know, you're wound pretty tight. Slow down for five minutes and we can grab my wheels."

Peter rubbed the spot where he got conked.

"Alright, but no games," he said. "We will take your Land Cruiser."

Deepend grabbed Peter's shoulder.

"Awesome. Just come by Mama Rosch's Guest House in the morning, but give me a few hours to get it running."

"Good," said Peter. "And we should try to find someone who knows the area."

"I got that covered too," said Deepend. "I know a Maasai guide."

Peter eyed him skeptically.

"We'll see."

Chapter Twenty-Six

Mama Rosch's Guest House

*D*eepend awoke on the porch at Mama Rosch's when the other tenants began to stir. Since negotiating his meals with Mama he'd been looking forward to the standard breakfast she offered her guests. He climbed out of his ragged sleeping bag and jumped to his bare feet.

His dirty socks hung on a line above the boots which were standing on the edge of the porch. The socks still smelled so badly that he almost left them, but then he remembered the blisters that resulted when he last tried to forgo socks and he put them on after all. He banged the boots together and shook them upside down, then held his breath as he pulled them on.

He walked along the porch with his boots unlaced.

A few travelers were cooking their own food on small propane camping stoves.

"Suckers," he taunted as he stepped over them.

"Oh, you're a big man now that you can afford breakfast," said an Australian who had some oatmeal cooking.

"That's right," said Deepend.

He crossed the yard and entered Mama's little house, cautiously side-stepping Wolfie who was sleeping in the doorway to take a seat at a large dining room table. Five other travelers joined him, and they sat sipping coffee and eating toast and eggs while Mama cooked in the kitchen. After the meager meals on the *Mongrel* he felt like he was sitting down to a Thanksgiving buffet.

"It's so nice to eat food that's not covered in fuckin' dust," he said to an English traveler who sat on his right.

Mama appeared with a plate of fried eggs, and Deepend pounced on it. The English guy, who had been reaching for the plate, watched with his mouth open as Deepend cleared off every egg on it and started filling his mouth.

"How about leaving some for us?"

Deepend spoke through a mouthful of egg. "Hey, she's still cooking. What the fuck?"

A few minutes later Mama reappeared with a tray of bacon, and an Australian traveler who sat opposite Deepend intercepted it and made sure everyone got some before it went near the American.

"You guys are fuckin' hilarious," said Deepend, chewing.

Mama came up to the table and stood with her hands on her hips. She looked at Deepend's plate. "My goodness, Francis, I fear this will be an expensive Land Cruiser before you are gone."

Deepend blushed.

"Mama, I told you it's Deepend now."

She laughed and went back into the kitchen, only to return a minute later with a tray of cornflakes.

Deepend noticed that the Englishman on his right kept staring at his U2 shirt with tour dates from a concert in Scotland.

He glared at Deepend. "Have you ever been to Great Britain?"

"No," said Deepend through a mouthful of cornflakes.

The man nodded. "Ever see U2?"

Deepend shook his head.

The man planted an elbow on the table and turned halfway to face Deepend. "Then where'd you get that shirt, mate?"

The American reflected for a minute, then admitted, "I found it on the line."

The English guy's face turned purple.

"That's my bloody shirt! You've got some nerve stealing it while I set it out to dry!"

With a shrug, Deepend peeled the shirt over his shoulders and tossed it at the guy. He laughed as he stuck a piece of bacon in his mouth. "I don't know what you're so sore about. I left another shirt in its place."

Out the window they could clearly see the clothesline. In the middle, alone, the dirty rag that Deepend had been using as a shirt hung like a decayed bat.

"I guess I've just gotten too lazy to wash anything," said Deepend. "I'm pretty much ready to go home."

"Well, it won't be soon enough for me," said the Englishman as he roughly pushed back his chair and stood. "And stay away from my laundry."

As the guy stormed out of the kitchen Deepend looked over the other travelers.

"That guy was a fuckin' wanker."

After breakfast, Deepend grabbed a spot on the edge of the porch where he soon talked someone into sharing a smoke. He was laying back in the sun, mildly stoned, when Mama came around to collect money.

"Who owes me money?" she shouted as she raised a large notebook.

The suddenness of her cry startled Deepend and he fell right off the porch.

Mama stood looking down at him, her hands on her hips.

"Francis, how could I have forgotten you?" she said, laughing.

She turned to an Irish guy who was trying to hide his face in a novel. She stared down at him. "You came here yesterday, didn't you?"

He nodded and she shook her head.

"Why didn't you write in the book when you arrived?" she asked. "Such a simple thing."

She opened the book and handed it to him and he quickly signed in and handed her his money.

Deepend got up, rubbing his shoulder, and sat back down on the porch. Mama leaned on one of the vertical posts that supported the simple roof and sighed.

She said, "Someday I want to be like you travelers — you *wazungus* — and sit on the porch all day."

She turned and moved along, then lowered herself down and gently shoved two travelers out of her way.

"I'll do nothing! No laundry. No cooking. Life will be good, eh?"

She looked along the porch and noticed that at least half of the travelers were busy at work deseeding marijuana.

"And why so much drugs here?" she asked them.

Everyone looked away, not wanting to get in trouble, until a long-time regular named Harry said, "Mama, the money changer was closed yesterday and the fruit market was open this morning."

"Oh! I see," she said with an exaggerated tone. "So you change money today and go straight to the market to buy some ganja."

The man stared back and then nodded.

Mama shook her head.

"Why is my life not so easy? Tomorrow I'll stay on the porch with you. It's better than cooking and cleaning, I think. I'll stay here. Tomorrow you make the breakfast."

"We love you, Mama!" shouted one of the travelers. "If you need help you just ask us."

She laughed deeply, and held her stomach as she leaned back. "I have seen you help in my kitchen. You cook just a little, you do no dishes, and when you leave my shelves are empty."

Deepend crouched by Mama and said, "Mama, I need to take my wheels for a few days."

She looked at him sternly.

"You come back with my Land Cruiser. I am putting my trust in you, Francis."

Deepend sheepishly looked at the ground.

"I'll come back, Mama. You don't have to worry about me."

She smiled as she reached over and ruffled up his curly black hair.

"The keys are in it. You should check the battery — there are jumper cables by the shed if you need them."

Deepend was working on the Land Cruiser when he saw Jacob — the young Maasai he'd met the day before — peeking over the gate. His eyes were fearful as he surveyed the compound. On the inside of the gate Wolfie growled and watched his every move.

Deepend closed the hood of the Land Cruiser and turned the keys. The engine fired right up. He left it idling while he walked through the gate and into the street.

Wolfie poked his head out through the open gate for a second and Jacob almost fled, but then Deepend closed the gate and locked the dog on the inside of the compound.

On the street Jacob greeted him happily.

"What would you like to do today, sir?" he asked.

Deepend put on a professional face.

"I want you to guide me to a Maasai village."

Jacob nodded, enthusiastically. "I know just the village, and it is not far."

Deepend shook his head.

"No, it's a particular village my friend wants to see. He'll tell you where it is."

Jacob said, "This I will gladly do. Do you want them to take you on safari?"

"I don't think so, this is personal business."

A bit confused, Jacob looked to the street as a taxi arrived and Peter got out. Peter had slept little the night before, and his head still hurt from the lump the bouncer at the Modern Green

Bar had given him. He didn't have much faith in Deepend producing a vehicle, but had decided to check it out anyway.

Peter looked at the young Maasai on the sidewalk next to Deepend, and the youth stared into his eyes for only a moment before he quickly looked down. He wouldn't meet his eyes again and moved back, shaken.

Here we go again, thought Peter.

"This guy says he can guide us to a Maasai village," said Deepend to Peter.

Peter stared at him. "Not just any village. I do not know its name but I can describe it."

Jacob stared at the ground and nodded.

"And I need to talk to a Seer named Laibon," said Peter. "I have something I have to discuss with him."

The young Maasai held up his hands defensively.

"Of all things, this I cannot do."

Peter held up a US note. "I will give you fifty US dollars for this and it should only take a day."

Jacob shook his head. "I have a family connection to this place. I am a disgrace there. They would most likely stone me."

Jacob nearly choked on his words. He covered his eyes and stared at the ground and spoke in a voice that was barely a whisper. "The fire in the hut of my mother has gone cold. She lives off the charity of others. I cannot go back."

Peter sensed something familiar about Jacob, although he couldn't seem to remember him from his dreams.

He decided to be blunt.

"It concerns the one they called Lekai. Did you know him?"

Jacob wouldn't look up from the ground as he nodded.

Peter continued, "I have a promise to fulfill in his name."

Suddenly bitter, Jacob asked, "What do you know of Lekai? Why do you wish to speak with Laibon?"

"What I have to say is for Laibon alone," said Peter. "Will you take me or not? You could use the money to help your mother."

"You and I have met before," said Jacob, quietly. "Lekai was my brother. When you met me I still used my traditional name, Kakuta."

Peter remembered Kakuta jumping out of the bush, and Lekai standing nearby with his spear raised.

"Yes," said Peter. "I remember you."

"I will take you," said the young man. "But keep your money. And we must leave soon if we are going to get there before dark."

Peter turned to Deepend.

"When will your Land Cruiser be ready?"

He smiled proudly. "Just give me ten minutes."

Chapter Twenty-Seven

The Abandoned Manyatta

*T*hey rode along in a severely beaten up Land Cruiser; the two travelers sat up front, with Peter driving. Jacob had taken the back, leaning forward between the seats.

Peter wore a short-sleeved button-up shirt, and Deepend had on a T-shirt advertising the *Dreamtime Guest House* in Cairns, Australia. He'd told Peter about the incident with the English guy at breakfast and Peter wondered if Deepend had stolen that t-shirt as well.

The ride was rough and the Land Cruiser shook violently when it hit one of the many potholes. Peter wondered if there were any shocks or springs on it at all. Jacob was half-standing in the back to brace himself against the next impact.

The noise of the impacts was deafening and Peter felt like he was back on the *Mongrel*. He looked at Deepend and shook his head.

"What'd'ya want for nothing?" said Deepend. "It won't go into four wheel drive, but we did throw in a new back seat."

Peter turned to Jacob and his expression became somber.

"I'm looking for a *manyatta* — a village — and all I know is it is near a large volcanic cone with a river running along its backside."

Peter stared into the void as he spoke. "In my mind I've dreamt of it for hours on end—I've walked through its thorny enclosure a thousand times—but I have no idea of its location."

With a desperate look, he asked, "Do you know of it?"

Jacob nodded gravely, fearfully. "I know it well; it was to be the home of Lekai and his men before…"

He paused.

"…things fell apart."

He nodded ahead, in the direction they were going.

"Keep driving, I will tell you when to turn off. You still have some distance to cover."

Jacob looked up at Peter, a mix of emotions on his face. Peter had seen the usual expressions of fear and mistrust in Jacob, but what confused him was that he now also saw hope. It flickered lightly, but seemed to grow throughout the journey.

"Hey, let's gets some beer!" said Deepend when they passed a small shop, but Peter drove on.

"Not today, Deepend."

Deepend had a feeling there was no pushing the issue.

They drove through the morning and stopped at a roadside stall where they each had a bowl of *ugali*—a porridge made from maize and small bits of meat.

They ate silently, climbed back into the Land Cruiser and continued on their way.

The road did not improve. Potholes pockmarked the asphalt, and at times, pedestrians spilled onto the roadway, forcing Peter to slow even more. The drive was taking longer than he'd expected.

At least the directions that Jacob called out every so often were easy to follow, and there was none of the craziness that would have come with Deepend behind the wheel.

Although Peter had wanted to get to the *manyatta* by noon, it was late in the afternoon before they got close.

From a distance they spotted the cinder cone of the volcano. Peter sucked in his breath sharply. At almost eight hundred feet it dwarfed the surrounding hills, and its black flanks made even the lush vegetation at its base appear desolate.

Peter had rolled up his window to keep the dust out, but as they got close he rolled it down again. The air was dry and smelled of sulfur.

"Is that thing active?" asked Deepend as he craned his neck to see the top.

"No," answered Jacob. "He has been dead a long time."

"What's in the cone?" asked Deepend eagerly.

The young Maasai shook his head.

"I do not know. It is an evil place—it is taboo—and we are not allowed to go there."

Deepend grinned. "Well, I'm fuckin' going there."

Near the top of the cone the ash was red and yellow, but the closer they got the more that faded from view and all they saw was the dark, lifeless black of the steep slopes.

It was so black it appeared to suck up all the light around it.

"You will park there, by that path," said Jacob as they approached a turnoff with space for a dozen vehicles. A trail led off to the right, around a low shoulder of the cone, rising two hundred feet before dropping behind the volcano.

Far to the west the sun was approaching the horizon.

Peter parked the vehicle and grabbed a small backpack from the back seat. After he stowed several plastic water bottles they started up the path that circled the volcano.

The lingering heat of the day was still intense—it seemed much hotter now without the breeze that they had enjoyed in the vehicle. The sun was softening, turning to orange, but the rock and cinder had been baking in its rays all day and now the volcano spat back the heat as if it didn't want to be tred upon.

The hot air singed their lungs, and they were glad to see the trail eventually lead to the shaded side of the cone. And when they reached the shade they caught their first glimpse of the *manyatta*.

Despite the harsh landscape, Lekai and his men had chosen a good location. In the afternoon the volcano's shadow sheltered them, and a small river flowed by the far side of the circular structure.

Peter stood looking down on Lekai's *manyatta*, his body reviving a bit in the shade. He'd dwelled so long on the mystery of this image from his dreams that he felt numb looking at the real place.

He opened his pack and took out one of the water bottles and drank. His thirst was unquenchable and he downed the contents in one long swig.

Upon closer inspection he saw that the village was in grave condition. Most of the huts had collapsed, and the circular fence of acacia thorns — or *kraal* — that provided protection from lions and hyenas had huge gaps in it.

As the sun sank lower the shadows thickened.

Peter shook his head, as if trying to wake. He fought off an irresistible urge to sleep. And then a door opened in his mind and it flooded with a mix of images from his dreams.

He stumbled backwards and sank to his knees.

In his mind he saw warriors pacing in the darkness, approaching each other, saying nothing. The look of devastation on their faces was horrible to witness.

He saw Lekai sitting in a low hut with Laibon. The words of their discussion were inaudible to him, but their expressions were somber and he knew what they were talking about.

He watched smooth stones slipping through aged fingers — one by one — and each one was accompanied by a word of greeting from the voice of Laibon.

And then he heard two gunshots, followed by one more.

In his mind they echoed loudly over the surrounding hills, but as he realized that Deepend and Jacob were leaning over him he knew that he had only imagined it.

"I'm okay," said Peter, but Deepend didn't buy it.

Jacob looked equally uncomfortable.

Deepend glanced down at the abandoned *manyatta*.

"That place looks spooky."

252

On the main road Conrad parked his red pickup next to Deepend's Land Cruiser. The sun had set and it was now dark. He looked around to make sure there were no witnesses and, satisfied, got out.

"Time to finish the job," he muttered.

Before he started up the path he checked his pistol to make sure it was loaded and stuck it in his belt.

By the village gate Peter stood silently, but his eyes were now filled with determination and his face was that of a warrior about to go into battle. He had dealt with nightmares and guilt for ten years, and one way or another it would end tonight.

He thought of Lekai, and the friendship that they had, and he told himself that he had nothing to fear. His face grew dark, and somehow became less Peter and more a proud Maasai warrior.

Jacob silently backed up and disappeared into the darkness.

Deepend looked at Peter, horrified. "Oh my God! You're fuckin' possessed!"

The long, sad call of a Kudu horn coming from the dark village intercepted Deepend's shriek.

Peter turned silently to enter the enclosure.

"I don't like this at all," said Deepend in a shaky voice.

As Peter approached the *manyatta* he saw a fire burning near the far wall of the *kraal* with a solitary figure standing in front of it.

Peter walked towards him and as he got closer he recognized the man as Laibon.

The Seer looked ancient and tired as he said, "Hello, Peter. I have been waiting for you."

Peter stared at him in confusion.

Laibon smiled proudly and added, "And there is someone else who has been waiting as well."

Laibon pointed to the shadows.

Out of the darkness stepped two people Peter knew well, but he questioned his senses as he found himself looking upon his mother and father.

As they moved closer to the fire Peter saw the woman was actually Pilar. He smiled at her, relieved that she would be there to witness the end of the nightmare he'd been living.

But next to her stood Peter's father, Simon, looking at him with a warm smile on his face.

Peter ran to him. They embraced and Peter found his mind flooded with memories and emotions. A weight had been taken off his chest and as he hugged his father he felt that burden being replaced by love.

Finally, Peter stepped back, holding his father's shoulders, and asked, astonished, "How can this be? They said you were dead."

Peter looked into his father's eyes, feeling the regret at his loss fade away. Throughout his journey north he'd felt utterly alone inside even though he'd been around people most of the time; and it hadn't been until he'd believed his father dead that he realized just how much he needed him.

Simon smiled, and subconsciously rubbed an injury on his right side, by his ribs.

"It turns out I didn't kill Red Beret after all. I don't know why he waited so long, but he came for me, and we had quite a battle."

Peter nodded, and waited for his father to continue.

"Well I gave him a good run, but eventually he blew up my truck. I was thrown from it into a river and he thought the crocs got me. I hid in the bush and watched him search for my body."

Simon smiled at Peter. "I thought it best to let him believe it. I went back to South Africa to tell you the truth, but by that time you were gone."

Peter creased his eyebrows while he tried to process it all.

He asked, "How did you know I'd come here?"

Simon looked at Pilar.

"Well, it turned out that I was searching Nairobi for you at the same time as this young lady and we bumped into each other this morning at your hotel."

Pilar gently touched Laibon's hand as she said, "And then Laibon found us and brought us here."

Suddenly someone else stepped out of the shadows.

"Well, isn't this a nice reunion?" Conrad said.

Simon moved in front of his son, protectively.

"Eh? You sure are a difficult one to kill. Guess I'll just have to do it again...and your boy, too, this time."

He raised his pistol and was about to fire when Deepend dove at him. He stepped back and pistol-whipped him with the pistol's solid handle on the head. The American dropped to the ground, unconscious.

Again he lifted the pistol and pointed the barrel at Simon, but this time a Maasai throwing club whizzed out of the darkness, hit his hand, and projected the gun into the shadows.

Conrad screamed and grabbed his hand. The club had broken two of his fingers.

Jacob appeared in the light of the fire.

"You killed my brother, Red Beret. I will not allow you to kill again."

The young man stood defiantly and added, "Not here. Not today."

Conrad twisted his face into an evil, pained grin and took out a large knife with his left hand.

He brandished the sharp blade in his left with surprising dexterity. "Sorry to disappoint you all, but there are many ways to kill a man."

He stepped toward Jacob, and the young man shouted, "*Eeuo!*" (It has come!)

Peter looked up sharply, startled that he could actually understand the Maasai words.

It has come, he thought. Finally, it has come.

From the shadows appeared silent black figures. In the darkness it was impossible to tell how many they were.

Jacob pointed at Conrad and shouted, "This is Red Beret! He killed Lekai."

A look of fear came over Conrad's face as the black figures began to call out. Some shouted their war cry; others imitated the low, coughing grunts of a lion.

Conrad backed up, trying to look calm, but his eyes betrayed his panic. He frantically peered into the darkness.

Suddenly he turned and ran toward the village gate by the path back to the parking lot.

The black figures followed.

Chapter Twenty-Eight

The Eye of Enkai is Large

Conrad was scrambling through the loose cinder of the volcano, but with every step he took he slid back a half step in the gravel, and soon he was sinking in up to his knees.

He cursed as he looked around for an established trail, but there was none. With no other options, Conrad climbed ahead frantically.

Initially he'd started for his pickup, but when he realized that more Maasai were heading towards him from the parking lot, he had diverted to the cinder cone.

Behind him a dozen warriors hesitated. They glanced at each other for assurance before climbing the forbidden cone.

"I should have killed you all!" he shrieked.

As one they slowly pursued him, crawling up the long hill like panthers in the dark.

He doubled his efforts when he saw that they were slowly closing the distance.

Panting hard, he finally reached the top and disappeared over the rim into the darkness.

Just under the rim of the cone one of the Maasai motioned for everyone to stop—they could go no further. With another gesture they began to fan out in each direction to surround the cone.

Then a horrible scream emerged from the crater.

It was followed by another.

The black men looked at each other, and despite the taboos they'd been taught, they crept a bit higher to cautiously peer over the rim down into the cone.

What they saw took their breath away.

Twenty feet below, in the crater of the cone, Conrad lay pinned by a large lion, its jaws clamped on his throat. Even from this distance and in the dark of night, they could clearly see the whites of his eyes and the terror on his face.

Conrad still fought.

Desperately, he punched the animal in the face. The lion raised its head and roared loudly, then pinned Conrad's arm with its paw. An excited murmur rose from the Maasai as they saw the lion's paw was white.

Conrad tried to scream but could only manage a gurgle through his mangled throat.

The lion lowered its head to Conrad's face and roared again.

The dark night echoed the proud sound. A moment later the lion roared again and this time there seemed to be a note of sadness that made Peter remember the day they'd found the cub, not far from its dead mother.

Conrad whimpered.

And then the lion clamped down on his throat again and even that small sound ended.

The last image Conrad saw on this earth were the lion's yellow eyes, only inches away.

One of the Maasai spoke.

"*Elala onu Ai.*" (The *Eye of Enkai* is large.)

Back at the fire Simon had roused Deepend and was examining the welt on his head. He would most likely develop a bad black eye, too, but otherwise appeared fine.

Deepend didn't remember much. He was sitting by the fire rubbing his head when Conrad's scream ripped through the night. Then another one.

"What the fuck is this place?" he asked fearfully.

Suddenly Peter stood and stepped back, away from Deepend. His expression was uncertain and he looked confused.

Simon grabbed his elbow to help steady him.

Laibon walked over and looked into his eyes.

The light of consciousness began to fade in Peter's eyes and he smiled.

"It is almost over, Peter. You must rest for now."

Laibon motioned for Simon and Pilar to help him lead Peter away from the fire. They sat down with him in the shadows, silently awaiting what would happen next.

Chapter Twenty-Nine

Carry the Tribe

*L*aibon stepped out of the shadows, his figure lit up by the fire. He was angry and the emotion made him look younger, and stronger. He was shaking his staff as if getting ready for battle.

He shouted, "*Oyiote!*" (I have a riddle!)

And then, defiantly, he added, "*Oyiote, olemeiruk!*" (I have a riddle! Unbelievers, come forth!)

For a moment all was silent. Then out of the darkness on all sides emerged the former warriors of Lekai's *moran*. Sendeyo was first among them, then Tiyo and Kulet appeared, and then the rest of them. A few were in traditional dress, but most wore ragged western clothing.

Laibon yelled again, "*Oyiote!*"

At once all the Maasai present responded in unison.

"*EEUO!*" (It has come!)

Their call was loud and strong, like a dozen lions roaring at once. And it carried the pride of a lion defining his territory.

Laibon walked around the fire, pouring milk from a gourd by his side into his hand, and then sprinkling it on the heads of the warriors and chanting.

"The time of *Ol-maitai* is ending," he said. "The spirit of Lekai will return soon. Did I not tell you of *Ol-maitai*? Ten years of bad fortune. And now it is ten years since the death of my apprentice!"

The men all bowed their heads.

"You should be ashamed!" he shouted. "Did I not advise you to follow the path *Enkai* had set down? Did I not tell you to stick to the traditional ways?"

He shook his head, and muttered to himself. "I warned you all, but none listened and you left this place."

He looked around at the dilapidated *manyatta*.

"This was to be your home," he said sadly.

Laibon slowly walked the circle, and as he passed each man he paused and they raised their head. He made eye contact and held it until he had seen what he was looking for.

"Lekai will return but he will not be Lekai. Look for the light behind blue circles and there you will find Lekai. Were these not my words?"

Examining the warriors again, he called, "Who amongst you has seen the *wazungu* from the south? Who has seen the light of Lekai behind his blue eyes? Is this not the light behind blue circles?"

Some of the warriors yelled their war cry, others nodded enthusiastically.

Laibon raised his hands over his warriors.

"*Olemeiruk!*" (Unbelievers!)

Then, with a look that spoke of *Enkai* Laibon pointed his staff at the shadows by the fence and shouted.

"Behold, Lekai has returned!"

In the shadows by the fence stood Peter, but what walked out of the darkness was only part Peter, for those who looked into his eyes saw Lekai.

It seemed by Peter's expression and his stance that he slept, and moving in his body was a young Maasai warrior, Lekai.

Lekai nodded to Sendeyo as he passed him, and then to Tiyo and Kulet. They smiled back in response. In all of his movements and gestures Peter appeared to be Maasai.

He walked to Laibon's side and waited patiently as the warriors formed a circle around him.

One by one Lekai embraced each of his brothers as they came forward to greet him. Sendeyo he held the longest.

When all the warriors had greeted him Laibon directed their attention to a large gap in the *kraal* and through it Jacob entered the *manyatta* and approached the fire.

He made no eye contact with Laibon, or any Maasai.

When he did lift his head it was in Lekai's direction.

Looking into Lekai's eyes, Jacob rushed forward and embraced him. Then he stepped back, his expression puzzled.

"One head cannot contain all knowledge, little brother," said Lekai's voice from Peter's mouth.

Lekai looked over the other warriors.

"I am sorry, my brothers, for I knew not the twisted journey *Enkai* had set before me. The *Eye of Enkai* is truly large."

The Maasai warriors all nodded as they looked at Peter. Several held talismans in their hands and they squeezed them tightly, others mumbled prayers as they looked to Laibon for guidance.

Lekai then reached into his backpack and produced the *Eye of Enkai*.

The warriors gasped.

He held it out to Laibon who took it, smiling.

"It was not I, but Peter, who has returned the *Eye*."

Laibon looked into Lekai's eyes, and then embraced him.

"Lekai has returned and restored his *moran*. Now it is time for Lekai to sleep. The spirit of Lekai has a new awareness and that awareness is Peter; it has all been foreseen. Sleep, Lekai, and follow the line *Enkai* has laid down."

Lekai smiled from inside Peter, and then addressed the warriors one last time.

"*Entanap olosho!*" (Carry the tribe!)

Then the light of Lekai slowly sank below the surface until it was just Peter who stood there silently. With a start he seemed to wake, and he looked around awkwardly, uncertain of where he was.

The warriors stared down at the ground.

Laibon stared for a minute, and then put a reassuring hand on Peter's shoulder and asked, "Peter, are you okay?"

"Ya, I think."

The old seer smiled at Peter and nodded. "The *Eye of Enkai* has finally been returned," he said.

Peter stared at his feet. "I only hope I haven't done any damage by waiting so long to return it."

Laibon said, "It is better that the *Eye* was safely hidden during *Ol-maitai*. We could have lost it for good."

Laibon gave Peter a reassuring smile.

The Seer then whistled and motioned for Simon and Pilar to join them. Deepend remained where he was. "I'm good here."

When they reached the fire Laibon held up the *Eye of Enkai* and the warriors cheered.

"Although to you Lekai has returned to the spirit world, to me he only sleeps. I look at the *wazungu* and I see him clearly. I can hear Lekai in his voice. In times of need he will assist us."

Jacob stepped forward, timidly. "Grandfather, I also see Lekai as if he never faded. To me there is no difference. I apologize for my disrespect and lack of belief. My brother has returned home as predicted."

Laibon placed his hand on Jacob's shoulder.

"Come, Kakuta, let the past be and stand by my side."

Peter cleared his throat and Laibon looked at him.

"There is another matter," he said shyly.

When Laibon nodded for him to proceed he said, "I would like to speak of Lekai's death."

The warriors fell silent again but then Sendeyo stepped forward and spoke.

"None of us were there when Lekai died. We knew Red Beret was involved but nothing more. We have never spoken of it because it is a mystery to us."

Peter tensed and sucked in a breath of air. Apprehensively he said, "Well, I was there. I saw it."

He stopped, afraid to continue until he saw the encouraging look in Simon's eyes.

He said, "Lekai died a warrior's death. But just as he was about to kill Red Beret I distracted him. It was because of me that he died."

Simon stepped forward, ready to defend him, and placed his hand on his son's shoulder.

Laibon asked, "And what did Lekai do when he looked at you?"

Peter stared at the ground, feeling lost. The fire crackled nearby and he looked into its depths. He remembered sitting by the fire with Lekai the night before his death and he reflected on their conversations that night. The world had seemed so bright that night — so positive.

The warriors watched silently as he returned to that horrible day. In his mind he watched it all play out again and his face reflected the emotions. And then he remembered the final moments when their eyes had met across the clearing.

Laibon watched as well, and he noted how Peter's expression of anguish changed at the last minute.

He asked Peter again, "What did Lekai do when you shouted to warn him?"

Peter's lips quivered slightly and he had to wait a minute before he could speak. When he did there was a look of wonder in his eyes.

He looked at Laibon. "He smiled."

"That's right," said Laibon. "He smiled, because he already knew that you would complete his journey."

Tears flowed down Peter's face and Pilar stepped to his side and held his hand. Many of the warriors by the fire were crying, but they also smiled.

Encouraged, Peter added, "My father followed the man that killed him, and he believed he got vengeance for Lekai. All these years we thought Red Beret was dead."

Sendeyo took a deep breath and said, "Well, he is now, so the spirit of Lekai is truly free."

Peter said, "Tonight by this fire I would like to tell the story of his brave death."

Several of the warriors nodded, somberly, and then others picked up a guttural chant. As it grew in volume Sendeyo addressed the fallen warriors. "Brothers, the time has come to rebuild our village."

Laibon stepped forward with his arms extended, motioning for the warriors to slow down.

"By the light of day you can rebuild your home. Tonight we will listen to the story of Lekai."

The warriors nodded.

Laibon grabbed his staff and slammed its base into the earth.

"But not like this!" he shouted.

The warriors looked baffled as they waited for their Seer to explain himself.

Laibon glared at the warriors and shook his head.

"Look at you!" he shouted. "You look like a bunch of *wazungus!*"

The men glanced at each other and suddenly looked at the western clothing most of them wore with disgust. Those with button-up shirts quickly took them off and tossed them into the fire.

"Good," said Laibon. "I know some of you have things hidden or buried here. Go find your belongings and return to me. I will not allow Peter to tell his tale until you once again look like Maasai."

As one they stood and left the fire.

Soon only Peter, Deepend, Pilar and Simon sat by the fire. Laibon had allowed it to die down to a bed of hot coals. The Seer walked to where Deepend now lay on his side and placed a wet cloth on his swollen head, then returned to the fire.

Peter looked at the coals and thought over the events of the last forty eight hours. It all seemed a blur, but it no longer left him bewildered. It was over, he thought, and with this realization he felt a lightness that had been missing for years.

He smiled.

Life no longer seemed a burden and he felt happy for the first time in years.

Pilar noticed the change. She watched as Peter lifted his head and looked around, happy. She elbowed Simon and nodded at Peter.

When he looked over Peter saw them both staring at him.

They were grinning.

"What´s up with you two?" he asked.

Pilar snuggled closer to him. "I do not think I've ever seen you smile. I didn't realize it until now."

He shrugged it off. "I must have smiled at least once with you."

She raised her eyebrows and shook her head, but then she started laughing.

"But you certainly can smile now!"

"Look at him!" she said to Simon. "He is like a boy he smiles so much."

Simon watched his son and knew exactly what she was talking about. He did appear different now. For years Peter had been a shell of a man and he'd known a part of him had died with Lekai.

Now he was back.

Pilar looked into his eyes. "And now what will you do?"

Peter picked up a stick and stirred the coals.

He looked at Pilar. "I was thinking about going to the island of Lamu."

"Oh, really?" said Pilar as she raised an eyebrow. "And what will you do there?"

Peter fidgeted. "I was hoping to spend time with you."

"You make me chase you across Kenya and you still think I want you to go to Lamu with me?"

For a brief moment the smile left his face, but then Pilar broke out laughing. "Of course I will go to Lamu with you."

She looked at Simon. "But what of your father?"

Simon leaned over and roughed up his son's hair. "Oh, I've got time for a break on Lamu." He glanced at his son and Pilar and added, "But I'm getting my own room."

Later, by the fire, the warriors had returned and sat in a circle around the warm coals. Most had put on their traditional clothing and Peter found himself surrounded by men in red and orange garments.

Those with ochre or beadwork had shared it, and they were facing each other in the firelight as they helped each other with their makeup. Sendeyo helped to pull back a warriors hair and mold it into shape with red clay. Soon they were all adorned properly as warriors in full battle decoration.

In the firelight they look fearsome.

Laibon returned wearing a worn leather garment made of cowhide, and his face was now covered with ash and paint. In his arm he carried a painted piece of leather. He stood inside the circle, close to the fire, and gestured for silence.

The men looked at him with firelight sparkling in their eyes.

He took the *Eye of Enkai* and poured its contents on the strip of cowhide — painted orange — that he'd laid out.

As the stones passed through his fingers he looked at the future. "The time of bad fortune is over," declared Laibon, "now we will begin a new cycle."

He turned to Peter.

"My apprentice has returned, and later tonight we will celebrate this reunion. Yet this is not forever. Lekai is now of two worlds and we will have to share him, and get to know the one called Peter."

Laibon let another handful of stones pass through his hands.

"If we need Lekai he will return. And we will be there for him as well if he ever needs us."

Having said his piece, Laibon nodded, more to himself than the warriors, and then sat beside Sendeyo.

The warriors started to dance. They crouched low and circled, making deep guttural sounds. Their war-like cries came in rhythmic bursts, as the dance picked up energy; soon they began to jump.

Laibon laughed and blew his kudu horn as the warriors sang and danced life back into their forgotten home.

Chapter Thirty

A New Day

*P*eter and Kakuta sat on the side of the crater while the horizon lightened. They were just off the footpath that circumnavigated the crater, a few hundred feet above the plain, and they were waiting for the sun to show itself.

Peter looked down at the plain that stretched off on the other side of the river and thought of the morning on which he had first seen Lekai, spying from under a bush on a hill overlooking the vast Serengeti.

For now the land was still hidden in shadows and they could only make out the isolated acacia trees. A cool breeze blew past them and Peter stretched and then yawned. "I don't understand why I was chosen for this," said Peter. It had been a long night and he'd yet to get to sleep.

"I know I was responsible for Lekai's death, and he was my friend, but why me?"

Kakuta grabbed a handful of cinder and let it fall through his fingers. He looked Peter in the eye and said, "I am to be Laibon's new apprentice. When I said I could see Lekai, he knew I was in touch with the mystic, like my brother, but still it is a mystery to me as well."

With a smile he added, "After all, I am only an apprentice to a Seer, not a Seer."

Peter remembered Lekai saying something similar and said, "Not yet."

Kakuta grinned and repeated his words. "Yes, not yet."

The two remained silent for a while. Then Kakuta said, "Often when the warriors surround a lion it comes down to two men. One man makes the lion angry with his spear. Then when the lion attacks, another man steps forward and grabs the lion's tail."

He had stood to act this out, dropping his spear as he reached forward with both hands to grab the imaginary tail.

"You see? He has to drop his spear if he wants to help his brother. This man also has a special place in our society; he is often greater than the man who kills the lion because once he has dropped his spear he is vulnerable and it is up to the other members of the *moran* to protect him."

He smiled at Peter.

The explanation made Peter feel better.

"But why the journey?" he asked. "Why the dreams and the long trek here after ten years?"

Kakuta pondered this. "Maybe Lekai felt you needed the journey to find the teachers to guide you here."

Peter considered this, but shook his head.

"I don't see where that would make sense. I've met many people on this journey, but no teachers."

Kakuta looked at him. "Laibon teaches us that everyone has a lesson to teach. Was there nobody you met who taught you on your journey north?"

In the cool morning air Peter recalled his journey from South Africa, and those he'd traveled with. In the distance the sun hovered just under the horizon, painting that distant line gold.

He thought of Henry, the Rastafarian, sitting under the silver glow of the full moon while Victoria Falls roared around them, and his words: "The mystic is a powerful thing, *mon*, but you should not fear it. It is the unknown, and you should embrace the unknown if you want to be free."

Then his thoughts turned to Q-tip who warned him before they parted ways in Lusaka.

"Hear my words, Peter," he had said, "you take care if you continue to chase the fire. For the fire is quick!"

He smiled as he remembered Deepend slamming the kerosene lantern into Conrad, and then again when he'd tried to save him the night before from Conrad at the Modern Green Bar.

He remembered how Henry had remarked on Deepend's courage, and Deepend had added, "Yeah, and I'm as loyal as a dog."

And finally, he thought of Pilar, as she had kissed him on their arrival in Nairobi and said, "You should make room in your heart for love, and if you do, come find me."

Peter smiled. He was going to find room in his heart for love — in a few days they would be on Lamu.

At that moment the sun poured over the horizon and illuminated his face.

"Yes, I guess I did have teachers."

Peter stood, a new look of confidence in his eyes.

Kakuta asked, "What will you do now?"

Peter silently looked into the new sun. Then he smiled and said, "I think I may rest for a bit on the Island of Lamu."

Kakuta nodded and stood as well. Peter motioned for him to follow as he descended to the savanna.

In the cool air of dawn, on the plains below, the annual migration was in full swing.

Kakuta said, "Today I will go to fetch our mother; I will bring her here and build a hut for her."

They descended in deep steps, moving quickly, sliding more than stepping down the steep angle of the volcano.

Soon they were in the high grass, on the edge of a vast plain full of animals.

Kakuta continued, "I will make sure she never again has to depend on the charity of others."

Then, from behind they heard something large moving through the brush, snapping twigs under immense weight. The scraping of padded feet over hard earth was a sound that was all too familiar to Peter who turned and looked expectantly.

A short distance away a young rhino emerged from the bush. It looked in their direction and shook its head violently; the great horn cutting an arc in the sky.

Peter looked at Kakuta and smiled, and in his eyes there burned a strange light.

Then, with an almost playful air, he ran in the direction of the rhino.

Robert Louis DeMayo took up writing at the age of twenty when he left his job as a biomedical engineer to explore the world. Over the next fifteen years he traveled to every corner of the globe, spending almost eight years abroad and experiencing approximately one hundred countries. He is a member of The Explorers Club and The Archaeological Institute of America. During his travels he worked extensively for the travel section of *The Telegraph*, out of Hudson, NH.

For three years he worked as marketing director for Eos, a company that served as a travel office for six non-profit organizations and offered dives to the *Titanic* and the *Bismarck*, Antarctic voyages, African safaris and archaeological tours throughout the world. After, Robert worked for three years as a tour guide in Alaska during the summers and as a jeep guide in Sedona, Arizona, during the winter.

He was general manager at A Day in the West, a Jeep tour company in Sedona before he decided to write full time. He is the author of *The Making of Theodore Roosevelt*, a fictionalized account of Roosevelt's acquaintance with wilderness living, and *The Cave Where the Water Always Drips*, an adventure tale set in modern and colonial times of the Southwest.

Currently he resides in Sedona with his wife Diana and three daughters: Tavish Lee, Saydrin Scout, and Martika Louise.

Made in the USA
Charleston, SC
29 December 2012